A

MURDER

INTRUDES

A MURDER INTRUDES

A Susan Brooks and Walter Conway Mystery

BARBARA VALANIS

ARCHWAY
PUBLISHING

Archway Publishing books may be ordered through booksellers or by contacting:

Archway Publishing
1663 Liberty Drive
Bloomington, IN 47403
www.archwaypublishing.com
1 (888) 242-5904

ISBN: 978-1-4808-8857-9 (sc)
ISBN: 978-1-4808-8855-5 (hc)
ISBN: 978-1-4808-8856-2 (e)

Library of Congress Control Number: 2020907585

Print information available on the last page.

Archway Publishing rev. date: 5/1/2020

ACKNOWLEDGEMENTS

Many thanks to my daughter, Karin Fischer, my sister, Kathleen Seraphine, my granddaughter, Elizabeth Weis, and my friend, Dolly Moore for the thoughtful feedback they provided on early versions of this book. Special thanks to my beloved husband, Kirk, the inspiration for the character of Walter. His candid opinions always prompt me to critically rethink what I've written.

PROLOGUE

Life is like a river traveling to the sea. Gentle currents lead to quiet pools beneath trees and offer respite from the strong sun. Roiling rapids threaten to overturn our boat or dash it on unseen rocks just below the surface. Shallow water, boulders, or a tree that broke in a storm and fell across the stream can bring our journey to an abrupt end. Like the river, human relationships are rarely smooth, or predictable. Life's choices enhance or impede our journey down the river of life. People we meet along the way may turn our lives upside down. This is a story about life and its challenges.

— CHAPTER 1 —

Seattle, Washington
Wednesday, July 6

Susan Brooks glanced again at the Arrivals Board. Still no notice that Walter's plane had landed. She checked her watch, then the airport clock. Both indicated four thirty-five p.m.

Calm down, Susan. His plane isn't due for another ten minutes. What's wrong with me? My nerves are on fire. My stomach is churning. My heart is pounding. I'm short of breath. Be sensible! You're meeting your friend Walter. He's a kind, considerate, witty, and intelligent man. You love him. You're excited to see him again—it's been six weeks since you parted at the airport in Kona. Why this anxiety? You're reacting as if you're going on your first date!

Susan sat down and slowly took a deep breath. She closed her eyes and concentrated on relaxing, first each arm, then each leg. She repeated the process twice. Finally, she began to feel less anxious.

Of course, you're nervous, she reassured herself. *Walter is coming here so we can determine whether we want to spend the rest of our lives together. He'll be living in your house for the next four weeks, the house where you and Scott lived for more than*

3

thirty years. Why do you feel like you're betraying Scott by having Walter here? Scott has been dead for almost five years. You're still alive. You deserve to be loved and to have a companion during your remaining years. Walter loves you. He's an amazing man and a wonderful human being. Get a grip before he arrives!

She glanced again at the Arrivals Board. It changed to indicate that the flight from Honolulu had landed and would dock at Gate 32. Susan concentrated on remaining calm. *Only a few minutes until the plane arrives at the gate. Walter travels first-class, so should be among the first to deplane, then another five minutes to reach the arrivals area. This ordeal is almost over.*

Susan joined the crowd where the arriving passengers would exit. When the first small group entered the reception area, she moved to her right, directly in line with the entryway. She stood on her tiptoes, focusing on the incoming crowd. Then, she spotted Walter and waved. Walter grinned when he saw her, rushed forward, and wrapped her in his arms. The familiar feel of his arms holding her tight against him drained away her anxiety. They held each other, oblivious to the passengers surging past them.

Finally, Walter released her. "I thought I'd never get here! I missed you these past six weeks, Susan, and I worried whether the separation would change things between us."

"I've missed you too. I also fretted about whether things would change. Now that you're here, those worries seem foolish. Seeing you, feeling your arms around me, it's as if we never parted. Everything feels right with the world!"

"My darling, Susan. I hope to keep you happy for the rest of your life. Now, perhaps we should move out of the traffic flow and head for baggage claim?"

Susan nodded. "Let's find your luggage and get out of here. I want you to myself." She smiled warmly, all recent anxiety forgotten. She slipped her arm around Walter's waist and led him toward baggage claim.

Thirty-five minutes later, Susan pulled her car onto the interstate highway, heading north. Traffic was moderate and moving at the speed limit.

"Congestion will increase when we reach the outskirts of Seattle, about ten miles north of here. We'll be in the middle of rush hour, with lots of slow-downs, even outright stoppages. My house is northeast of the city, on Lake Washington. If you're hungry, we should consider stopping somewhere for dinner."

"I'm starving! It's been hours since lunch on the plane, and it wasn't substantial. Is downtown likely to be crowded?"

"Yes, and parking a problem. If we exit south of the city and go to one of the hotel restaurants on *Pill Hill*, we can avoid traffic and parking issues. Several have acceptable food."

"Sounds good. We can also get reacquainted on neutral ground. I wouldn't be surprised if you feel a bit anxious about having me stay in the house where you and Scott lived for so many years."

"Walter Conway, I can't believe you know me so well!"

"When we were in Hawaii, you sometimes said that being with me felt like a betrayal of Scott. I understand that feeling. Remember, Susan, I'm also widowed. I frequently converse with Marge in my mind, explaining to her that I still love her, and asking her to approve of my evolving relationship with you. Although you and I lost our spouses many years ago, we were married longer than we were either single or widowed. Our marriages were happy. Memories of those years are alive and comforting. Although we've committed to trying to build a future together, it's only six months since we met. We're in transition, feeling our way in this relationship. I believe, however, that our spouses would want us to move on and find happiness again."

"I agree with those perceptive words of wisdom, Walter. Here's our exit. This service road runs up to *Pill Hill*. Let's have dinner at the Hotel Sorrento. I've never had a bad meal in their Dunbar Room."

Over dinner Susan and Walter revisited their happy days together in Hawaii. Generous servings of succulent roast prime rib, the formal elegance of the dining room, and a background hum of conversation over the quiet notes of a piano, relaxed them, and facilitated a return to their previous comfortable companionship. Following dinner, they resumed their drive to Susan's house. North of downtown Seattle, Susan exited for Lake Washington.

"This is the only bridge that will take us to where I live. It often resembles a parking lot, so I frequently yield to the temptation to stay home. I love the peace and quiet of living on the lake and could easily become a recluse. Your presence will encourage me to get out and about as I show you some of my favorite spots in Seattle."

"In that case, I'll consider myself a positive influence. If you don't mind, Susan, I'd like us to have a few days together in peace and quiet before we begin sightseeing. I want you all to myself for now. Are there local spots where we can take a walk or find something to eat if we don't feel like cooking?"

"Of course. We've lots to catch up on." Susan turned onto a leafy two-lane road that followed the shoreline of the lake, and then into a driveway surrounded by woods.

"Here we are. I love my house and it's setting, but the damp climate takes a toll. I fear that its age is showing. Upkeep is becoming an issue. Scott and I built it more than thirty years ago as a home in which to raise our family. Now, it's much more house than I need."

"I'm surprised by the modern design," commented Walter. "Not what I expected. I pictured you living in a cozy cottage in the woods overlooking the lake. Instead, it's all angles and big windows. I can't wait to see whether the interior also differs from my expectations."

Susan helped Walter carry his luggage up the flagstone walkway to the front entry. "Here we are." Susan held the door open so Walter could enter. "Tell me. Is it anything like you expected?"

"Wow! What a view! Those floor to ceiling windows facing the lake and the skylights let in so much light, despite the trees all around the house." Walter looked around. "That view, and the angles of the vaulted ceiling, create a sense of drama and space. The wooden ceiling beams echo the wooded setting. The way you've decorated the interior has a traditional feel that draws one's focus from the modern architecture. The decor provides a feeling of calm and comfort. The calm and comfort are what I expected. I really like it, Susan."

Walter walked to the windows and gazed at the lake. "You have a boat dock. Do you have a boat?"

"We had a motor boat. I prefer quiet to the noise of motors, so I sold it years ago, and replaced it with two single kayaks and a canoe. Those also give me some exercise."

"I also prefer the quiet. Hopefully, we can spend some lazy, romantic afternoons out on the lake. Now, would you show me to the guest room so I can freshen up, then change into something more appropriate for this climate?"

Walter thought he detected an expression of surprise and relief on Susan's face. "What? Did you think I'd expect to move into the master bedroom with you? Didn't I promise you that we'd take things slowly and let our relationship mature in its own time?"

"You did, Walter. But, I wasn't sure what you'd expect for sleeping arrangements."

Walter walked to Susan, put his hands on her shoulders, and looked directly into her eyes. "Susan, dearest one, it's not a matter of what I expect, but what you are ready for. I love you. Of course I'd welcome a physical relationship. But, I understand that your feelings of betraying Scott are holding you back from physical intimacy. I'm sure you feel his presence strongly here where you lived together for so many years. Overcoming those feelings will take some time. Unless he was a jealous, self-centered bastard, he would want you to find happiness. After all, you may live another twenty-five or thirty years. I'm willing to wait, but not forever.

Susan smiled. "Walter, I love you. Your way of seeing things is so logical. I never thought about living so long." She hugged him. When she released him, she glanced upward. "Scott, are you listening? You were the love of my life, but it's been five years since you left me behind. I'll never forget you. I'm sure you're feeling jealous, but I have a life to live. And I have someone who loves me and can offer me some happiness for the remainder of my life. Please let me go."

Walter also looked upward. "Scott, I promise to love and cherish Susan. I won't let her forget you." Then he cupped Susan's face in his hands and looked at her seriously. "Susan, please, promise to tell me how you feel about any particular situation. We must share our feelings and expectations to avoid misunderstandings. That's crucial to our relationship. Agreed?"

Susan nodded. He kissed her lightly on her forehead. "Now, where is the guest room?"

— CHAPTER 2 —

Thursday, July 7

Susan sat on the deck with a cup of coffee and the newspaper. It was cool, but pleasant with the morning sun warming her skin. As usual, she had risen early, showered, dressed, and then put on the coffee. She set the timer to keep it warm for Walter. Come to think of it, she wasn't sure if he drank coffee first thing in the morning. She had never been with him in the morning.

Maybe he prefers tea. I guess I'll find out when he gets up. He once told me that he's not an early riser. I like having time to myself in the morning, a chance to have my first cup of coffee, read the paper, and collect my thoughts for the day ahead.

As Susan turned to the last page of the newspaper, she heard the sound of the sliding glass door. She looked up to see Walter, dressed in jeans, a white polo shirt, and bare feet, holding a coffee mug. *He is so handsome!* Susan's heart skipped a beat.

"Good morning, Sweetheart. What a lovely day! May I join you?"

"Of course. Good morning Walter." She smiled at him, stood, and gave him a hug. As she released him, Walter pushed back a loose strand of hair from her face, then kissed her gently.

"How do you manage to look so fresh and alert in the morning, Susan? I always feel a bit sluggish when I wake up."

"I've always been an early riser. A cup of coffee and some quiet time with the newspaper usually put me on track for the day. Did you sleep well?"

"Better than I've slept in ages. I'm not used to the cool nights, so I snuggled up with a blanket and fell into this lovely, deep sleep. I'd heard that one sleeps better when it's cool. Living in warm Hawaii, where my only cooling comes from a fan or the ocean breeze, I never really tested it. After last night, I'm a believer! And as for your guest room bed, it has the most comfortable mattress I can imagine."

"I'm pleased you slept so well. I see you got some coffee. Do you usually have coffee in the morning, or do you prefer tea? I can make you some."

"I usually have tea when I get up, and then coffee with breakfast. I've already poured myself a cup of the coffee you had warming. Hopefully, it will wake me up. I need to adjust to the four-hour time difference. Sorry I'm so late."

"No need to apologize, Walter. I'm glad you slept well. I've enjoyed perusing today's *Seattle Times*. It's a beautiful morning for enjoying the Northwest sunshine. You'll find that it feels less harsh than the Hawaiian sun.

"I'm sure you're hungry. Make yourself comfortable. I'll fix us some breakfast. Would you like something light like toast, cheese, and fruit, or a hearty breakfast of eggs, toast, and sausage or bacon with a grilled tomato?"

"This morning, I'll accept your offer of a hearty breakfast. While you're slaving in the kitchen, I'll laze here in the sun and enjoy your beautiful view. I'd prefer sausage to bacon. But, in the future, Susan, I want to assist with preparing breakfast, and sometimes to make breakfast for you. I don't expect you to wait on me. This is a partnership. Besides, cooking together will be fun."

"Yes, it will. This morning, however, it's my pleasure to wait on you while you adjust to the new time zone, climate, and surroundings. Do you need anything while I'm cooking?"

"No, I'm fine, thanks. I helped myself to milk and sugar for my coffee."

"Good, I want you to feel at home. Enjoy the newspaper. I won't be long."

About twenty minutes later, Susan emerged from the kitchen carrying a large tray. "Breakfast is ready, Walter." While he stacked the newspaper on an empty chair, Susan put down place mats and cutlery, and then set out orange juice, condiments, and two plates heaped with food.

"I'll get the fresh pot of coffee. Is there anything else you need? I hope you don't mind that I plated the food, rather than serving it family-style. This approach saves on dishes and trips between the kitchen and the deck."

"Good thinking. It looks scrumptious. Thank you, Susan."

Over breakfast, they discussed the news. "Walter, did you see the article about people competing to purchase low number license plates? I can't believe people's priorities."

"No, I missed that one. What's going on?"

"Apparently, in many states, a low number on your car's license plate is a status symbol. People pay huge amounts to obtain one. A retired dentist in Alabama bought a second-hand Mercedes Benz at auction. He paid just under seven thousand dollars for the car. Subsequently, he bid something like two hundred and forty-eight thousand dollars to obtain its license plate with the number twenty on it! That's probably more than the median price of a house in that state. He then sold a plate he already owned with the number one hundred fifty-eight to the man who had been bidding against him. The man paid sixty-eight thousand dollars."

"That's outrageous! You're serious? You said this guy is retired. I wonder if he thought about the effect of inflation on his savings. Of course, if demand for license plates with low numbers continues, I suppose it could be considered an investment."

"Perhaps I should sell my Hawaii condo and buy a low number license plate," said Susan with a grin. "It might be a better investment."

"But not half as much fun. We had some lovely times at your condo. Seriously, what is it with people that they need these external symbols of status?"

"I wish I knew, Walter. Another article said that manufacturers of status accessories destroy unsold stock at the end of each season to retain brand exclusivity. I think that means so they can charge outrageous prices for their goods. Can you imagine spending three thousand dollars or more for a purse or a pair of shoes? For many people, that's three month's income! One handbag was advertised for sixteen thousand dollars. Wealthy women may own dozens."

"Don't you think, Susan, that those folks would feel better about themselves if they used their money and talents to make a difference in the world?"

"That's an interesting thought, Walter. Would you want to be super-wealthy? I wouldn't. I like the anonymity of the middle class. Possessions aren't important to me. I'm grateful to have money for necessities, with extra to spend occasionally on travel or entertainment. I like stylish clothing, but at a reasonable price. I don't need a tag indicating that it's designer-wear. I've never been especially fond of shopping. Large social gatherings make me uncomfortable. Can you imagine shopping and attending social events as the focus of your life?"

"I'd go mad!" Walter grinned. "My sensible Susan. I appreciate that you don't value material things and share my view that money and talent should be used to improve the world. My volunteer work with the planning board in Hawaii lets me feel I'm making a contribution to the community. You contribute through your work with the children's reading group at the local library. I look forward to when we get our lives settled and can become more involved. Hopefully, we'll find something we can enjoy doing together, using our talents to improve the lives of others."

"Enough serious discussion for this fine morning, Walter. Let's decide how we want to spend our day. Would you like to take advantage of this beautiful summer weather to go canoeing and fishing?"

"I'd love to catch a fish for dinner."

"You have to promise to scale and filet it, Walter. Then I'll cook it for you. I don't do scaling."

"I promise. I'll cook it for you, if you'll prepare the side dishes."

"Deal! Let's do these dishes and get on with our day."

Walter caught an eighteen inch large-mouth bass. He scaled and fileted it while Susan changed her clothing for a trip around the area to familiarize him with their surroundings. They enjoyed a late lunch at a nearby bistro, and then stopped at the wine store. When they arrived back at the house, Walter yawned. "An afternoon nap is in order. I'm not yet adjusted to this time zone."

Later, they strolled hand-in-hand through the neighborhood. Walter was fascinated by the lush Northwest flora. Because he had lived in Hawaii for so long, he was unfamiliar with the northwestern azaleas, rhododendron, Oregon holly, Douglas firs, ferns, and mosses. They spotted a deer family grazing on a sunny patch of lawn while a blue heron watched curiously from the water's edge. The sight was the highlight of their walk.

Dinner preparation led to laughter. They repeatedly bumped into each other in the compact kitchen. "We'll need to establish some traffic patterns to avoid these constant collisions, Susan." A long kiss followed.

"You make colliding an experience to enjoy, Walter."

Dinnertime was filled with talk about memorable experiences they had shared in Hawaii. They recalled their initial meal together at Walter's house after he rescued Susan from the golf course because she sprained her ankle. That night they had discussed the challenges of adjusting to the death of their spouses. Those discussions had led to an empathetic companionship, which later blossomed into love.

Then there was the first dinner at Susan's condo. Neither of them had ever seen the fabled green flash, purported to occur in Hawaii at the moment the sun dips below the horizon. They both saw it that evening as they watched the sunset together.

Susan could hardly stop laughing at Walter's comic description of how he had driven off the flock of ducks at the Punaluhu black sand beach. Not content with Susan's offer of picnic leftovers, the ducks had attacked the cooler and picnic basket looking for more food.

They ended their evening on the deck, chatting under a starlit sky. Classical music played softly in the background. It was a replay of many evenings they had spent in Hawaii.

— CHAPTER 3 —

Monday, July 11

Susan answered the phone on the second ring, hoping that it hadn't awakened Walter. The caller was her daughter.

"Hi Kristin! How are things in North Carolina?"

"Everything's fine, Mom. The boys are with friends, and Jim is at work. I'm taking advantage of having time on my own to catch up on household chores. I always seem to be behind. How are you and Walter? Is the visit going well?"

"It's been wonderful to be with him again. We were both a little nervous at first. Once we got reacquainted, we fell back into our previous comfortable relationship. We've stayed at home the past few days, resting, eating, reminiscing about Hawaii, boating, taking walks, reading, listening to music. It took me a while to stop feeling strange that it was Walter in the house, and not your father. I think I'm past all that now. Tomorrow, we'll play tourist in Seattle. I want to show Walter some of my favorite places. He's never been to Seattle before."

"Should I ask whether the romantic aspects of your relationship have evolved?"

"You should not. That's between Walter and me."

"I understand, but I also need to be practical. When you

15

two start visiting each other's families, you'll need to let folks know about sleeping arrangements. When you visit us, if you need separate rooms, you'll need to stay at a hotel. We've only got the one guest room. Something to think about."

"Yes, you're right. Maybe we should just plan to stay at a hotel in any case. Walter and I will have to discuss it. We haven't talked about when we plan to travel. Its early days for us at this point. We're still feeling our way along this journey."

"Enjoy the trip, Mom. I've got to run and get this housework done before my gang gets back. Just wanted to say hello and be sure everything is okay. Say hi to Walter for me."

"Will do, Kristin. Thanks for calling. Love to everyone. Bye."

Susan was deep in thought as she hung up the phone. "Good morning, Susan."

She turned to see Walter entering the room. "Good morning, Walter. That was Kristin on the phone. She says hello."

"Thank you for delivering the message. What's wrong? You look like you've been knocked aside the head."

"Oh, Walter! Kristin asked about sleeping arrangements when we visit them. Her question brought back to me all the unresolved aspects of our relationship."

Walter put his arms around her and held her close. "Relax, my love. There's no hurry about visiting family. We've only been back together a few days. The present is what's important. We agreed to take it one day at a time, remember?" He kissed her forehead before releasing her.

"Thanks Walter, for keeping things in perspective. You're so good at focusing on the present. I jump ahead. The pending decisions bring me to the brink of panic."

"My mother used to call that behavior borrowing trouble."

Susan kissed Walter on the cheek. "Point taken. I'll keep reminding myself, one day at a time. Now, how about some breakfast? If we're going sightseeing downtown today, we should get moving. Rush hour traffic will soon abate. If we time our trip during the lull, we'll have time to look around, and then head home before the afternoon rush hour."

"My practical, Susan. There is an alternative. We could leave at our leisure, do our sightseeing, then have dinner downtown, and return home after the rush hour. That way we can enjoy our breakfast and still have time for a day of sightseeing without worrying about the traffic. What do you think?"

"Walter, that's a great idea! You have a way of offering possibilities that I don't see. I've become rigid in my thinking. Hopefully, your flexibility will rub off on me."

"I'm not sure if it's flexibility or the demands of age. I'm a slow starter these days. Let's settle for cereal, fruit, and coffee for breakfast. While we eat, you can brief me on what we should plan to see today. I'll get the cereal and coffee ready if you'll prepare the fruit."

They were soon settled at the table on the deck. "How does this sound as a plan for our day, Walter? We could begin with a stroll along the waterfront park. A walk might feel good after the drive to town. Then, I'd love to sit on a park bench and watch the boat traffic for a while. I've always been fascinated by boats."

"How about you sit and watch the boats and I'll watch you?"

"Oh! We don't need to watch the boats if you'd….."

"I'm teasing you, sweetheart. I'd enjoy watching the boats with you. I think it's charming that you can find pleasure in such a simple activity. I love that about you. What do we do after boat-watching?"

"We walk up the hill to the Pike Place Market. There we graze on exotic food as we explore. That can serve as lunch. If we feel up to it afterwards, we could wander around downtown to give you a feel for the city. Downtown Seattle is quite hilly, so it requires some energy. We'll save the Space Needle, the aquarium, the underground city, and other indoor venues for days with less desirable weather. One day we should take the ferry to Bainbridge Island and poke around over there."

"I've heard of the Pike Place Market. I'll see if it lives up to its reputation. The rest of your plan for the day sounds enjoyable, even climbing the hills if it doesn't get too warm. Do you have somewhere to suggest for dinner? I'd love some fresh seafood."

"In that case, I'd suggest Elliott's Oyster House. I'll call before we leave here and make a reservation. Meanwhile, if you'll clean up the breakfast dishes, I'll get myself ready to go."

Susan and Walter were ready to rest when they arrived at Elliott's Oyster House for their six o'clock dinner reservations. It had been a full day of exploring Seattle. The brilliant sunshine had produced an unusually warm day. Walking all afternoon left them hot and tired, even with several stops for liquid refreshment.

The waiter brought their wine and large glasses of water. They ordered dinner, but asked the waiter to wait a half hour before serving. They wanted to relax and enjoy their wine.

"What do you think of Seattle, Walter?"

"It's an interesting city. Somewhat difficult to get around because of the hills and the traffic, but full of life. The setting is spectacular, on the waterfront with those snow-covered mountains in the distance. I was surprised by the number of homeless people in several sections of downtown. It's tragic that so many of the homeless are families with small children. Why can't a country as rich as the United States of America do better?"

"I wish I knew. Seattle has struggled to deal with their homeless. When tourists complained about panhandling, city officials made it a criminal offence to sleep on park benches or the ground; it was even illegal to sit on the ground in certain areas downtown where tourists congregate. Officials thought such regulations would drive the homeless away. It wasn't successful, and certainly did nothing to help those in need.

"The need for help was real, not just people being lazy. After the 2008 recession, many folks lost jobs and their homes. Several not-for-profit organizations stepped in to provide temporary shelter, clothing, medical care, and help in finding jobs. They lobbied for a kinder, more helpful municipal approach to the problem. Needs were far greater than the available resources. As you observed, Walter, the problem has not been solved."

"I want to do something to make a difference. But, I don't know what I can do, other than making donations, volunteering my time to caring organizations, and voting for politicians who put forth solutions. I know we've talked about this before, Susan. Why can't corporations become part of the solution? They should consider long-term consequences of their decisions, not just the bottom line. I know, I know." Walter held up his hand as Susan started to say something. "I realize that companies are under pressure from shareholders. Don't you think it's time they develop some backbone and push back? This country could benefit from some long-term planning by government, corporations, and individuals."

"Maybe you should run for public office."

"Heaven forbid! I'd never get elected. I have no talent for diplomacy."

"Do you remember, Walter, before the advent of credit cards when people were forced to plan ahead and save for a rainy day? If you didn't have cash, you couldn't buy anything; only cars and houses could be bought on credit."

Walter chuckled. "I remember when things were hard for my parents. They didn't have much cash. Mom's old tub washer with the wringer on top died. For several months she had to drag the laundry to a friend's house about a half mile away. Mother piled it in my red wagon, and put my baby sister on top of the laundry bags. I had to run along-side all the way. After she washed it, we'd drag the wet laundry home to hang on the line in the backyard to dry. She was thrilled when they finally saved enough to purchase a new washer, a newer, spin-dry version, without the wringer!"

"People in those days made the most of what they had. They repaired rather than replaced. I spent hours darning my Dad's old socks. We passed clothing from child to child. We grew our own fruits and vegetables and canned most of it for the winter. Mother washed aluminum foil and plastic wrap for reuse. She was an environmentalist before her time, except she did it to save money. Today, we live in a disposable society. Not good for the pocketbook or the environment. As long as our economic model is driven by growth and consumption, nothing will change."

"I fear you're right. In any case, back to my impressions of Seattle. Pike Place Market lived up to expectations. I enjoyed the bustle, the variety of food and other merchandise. It's nice that they provide places where people can linger and soak up the atmosphere. Did you notice the gentrification occurring in that part of town?"

"Yes, it made me realize how long it must be since I'd last been there! I haven't come to town much since Scott died."

"Seattle must have more cultural venues than Symphony Hall, which we passed in our meanderings."

"Yes, there is the opera, the art museum, and several small playhouses."

"Perhaps we could plan to attend a concert, play, or the opera while I'm here? We both enjoy music and the theater. Those are the aspects of urban life that appeal to me."

"Of course, Walter. We can check and see what is going on. I did get us tickets for a symphony concert early next month. I should have mentioned it sooner."

"That was thoughtful of you, Susan. I look forward to an evening at the symphony. The Seattle Symphony is an excellent orchestra. I'd also enjoy visiting the art museum. Isn't there a Chihuly Museum somewhere near Seattle? I'd love to go if it isn't too far to travel. His glass work is spectacular!"

"That's a great idea, Walter. I like his glass art. The Chihuly Museum and Park is not far from the Space Needle. The building is surrounded by a lovely garden in which some of his work is displayed. That would be a fun day's outing and far less taxing than climbing the hills of downtown!"

"Sounds good to me. I look forward to attending some cultural events and also visiting the aquarium. After a few more days exploring Seattle, I'll be ready to expand our horizons. Have you ever visited the Oregon Coast? I've heard that it's very beautiful."

"Many years ago, Scott and I took the children there. We visited the Olympic National Forest, and then headed south along the Washington coast. We drove all the way to Newport, Oregon. Scott and I visited the Oregon Coast several times on our own after the children were grown and away at college.

"Did you enjoy it? Do you think it's worth our making a visit?"

"Absolutely! I love the coast. You're a nature-lover, so I'm sure you'd like it. Both the Washington and Oregon Coasts are beautiful, with substantial undeveloped areas, and mountains that come right down to the sea. In some places, waterfalls pour over cliffs onto the beach. I prefer the Oregon Coast. Much of Washington's coast has high cliffs, with limited views of the ocean from the coastal road, because of the rain forest. While it's lush and beautiful, many sections of the coastal road offer little access to the interior of the state. There are few towns along the road and access to beaches is limited. In that regard, it reminds me of Hawaii, for instance the drive to Hana on Maui. Along the southern Washington coast, the road borders the sea and one can access wide, flat beaches. The weather tends to be overcast and damp. To me the beaches feel wild and desolate.

"Oregon's coast has many small, funky beach-towns, and easy access to the rural interior. Sections of highway on sea-side cliffs offer good views of the ocean, while sections at sea level open to river estuaries. The weather becomes sunnier and drier as you drive south. In general, towns are small. Most buildings are no higher than two stories. The ocean is the focus, with many state parks along the way. I really liked it."

"What would you think about us spending a week on the Oregon Coast, Susan? I'd enjoy being away from the city. It would remind me of our times out and about in Hawaii."

"What a lovely idea, Walter. I'd like that. Do you want access to restaurants, shops, and entertainment, or would you prefer a more isolated setting where we would cook in most of the time and spend days exploring the natural beauty of the coast? If the former, I'd suggest staying in Cannon Beach. For the latter, Neskowin is a good option.

"Tell me something about them."

"Cannon Beach, on the northern Oregon Coast is a charming town, visitor friendly, with lots of shops, art galleries, and restaurants, some bed and breakfasts, many small hotels and motels, and flowers everywhere. The rustic buildings, often painted in bright colors, add to the charm. It's always bustling in the summer. The beach is long and deep with a few monoliths off-shore. The best known, Haystack Rock, is a town landmark. Although it's a popular place that attracts folks from Portland, the beaches aren't terribly crowded. It also has a small theater with live performances.

"Neskowin is a tiny town located about twelve miles north of Lincoln City on the Central Coast. It's about a two hour drive south of Cannon Beach. It has several small resort hotels, one restaurant, a post office, a general store, and a golf course, frequently soggy. Newer developments occupy the hills north of town and east of U.S. 101. There are about twelve to fifteen residential blocks running north/south on the flatter land between the ocean and the road, adjacent to what I jokingly call beautiful downtown Neskowin. That area contains a general store, a restaurant, the post office, a realtor, and several small timeshare hotels. Houses in the southern end are older, built as small vacation cottages. To the north, houses are larger, and more modern. Several small hotels sit on the beachfront. The third part of town, South Beach, a gated community nestled in the trees, has larger, modern homes and no commercial development.

"The town is popular. Owners of the timeshares usually use their allotted time. The small beachfront hotels are booked well in advance. Fortunately, many local homeowners rent to tourists in summer. The beaches in Neskowin, like in Cannon Beach, are wide and deep, and not crowded. The town also has its own monolith, called Proposal Rock."

"Both sound fascinating. Do you have a preference, Susan?"

"I enjoy them both. One or two days in Cannon Beach are plenty for me. I find it too civilized. For longer stays, I prefer being immersed in nature. I like to rent a house somewhere quiet, like South Beach in Neskowin, where the houses are set among big trees and there is little traffic. The beach, separated from the town to the north by Hawk's Creek, is very private, with lots of driftwood along the dunes at the rear. Tide pools surround Proposal Rock when the tide is out. Petrified tree trunks, several inches to a foot high, can be seen poking out of the beach sand at low tide. Exposed some years ago by a big storm, they had been buried, supposedly for hundreds of years.

"It sounds idyllic! Let's get on the internet tomorrow when we're fresh, Susan, and look for houses for rent on South Beach."

"It is pretty special, and a good base for exploring other areas. North of Neskowin, a stretch of road runs from the oceanside highway east into the interior. Along that road, a mile or so inland, is an area with huge sand dunes surrounded by forest—a fascinating oddity. Another stretch of road west of Tillamook, Oregon, called the Three Capes Drive, follows the coastline north past bays, estuaries, and several small towns. The scenery is varied and spectacular, definitely worth seeing.

"Lincoln City, south of Neskowin, is handy for grocery

shopping at a reasonable price. It has a large outlet mall, some restaurants, and lots of small shops along the main drag. It also has a sizable lake, and several marinas where you can rent watercraft. Newport, further south has an aquarium, a maritime museum, and a large harbor with fishing boats, restaurants and shops. South of Newport is the sea lion cave, and the National Sand Dunes, which are spectacular! Listen to me. I'm getting carried away."

"Your enthusiasm is catching. It sounds like a week will hardly be enough time to do it justice. I can hardly wait to start planning our trip."

They were interrupted by the appearance of the waiter with their dinner. Agreeing to resume their discussion of the Oregon trip the next day, they turned their attention to what looked to be a delicious meal.

— CHAPTER 4 —

Irvine, California
Tuesday, July 19

Juanita lowered herself carefully into her favorite armchair. Her grandson, Miguel, shifted her walker to the side of the chair, careful to assure that she could reach it. He brought her tray table and positioned it over the armrests. Then, he returned to the kitchen for plastic cutlery and a paper plate containing her dinner—a cheese quesadilla, some refried beans, and a small lettuce salad.

"It's only a simple meal, Abuela," apologized Miguel.

"It's more than I could easily prepare for myself, Miguelito. Thank you for looking after me. May I have some iced tea with dinner?"

"Of course." Miguel brought her a paper cup of iced tea and a plastic bag. He placed the tea on the tray table and tied the plastic bag next to the handle of the walker. Then he retrieved the TV remote and laid it on the bed next to the armchair, within easy reach for his grandmother.

"When you're finished eating, put the remains of your meal into the plastic bag, Grandmother. That way, when you go to the kitchen, you can just dump the bag into the trash bin. I'm sorry I have to leave you now. I'm supposed to meet Henry at the gallery at six and am already running late. I'll lock up on my way out." Miguel kissed his grandmother and turned to go.

"Don't be too late," called Juanita, just as she heard the door close. She shrugged and returned to her meal, enjoying every morsel. She didn't get much to eat these days. Since her stroke, it was difficult to cook for herself. Miguel helped when he could, but wasn't around much lately.

Juanita's thoughts drifted to the past. *How my life has changed since my dear Manuel died! For thirty-five years we did everything together. Our life was busy, filled with family and friends. These last thirteen years, I've been mostly by myself. It's partly my own fault; I pushed people away after Manuel's death when I was so depressed and unhappy. Then, the 2008 recession hit this neighborhood hard. House prices still haven't recovered.*

Neighbors moved away after the banks foreclosed. Speculators moved in. Now, there are more renters than owners. Many houses aren't maintained; even mine needs attention. Young men hang around in the street, smoking, drinking, shouting, sometimes fighting. Burglaries in the neighborhood eventually drove away my remaining friends.

This house has become a liability. It's old, and expensive to maintain. It needs exterior painting, and soon, a new roof. It's too big for me. I haven't been able to access the second floor since my stroke. I can't manage the front steps or public transportation by myself, so I'm a prisoner in my own home. Nights frighten me. Once familiar creaks and groans now sound ominous. I probably should sell. But, Manuel and I built this house for our family when the area was being developed. Fond memories of my life here with Manuel and the children are almost all I have left these days

I crave companionship, people my own age. My children are busy with their own lives. Carmelita's home is two hours away by car. Her full time job as a dental assistant, and caring for her three children make it difficult for her to visit me.

I enjoy the yearly visit from Marta and her family. Unfortunately, the cost and time involved make more frequent trips from Florida difficult. Even connecting by phone is challenging because of Marta's busy schedule and the three-hour time difference.

Miguel's father, Sergio lives only fifteen minutes away. Since Manuel died, he's been obsessed with developing his father's landscaping and yard care business. Last I heard, he had sixteen employees! I miss seeing his younger children, Delia and Fernando, and his wife, Dolores. I always enjoyed her company. I regret that he broke off our relationship and forbade his family to visit because I allowed Miguel to move in here.

Miguel has been a bright light in my life. I've always loved him. He was a shy and lonely child, who loved hanging out in the kitchen, helping me to cook and listening to my stories of life in Honduras. Tragically, Sergio believed that Miguel's preference for sketching and reading over sports was not macho. Sergio's insistence that Miguel spend time with boys in his neighborhood, rather than pursue his own interests probably contributed to Miguel's involvement with drugs.

Sergio was so cruel to Miguel. Imagine, refusing to allow your nineteen year-old son to move back into the family home because he served a year in prison for drug possession! How could I not help my favorite grandson when he begged me to let him live here until he could get a job and afford a place of his own? His offer to help with maintaining the house, running errands, and doing the heavier chores like vacuuming and window washing was a bonus. I welcomed his company. I still do.

I'll never forget the day when Sergio heard that Miguel was living here. He came to the house and pounded on the door. When I opened it, he stormed into my home.

"Mother, why didn't you talk to me before allowing Miguel

to move in here? You must have realized that I had a reason for not allowing him to live at home! He's a druggie and a sissy. He would be a bad influence on his siblings. He needs a dose of life. It will do him good to struggle while he tries to make something of himself. You should throw him out."

"Sergio! Miguel is young. He made a mistake and has done his time. Life will be difficult enough for him. Businesses are reluctant to hire a convicted felon. If he's living on the streets he'll be exposed to more temptations. His life would be in danger. I think you've been unnecessarily cruel to your son. This is my house. I do not need to ask your permission to offer him a home. I'm lonely and need companionship. I see little enough of you since your father died. Miguel and I have always gotten along, and I think I can be a positive influence. He has agreed to help me around the house and with errands. This arrangement is mutually beneficial."

"Mother, if you insist on having Miguel here, you will not see anything of me or my family. I do not want them exposed to him."

"Sergio, you have become a hard man. Your father would be appalled. I know that I am. I will be sorry to be cut off from you and your family. I love you, and your wife and children. But I will not agree to throw Miguel out to live on the streets. As long as he remains clean, supports himself, and keeps his agreement to help me out, he may stay. I shall miss you and your family. Now, I think you should leave."

Sergio turned and strode swiftly to the door. He slammed it behind him as he left.

Miguel had managed to find work as a short order cook in a Mexican Restaurant. He didn't want a restaurant career, but few others would hire felons. Miguel figured he could save his earnings, then return to school to prepare for a better life.

One evening, Miguel came into the house carrying an armload of parcels.

"Look what I have, Grandmother." Miguel showed off his purchases, some cheap oil paints, canvas, charcoal, sketching paper, and an easel. "I decided to try my hand at art again. I used to love to sketch. If I can still do it, I'd like to take an art course."

"Good for you, Miguel. You were quite good at sketching when you were young. No reason you should have lost the talent."

Juanita had been pleasantly surprised by Miguel's early efforts. Soon he bought a book on portrait painting and asked his grandmother to serve as his model. Juanita smiled now as she remembered her amusement at the thought of modeling. She got into the spirit of it and dressed in a sultry red outfit, one of Manuel's favorites. She posed for Miguel in the evenings. Those times they shared while he painted her had been filled with conversation and laughter. Recalling that now lifted her spirits.

Miguel gave her the finished painting on her birthday, framed in an ornate frame that matched those on other paintings in her home. Juanita thought the portrait quite professional. It was one of her favorite possessions.

To encourage his talent, she bought Miguel a set of quality paints and brushes, and paid for him to enroll in evening art classes at the local community college. The professor, enthusiastic about Miguel's talent, encouraged him to show his work in the college art show. One of the paintings sold at the show!

"I owe it all to you, Grandmother," Miguel said that evening as they discussed the show. "Without your encouragement and financial support, I'd never have felt that I could become a real artist."

Subsequently, Juanita arranged to have skylights, overhead lighting, and storage units installed in the room over the garage, so that Miguel could use the room as a studio. He painted nearly every night, and on weekends. Eventually, he joined a local artist's cooperative and showed his work in their gallery. Occasionally, a painting sold.

Life had been good for both of them during those years. Miguel was building his career. Juanita was enjoying his companionship.

Everything changed again for Juanita two years ago, when she had her stroke. It left her with difficulty speaking, a weak right arm, and a right leg that barely moved. Miguel took a leave of absence from his job for two months to look after her and to run the household.

Juanita had been depressed and listless, with no interest in living. Miguel refused to give up. He encouraged her, served as her physical therapy coach, prepared her favorite meals, and read to her. He spent every free minute with her, trying to reignite her interest in life. Because she couldn't manage the stairs to the second floor bedroom, her hospital bed was in the living room. She had no privacy, and was frequently awakened by the sounds of Miguel coming and going, cooking in the adjacent kitchen, or cleaning the house. Eventually, Miguel persuaded her to remodel the room off the living room into a bedroom/bath suite.

Juanita gave Miguel her power of attorney so that he could handle the remodeling project and take over management of her finances. She, who had managed all the finances for her husband's business, simply had no interest anymore. Juanita also rewrote her will, making Miguel her major beneficiary, leaving her daughters and other grandchildren small legacies, but leaving nothing to her son, Sergio. She was still angry with him for cutting her off from his family.

Although Sergio visited her once or twice at the hospital after her stroke, neither he nor his wife had visited since she returned home. Miguel's younger sister, her granddaughter, Delia, sometimes came by after school with a friend, Monica. Delia risked her father's wrath, but was willing to take that risk. She enjoyed seeing her brother and loved her grandmother; she was determined to spend time with them.

After Juanita moved into the new suite, her outlook improved. Her sleep was no longer interrupted and she had privacy. She also exercised more regularly when she was alone in her room. Gradually, her mobility and strength had improved. Now, she could walk around the main floor of the house using a walker. Miguel rearranged the furniture to facilitate her mobility.

Cooking remained a challenge; she needed the walker for support when standing. Once Miguel returned to work, she relied on meal packages that Miguel cooked and froze. Because Miguel worked his restaurant job six days a week, starting at six a.m., and then sometimes spent evenings at the art cooperative or with friends, she was often alone. Miguel moved his painting gear from the studio into the living room, so they could chat while he painted. Sometimes Juanita would simply listen to music and watch him. Life settled into a routine. Juanita read when she was alone, and increased her use of the telephone to keep in touch with daughters. She had been content.

When *had things begun to change?* Juanita reflected on the past year. *I think it was after Miguel's friend, Henry, moved into the house. That was seven or eight months ago.*

One evening after dinner, Miguel told Juanita he wanted to ask a favor.

"I have a friend, Henry. I met him at the artist's cooperative. He is an oil painter, mostly modern stuff. He's not had much success selling his work and has been living in his car. He recently began working as manager of a local gallery. Would you allow him to live here in one of the unused bedrooms for a few months until he can save for a security deposit, and the first and last month's rent he needs to lease an apartment?"

I don't see why I shouldn't grant Miguel's request; Henry has a steady job at a gallery. Certainly a few months will be enough, even with today's high rents, for Henry to save a down payment and deposit on an apartment. Do onto others.... Juanita thought. *I'd be grateful if someone did this for me if I were in Henry's situation. I certainly have the space!*

So Juanita agreed to allow Henry to live in the house for three or four months.

How did it happen that eight months later, Henry is still here?

Two months ago, she had approached Henry about when he thought he would be moving into an apartment of his own.

"I'll move when I've saved enough," he had snapped at her. "Apartments are expensive. At the salary I'm earning, with the expenses of insuring and maintaining my car, buying painting supplies, and enjoying some time with my friends, it's taking a long time to save what I need. I haven't found an apartment I can afford." His words were defensive, but his body language was threatening.

Juanita was afraid of his belligerent attitude toward her. Even before she had raised the question of his moving out, he had seemed antagonistic when their path's crossed. He seemed annoyed by her presence. She considered asking him to pay some rent for his room and board, but decided she didn't have the courage to ask. Besides, that might delay his moving out.

When Henry was around, Miguel seemed to avoid her. Juanita found herself alone all day, and most evenings too. Henry and Miguel shared the upstairs studio for their painting sessions. If they weren't in the studio, they were in the living room watching TV or talking. Henry made it clear to Juanita that he preferred she stay out of sight when he was in the living room. When she pointed out that it was her house, he shouted at her and called her a stupid old woman. She saw Miguel cringe when he did that, but Miguel said nothing. Juanita became so uncomfortable around Henry that she spent most evenings alone in her bedroom suite.

The two friends ate few meals at the house these days. Miguel's help with shopping, food preparation, chores, and errands was now rare. On numerous occasions, Juanita found little or no food in the pantry for preparing a meal. Following her stroke she had lost weight, but her weight had stabilized when Miguel was looking after her. *Now,* she thought ruefully, *I look like a scarecrow. My clothing just hang on me.*

She seldom had time alone with Miguel. I*t seems that Henry is trying to keep me and Miguel apart. But why?* She couldn't imagine a legitimate reason. Henry had a short fuse, and seemed to dominate Miguel, who tried hard to please him. *Perhaps, Miguel is also afraid of Henry's temper.*

If it weren't for the visits by Delia and her friend, Monica, Juanita's life would have been miserably lonely. Delia usually managed to visit once a week. While the visits rarely lasted more than twenty minutes, they were the highlight of her week.

When Delia discovered the empty pantry, she offered to go to the store for her grandmother. Juanita explained that she had no cash in the house. Miguel had been paying her bills for her, so she had no checkbook. She had to wait for Miguel to go shopping. Delia was appalled! She wanted to give her brother a piece of her mind, but he was never around. Delia couldn't go to her parents for help; her father would be angry that she was visiting against his wishes. She was worried for her grandmother, and angry with her brother for his neglect.

From then on, Delia would sometimes bring food when she visited. Juanita was grateful, but felt guilty that the child was spending her allowance to feed her grandmother. The situation was becoming desperate. She would have to do something.

— CHAPTER 5 —

Oregon Coast
Saturday, July 23

Susan and Walter pulled up in front of their Neskowin rental house in South Beach. It was less than two weeks since they first discussed a trip to the Oregon Coast over dinner in Seattle. They had visited Seattle sights on two additional days after their first tour. While Walter had enjoyed the Chilhuly Museum and Garden and the Seattle Aquarium, he preferred to hang out at Susan's place on the lake. So, they relaxed and enjoyed Lake Washington for several more days.

Three days ago, they drove south to Portland, Oregon, where they picked up picturesque Route 26 for a drive through the mountains to coastal Route 101 southbound. From there, it was only a few miles to Cannon Beach. They stayed for two nights, exploring the town and soaking up sun on the beach. Their second night in town they attended the local production of Agatha Christie's *Three Blind Mice*, at the Cannon Beach Playhouse. This morning after breakfast they began their eagerly anticipated drive south to Neskowin.

Check-in time at their rental house was 3:00 p.m. The drive between Cannon Beach and Neskowin takes only about two hours, so they stopped for a stroll and window shopping in the small, tidy town of Manzanita. Before continuing their drive south, they also took a brisk, chilly walk on the wide, but very windy beach on the edge of town.

The scenery was spectacular as they wound their way south on the Three Capes Drive. Susan suggested they stop for lunch at a small seafood café by the ocean in the quaint hill town of Oceanside. She and Scott had once enjoyed an excellent meal there. Walter was not disappointed; their fish was fresh and cooked to perfection.

At ten minutes after three they pulled up in front of their rental house in Neskowin, Oregon. They gazed at the tidy clapboard house. "What do you think, Walter? It doesn't look too bad for a last-minute booking. We were very fortunate they had a cancellation."

"I like the setting. This community appears well kept and quiet. The house looks in good repair. Shall we check out the interior?"

"Here's the lock box code." Susan handed Walter a paper. "They told me it is on a pipe at the right side of the house. I always worry that I won't be able to find it or that the code won't work."

"There you go, borrowing trouble again! Complaints would soon appear on VRBO if they didn't follow through on what they said." Susan hung her head, and then followed as Walter walked around the right side of the house. "Here's the lock box, next to the side door of the garage." He handed to paper to Susan. "Read me the code, please."

Susan read off the numbers and a minute later Walter had the box open and key in hand. He led the way up a flight of wooden stairs to the front door.

"OK, fingers crossed? Here goes." He swung open the front door and they stepped in. "This is every bit as nice as it looked online. No musty smells, bright and cheerful with nice views. Well done, Susan."

"Yes, it is nice. The open floor plan feels spacious, especially with the big windows, high ceiling, and the skylights. The décor is casual, but attractive, appropriate for a place by the beach. It's clean and appears well maintained. I like the fireplace. That will be nice on a cool evening. They told me there is wood for a fire stacked behind the house."

Susan opened drawers and cabinets. "The kitchen is large enough for the two of us to work together. All the essential equipment for cooking seems to be included."

"You check out the rest of the house. I'll bring in the luggage and the beer from the car. I'd like to sit on a comfortable lounge chair on the deck with a cold beer before we go to the grocery for supplies. What do you think, Susan?"

"I like that great idea. I'm thirsty. A cold beer would be perfect."

Susan arranged two deck chairs side-by-side facing the ocean, and placed a small side table between them. She opened the umbrella, and positioned it to provide shade from the afternoon sun. By the time Walter returned with the beer, she found two beer steins and an opener. While he loaded the beer into the refrigerator, she opened two bottles, poured the beer, and carried it to the deck.

Soon, Walter joined her. "What a lovely view of Proposal Rock and the beach. There must be substantial storms here. Look at all that driftwood. I see what you mean when you say the beach isn't crowded. There aren't more than a dozen people on the entire beach, even though we're in the heart of the summer season. Having the main living area of this house above the garage gives us a nice view, while the dunes and trees along the beachfront road give us privacy from those on the beach. I think we did well, Susan. Here's to a wonderful week." toasted Walter, clinking glasses with Susan.

"To a wonderful week." echoed Susan.

Before long, they dozed off in the warm sun, their beer only half finished. About an hour later, Walter shook Susan gently and kissed her forehead. When she opened her eyes, he ran his hand lightly over her face. To Susan, it felt like the caress of a butterfly wing.

"Susan, I'm sorry to wake you. I feared that you might get sunburnt; we've been out here over an hour. Your face and neck are getting quite red."

"Thanks, Walter." She shook her head to clear away the fog. "I drifted off into the dreamiest sleep. Have you been awake all this time?"

"No, I slept for about forty-five minutes. Then I put our luggage in the rooms and unpacked my gear. I put you in the master bedroom. There's more room for your clothing in there than in the guest room. I'm always amazed at how much women take with them when traveling! I hope you don't mind sharing a bathroom. It has a separate entrance from the hall across from the guest room. The second bath and the second guest room, both downstairs, are quite damp and musty-smelling. Best to avoid them."

"I don't mind sharing the bath, but wouldn't you prefer the master bedroom? It has a queen-size bed. The guest room has only a double."

"Don't worry about me, Susan. I'll be fine. I'm a good sleeper. Why don't you unpack? Then we can go to the grocery store and pick up something for breakfast. Tomorrow, we can go to Lincoln City for a more substantial shopping. When would you like to have dinner? Where do you suggest we eat?"

"Questions, questions!" said Susan with a fond smile that caused Walter's heart to skip a beat. She got up from the lounge chair and hugged him. "You're so organized and considerate. I could get used to having you around. Our lunch was late, and substantial. I'd rather not drive to Lincoln City for dinner. That leaves Hawk's Creek Café, Pizza, or a frozen dinner from the little grocery. Any preference?"

"I'm not hungry yet, but would like something more than pizza or a frozen dinner tonight. So, Hawk's Creek it is."

"In that case, after our grocery run, why don't we take a leisurely walk on the beach? Hawk's Creek gets very busy during summer dinner hours. It's a small place and they don't take reservations. The rush starts early, around 4:30. Let's return for dinner about 6:30. By then, the crowd should have thinned and the wait for a table shouldn't be too long."

"It's a plan. Shall we do a grocery list?"

Susan handed him a pad and pencil she had found in a drawer. What do you want for breakfast tomorrow?"

"Who knows what I'll be in the mood for? How about we pick up some eggs, bread, butter, jam, cheese, cereal, milk, orange juice, and fruit? Oh, and we'll need some tea and coffee. That gives us some options. And I'd like to get some ice cream to have while we sit in front of the fire tonight."

Susan chuckled. "I hadn't realized that mood was such a guiding force in your life. It is nice to have options. The store should have ice cream from the Tillamook Creamery. It's delicious--as good as that we had at *Tropical Dream* in Hawi when we were in Hawaii."

The next few hours passed quickly, with grocery shopping, the walk on the beach, and a quick shower before heading to Hawk's Creek Café for dinner. Walter was pleasantly surprised by the quality of their meal, unexpected for a tiny restaurant in rural Oregon. After dinner, they watched the sunset and enjoyed the ocean breezes from the deck of their rental house. Once the sun dropped below the horizon, the temperature dropped rapidly, so they moved indoors. Walter fetched wood and started a fire. Now they were sitting side by side on the comfortable sofa, watching the fire dancing in the fireplace.

"It's been a lovely day, Susan. I understand why you love the Oregon Coast. It's absolutely beautiful! The small towns are charming. The beaches are pristine and empty. I love the cliffs and forest bordering the beach. And I like the cool weather. The fire is a treat, and very romantic. Much better than central heating!"

"It has been a nice day. This remote setting recaptures the comfortable intimacy we enjoyed on our Hawaii excursions. I find the fire soothing, hypnotic, and romantic."

Walter casually draped his arm over Susan's shoulder, hoping she wouldn't pull away. She cuddled closer, resting her head on his shoulder. Walter sighed contentedly and rested his head against hers. "This feels so natural, like we are meant to be together," Walter whispered in Susan's ear.

"Ummmm, so nice," was Susan's drowsy response.

They sat quietly, enjoying the fire and their physical closeness.

Sometime later, Walter stirred. "I don't suppose I could interest you in some ice cream?"

"Only if you promise to cuddle up again after we finish it."

"That's a promise I'll be delighted to keep. Which flavor would you prefer?" Unable to settle on a single flavor, they had bought several pints.

"I think I'd enjoy the strawberry tonight."

"Your wish is my command."

Walter headed to the kitchen. He returned with one bowl of strawberry ice cream and two spoons. He handed one spoon to Susan. "I thought we should get used to sharing."

"So, you've decided that we're a permanent team?"

"Isn't that what we both said we wanted? Maybe I'm just trying to move things along. Oh, but this is good ice cream! You were right." Walter dug his spoon back into the mound in the bowl and moved a second huge spoonful to his mouth.

"Hey, Buster!" exclaimed Susan as she watched Walter eat yet another huge spoonful. "I though you said we were sharing this. If I don't eat fast, I won't get any. "

"Sorry." He watched Susan take several dainty bites. "I guess I was anxious to move on to the next course."

"The next course?" asked Susan taking another spoonful.

"You did make me promise we'd cuddle up again, did you not?" Walter scooped up the last of the ice cream, put his spoon into the empty bowl, and set it on the coffee table. He turned to Susan and cupped her face gently in his hands. They gazed into each other's eyes. Susan fought her instinct to pull back as he moved toward her. First, he gently nibbled her lips. "Better than strawberry ice cream!" Then, he gently covered her lips with his own, slowly deepening the kiss. Susan moaned deep in her throat, trembling as feelings she hadn't experienced in years rushed through her. She opened her mouth in response to Walter's searching tongue, wrapped her arms around his neck, and pulled him closer.

Walter turned his attention to her ears, then her throat, teasing with his tongue and his breath. Susan moaned again as warmth flooded her body. She gasped as he continued exploring her body. Abruptly, she stood, took his hands and pulled him upward from the sofa.

"Come," she said, leading him toward the master bedroom. "I want you to make love to me, please!"

Later, they lay together with Susan's head resting on Walter's chest, his arms wrapped around her. She was dozing. Walter gently disentangled himself, lifting Susan's head to her pillow. As he sat on the edge of the bed, Susan cried urgently. "Don't go! Stay here with me."

"I'll be right back dearest Susan. We left the fire burning. I need to make sure it has died out."

A few minutes later, Walter returned. "I banked the fire and closed the screen. It should soon burn out. But my need for you is still burning brightly. Where were we before I left?" he reached for Susan.

— CHAPTER 6 —

Sunday, July 24

Susan lay quietly, gazing at Walter. She smiled, remembering the night before. He had been a wonderful lover, kind, considerate, gentle, taking his time and wanting to please her. This morning she felt like a different person.

It had been years since the last time she had made love with Scott. Her sense of betraying him had made her fearful of taking this step with Walter. She had also worried about whether Walter would be disappointed in her as a lover.

What is it about me that I always worry about what might go wrong, rather than anticipating the possibilities? No more, she vowed.

None of her fears had been realized. Here she was next to the man she loved. He had not been disappointed with her. He had wanted more. She felt like a contented cat. Slowly, she stretched, working the usual morning aches from her joints. Walter slumbered on.

Susan glanced at the clock on the bedside table. Eight-ten a.m., later than she had slept in months! Knowing that Walter would probably sleep for another hour or more, Susan eased from the bed, grabbed her robe, and headed for the shower.

The warm water eased her achy joints. Susan felt fresh and invigorated. She slipped on her robe, afraid to rummage in the closet for fear of waking Walter prematurely, and headed for the kitchen to make coffee.

The wrap-around deck was shaded at this hour, except for one small sunny spot on the eastern portion behind the kitchen. Susan moved a chair into that spot and settled in with her coffee. She luxuriated in the warmth of the sun. No one was out and about at this hour. A small thicket of mixed pine and deciduous trees next to her spot in the sunshine hid the neighboring house and gave her privacy. She watched in amusement as a Steller's jay noisily scolded a cat dozing on the deck railing.

Susan thought again about the previous night. She recalled when Walter brought the ice cream in a single bowl and commented that they should get used to sharing. When she had replied that his comment seemed to assume a permanent future for the two of them, he had said something about trying to move things along. Her prior reluctance to engage in a physical relationship had been the primary impediment to a shared future. How she had wanted a physical relationship! Finally, last night she had shut down her concern that she was betraying Scott and gave of herself fully.

Walter had been extraordinarily patient and understanding of her feelings. Not many men would have been so undemanding. But, he had clearly decided that it was time for her to move past her inhibitions and commit all of herself to their relationship. She was grateful, both for his patience, and for taking the risk to push her. Now, the whole world seemed to lie before her. The final ties binding her to Scott had been severed. She was free to live her life without feeling that she was betraying her past. It was extraordinary!

Susan returned to the kitchen for another cup of coffee. She debated looking in on Walter, but decided to let him sleep. Then, she heard the sound of the shower, so headed for the bedroom to dress. As she slipped into her sandals, Walter wandered in from the bathroom, a towel around his waist. His wet hair was askew, his body lean, muscular, and shiny with moisture. When he saw her his face lit up with a smile that radiated like the sun. Susan's heart skipped a beat.

"I thought I heard you in here. Good morning, Susan." He opened his arms and she moved into them. He kissed her long and deeply. Susan responded eagerly, letting herself drift in a rush of feeling. When he released her, he muttered, "If I weren't so hungry, I'd take you right back to bed! But, I'm starving, and I still feel a glow of contentment from last night. Please start preparing us a big breakfast. I'll dress, then come help you with the preparations. I assume you will have no objections if I move my things from the guest room into this one?"

"I'd be very disappointed if you didn't."

—— CHAPTER 7 ——

Friday, July 29

The week in Neskowin passed quickly. Susan and Walter spent their first day in Lincoln City, stocking up on groceries, buying hiking shoes at the outlet mall, and enjoying a late lunch. Monday they spent sunning, reading, and strolling on the Neskowin beach. Subsequently, they spent days sightseeing further afield. They visited the National Dunes Park near Florence. After they climbed up the 30 foot dunes to admire the panoramic view, they enjoyed the thrill of sliding back down. Next, they drove to the Sea Lion Cave. While the sea lions were interesting to watch, the smell of sea lion bodies and poop in the cave soon drove them away.

On the return trip, they stopped in Newport. Walter particularly enjoyed the marine museum. Susan preferred watching the boats coming and going from the marina while they lunched by the bay. "When I see the boats, I imagine the interesting places they have been and dream of taking an exotic cruise. Would you believe I've never been on a cruise? Scott never wanted to go; he said he gets seasick and can't swim."

"I'd be delighted to take you on a cruise, sweetheart, once we can fit it in our busy schedule."

Following dinner that evening, they carried blankets to the beach, built a fire from driftwood, and cuddled up by the fire. As they talked, they gazed in amazement at the night sky. So far away from city lights the sky was filled with more stars than they could ever have imagined, all sparkling like diamonds against the blackness. Eventually, the evening chill drove them to return, reluctantly, to the house.

The next day, they hiked the Cascade Head Trail. It proved to be a long, steep climb up the mountain, full of switchbacks, with several stream crossings. Both Walter and Susan had to stop repeatedly to catch their breath; neither had hiked in years. Where the trail emerged from the forest at the top, the sea glittered in the sunshine beyond a meadow filled with wildflowers. As they neared the edge of the cliff, they could see the shoreline running for miles in both directions, waves pounding the shore. It was spectacular! Susan began taking pictures with her mobile phone.

"Come, sit and snuggle with me for a bit," said Walter. He grabbed her hand to pull her down next to him amid the rich scent of wildflowers. "You've taken enough photos."

Susan resisted his efforts. "We'll be glad to have photos to remind us of our trip when our memories start to fade," she protested impatiently. "And I want photos to use as inspiration for paintings. It's unlikely we'll ever be here again."

"I look forward to seeing what you'll paint. But, sweetheart, this view is breathtaking, definitely worth the struggle to get to the top. Sit down and enjoy it for a while."

Susan, annoyed continued taking pictures. "Don't tell me what to do, Walter. I'll sit down when I've finished."

"I'm sorry, Susan. I got carried away. It's such a romantic spot. I want us to enjoy it together. Let's feast on the riot of color, smell the scents, and feel the warm breeze caressing our skin. Besides, we need to regain some energy for our downhill trip. We don't want to slip and fall on some of those wet, steep sections. We can't afford any broken bones!"

Eventually Susan dropped to the ground beside him. "I've taken enough pictures now. I'm ready to relax and soak it all in." She leaned against him and concentrated on the view.

Yesterday, they kayaked on the Nestucca River in Pacific City. The downstream leg to the ocean was relaxing, the return upstream was demanding. They relaxed over lunch at a café overlooking the river until they felt recovered. Following lunch, they poked around the shops in town. Susan's favorite memories of the day were of the river otters that poked their heads above the water as the kayak passed. That evening, they dined at the *Bay House* restaurant in Lincoln City, a favorite of Susan's for its excellent food and service. She also liked the quietly elegant interior, a contrast to the raw tidal mud flats of the Bay, which it overlooked.

Today was their last full day in Neskowin. They planned to explore the tide pools around Proposal Rock this morning. Last evening, Walter had checked the tide tables and announced that low tide would be at 8:36 a.m. It was now 7:45 a.m. and they were ready to explore.

Only a few other folks were about when they arrived on the beach. To reach the tide pools, Susan and Walter had to wade through icy cold river water that flowed swiftly between the beach and Proposal Rock. Once through the river, they could walk right up to the monolith. Above the trees clinging to its slopes, sea birds circled. A bald eagle sat on a large tree that leaned seaward on the south side of the rock. The tide pools at its base were filled with starfish, sea anemones, spider crabs, and other sea creatures. Some deeper pools contained fish that had been trapped as the water receded. On one side of the rock was a shallow sea cave. Mussels clung to its walls.

"So much life here!" exclaimed Susan. "Usually, it's unseen because the rock is inaccessible. Low tide exposes a whole new world. I'm glad we made the effort to get out here this morning."

"It was worth it," agreed Walter. "Each side of the rock seems to have a unique ecosystem."

Sometime later, Walter exclaimed, "Susan, look! The tide is coming in. That area by the rock was dry not long ago. Now it's being washed by waves. Nearly everyone is heading back across the river. We should soon join them. Otherwise, it may become dangerous to cross. Before we go, stand on that sandbar by the rock so I can take your picture."

Walter pulled his phone from his back pocket as Susan posed saucily before the rock. He snapped the picture and put the phone back in his pocket. Then he knelt before Susan.

"I love you, Susan Brooks. Will you marry me? Make me the happiest man on this earth. Please say yes!"

"Of course, I'll marry you, you wonderful, goofy man. I look forward to spending the rest of my life with you. Now please get up before you get soaking wet!"

Walter rose and reached for Susan. They wrapped their arms around each other and enjoyed a long, lingering kiss. Suddenly a sneaker wave knocked them to the ground. They arose sputtering, wet through and through. "Oh! That was cold!" exclaimed Walter.

"The Pacific Ocean is never warm here," observed Susan, laughing through chattering teeth. "Maybe you've noticed that you hardly ever see anyone in the water."

"Now that you mention it, I did wonder why most folks stayed on the beach and the children played mostly in the river."

"It has to do both with the cold temperature of the water and the fact that there can be dangerous rip currents just a short way out. I never go into the water here. Even in California, I find the water too cold. It's not warm like the Pacific Ocean is in Hawaii."

Walter put his arm around Susan's waist and helped steady her as they crossed the river to the safety of the beach. Back at the house they shared a steamy shower. Dressed in robes, they prepared breakfast. Following their meal, Susan began washing dishes. Walter briefly disappeared into the bedroom, and then returned to lend a hand.

When they had finished, Walter took Susan by the hand and led her to the sofa. "Please sit down, Susan." He sat down beside her and then handed her a small box from the pocket of his robe. Susan opened it and stared at the exquisite diamond ring.

"I was afraid to take the ring to the beach with me. I feared I would drop it in the sand and lose it. Let me put it on your finger, Susan." Walter took the ring from the box and put it on Susan's left-hand ring-finger. "Now it's official. We are going to get married and spend the rest of our lives together, my love!" They reached for each other and enjoyed a long kiss, then clung together, relishing the warm feelings that enveloped them.

When Susan finally drew away, she gazed at Walter with tears in her eyes. "You are the most amazing man, Walter Conway! You had this all planned when you suggested this trip, didn't you?"

"Well, I thought it might help you get past your concerns about betraying Scott if I could get you on neutral ground, away from the house where the two of you lived for so long. When you were telling me about the Oregon Coast and mentioned Proposal Rock, I thought it was too good an opportunity to pass up. I came prepared, just in case. I'm so glad it has worked out as I hoped. I'm a very happy man today, Susan."

"I'm happier than I could possibly have imagined, Walter. You are a special man. Your upbeat and flexible character supplements my weaknesses—a tendency to always see the negatives, and to be rigid in my thinking. You steer me around my fears, almost before I've realized what you've done. You make me feel safe, protected, yet adventurous. Being independent and dealing alone with what life threw my way was wearing me down."

"And I was getting tired of not having someone to look

after occasionally. Do you still want to spend our last day here sunning on the beach? We can take a walk before dinner for exercise. Tomorrow, we'll be back on the road again."

"Good point, Walter. A walk would be great. I'm happy to hang out in the sunshine the rest of the time. Shall we have a final dinner at Hawk's Creek tonight? We are running short on supplies."

"I like that suggestion. And I have another. Perhaps after lunch, we can discuss the possibility of breaking up our return trip. There's somewhere I'd love to see, and it's not a long detour from our route back to Seattle. We can look at the maps of Washington and Oregon and see what would be involved."

"What is this place?"

"The Columbia River Gorge. Have you visited there?"

"No, I haven't. It's somewhere I've often thought I'd like to go. What a lovely idea! I assume we'll stop overnight somewhere along the way."

"Absolutely. I thought we could stay in Portland tomorrow night, or even two consecutive nights. That way we can see the sights without wearing ourselves out. We're not kids anymore. If I don't rest during the day, I have difficulty staying up late."

"You make yourself sound like an old man, Walter. You've always seemed young and energetic to me. However, your comments made me realize that I don't know your age; it hasn't come up. I guess I always assumed we were about the same age. Just how old are you?"

"I do hope my age won't change your mind about marrying me. I'm sure I'm older than you are. I was seventy-three in April. What about you, Susan?"

"I'll be sixty-eight in September. So, as I thought, we're not far apart in age. Stop talking as if you're ancient, Walter. We'll get there soon enough. No need to rush. Let's concentrate on keeping healthy and maintaining a young outlook."

"You're right, of course, Susan. I didn't mean to sound like

I'm feeling old. I don't. On the other hand, I must make some accommodations in my daily routine. I intend to keep on enjoying life, especially now that you're to be part of it. Are you ready to soak up some sunshine? After lunch, we can plan our Columbia River Gorge trip."

"Perfect. I'll just change into my swimsuit. Meet you here with our beach gear in ten minutes."

Several hours on the beach passed quickly. Susan and Walter sat with their backs against a huge log that had washed up onto the sand. They watched as three children with shovels dug into the sandbanks of the river, trying to create a pool they could fill with water. The running water, and later the incoming tide, kept washing away their structure. Despite the setbacks, they were not deterred. Several dogs ran up and down the beach, splashed in the river, and then shook off the water, drenching some children who were building a structure with pieces of driftwood and their towels. The ocean shimmered in the sunlight. A gentle breeze attenuated excessive heat from the sun. Further up the beach, three boys set up a goal using driftwood, then took turns kicking a soccer ball and playing goalie. Susan and Walter basked in the sun and watched the activity. They reluctantly returned to their house for lunch.

After lunch, they perused their maps and travel guides to plan their trip to the Columbia River Gorge. Then they relaxed with a beer on the deck before taking a final stroll on the beach. They walked slowly, trying to prolong the experience and imprint memories of this beautiful place. By five-thirty that evening they were at Hawk's Creek Café for dinner. Later, they again shared a bowl of ice cream in front of a crackling fire. An hour later, they retired for the night, walking to the bedroom with their arms around each other.

— CHAPTER 8 —

Saturday, July 30

Morning brought a flurry of activity. Although check-out was not until noon, Walter and Susan had agreed to leave no later than ten o'clock. Instructions posted by the owners of their rental house specified that before leaving, tenants should wash and put away all dishes, wipe down surfaces, empty the refrigerator, wash and dry bed linens and towels, and put all trash in the outdoor trash bins. Up to two hundred dollars would be deducted from the security deposit for failure to comply with instructions. Walter wanted to take the hit. Susan preferred to comply with orders to avoid paying the penalty. Despite Walter's pleading, Susan insisted she would do as instructed. They almost had their first argument. Walter eventually gave in and helped with the chores. They left at 9:55 a.m., tense and tired. As they drove, Walter initiated a discussion on priorities.

"Susan, I understand that you're used to following instructions and hate to spend money unnecessarily on a penalty. Please, think about this. Having done all that work, we are now hot, sweaty, and tired. The maximum penalty we'd have paid is two hundred dollars. Isn't it worth two hundred dollars to feel fresh and relaxed for our long drive, and to leave with happy memories, rather than frustration and exhaustion? If money were a problem, I'd happily have agreed to do the work. But we're fortunate enough to have plenty for small luxuries. What is money for if not to make life easier and more pleasant?"

Susan looked at Walter thoughtfully. "Deep down, I know you're right. Something in my upbringing makes me very careful with money. I probably got it from my mother. As a product of the Great Depression, she always feared something would happen to leave her without enough food, or a place to live. Scott used to tell me that I was tight, not frugal, or careful, but tight. I never spent on material things or comforts. My friends enjoyed regular massages, pedicures, manicures, and new clothing and accessories every season. I was busy with my job and my family, so I didn't have much time for such things. I preferred to spend my time and my money on experiences. Activities with family and friends, travel, concerts, or the theater gave me long-term memories, not just momentary pleasure.

"I'm sorry to have annoyed you, Walter. I appreciate that you helped me to get the work done. In the future, I promise to deal with such situations intellectually, using cold logic to fight the feelings I experience when I spend unnecessarily. We should have discussed this last night; you could have made your point and I'd have had time to consider it. I'd rather part with the money than upset you. Forgive me, please."

"You're forgiven, Susan," said Walter, taking her hand in his and giving it a squeeze. "I love you. We're still getting to know each other. No doubt we'll have lots of surprises along the way. We generally share values, so if we discuss our feelings and why we do what we do, we should find mutually agreeable solutions. When we can't, we'll have to agree to disagree. As long as neither of us holds a grudge at those times, we'll be fine."

"Thank you for understanding, Walter. You're so caring and considerate. I love that about you. I'm grateful that you tell me how you feel when I do something you don't like. From now on, when faced with a decision on whether to spend money, let's ask the question, 'Does this enhance our quality of life or is it throwing money away?' I'm pretty sure that we can agree on the answer. Now, if you're too tired, I'll be happy to drive for a while."

"Thanks for offering, Susan. I'm okay for now."

Traffic remained light, and the trip through rural Oregon was relaxing, scenic, and pleasant, winding past vineyards, forested hills, and farms with cows and horses grazing. The road passed through several small towns with shops that were obviously empty or boarded up, reflecting a disappearing world. As they approached Salem, traffic picked up considerably. Scenic views were replaced by urban sprawl.

They arrived at their hotel in Portland at 1:15 p.m. After registering and putting the luggage in their room, they strolled around town. For lunch, they checked out the food truck scene for which Portland was famous. The range of choices was mind boggling! There was everything from hot dogs and burgers to chicken, seafood, sandwich wraps, barbeque, Southern cuisine, vegan, Thai food, Mexican food, Korean food, Chinese food, and more. They finally settled on Greek gyros, served with salad and tszsiki in portable containers. They sat on a bench in the waterfront park and watched the river traffic and pedestrian activities as they ate.

Afterwards, they wandered north toward Chinatown. There, they visited the fascinating Chinese garden. It was like entering a totally different world. When they left the garden, they wandered west on Burnside Street to Powell's bookstore, fabled to be the largest bookstore in the United States. The vintage building covered an entire city block. Inside were new books, used books, and antique books, a collection too vast to see, even if one spent a full day at the store. After browsing for an hour, they purchased several books. These they carried to the in-house café, where they relaxed over cappuccinos before they returned to their hotel for a much-appreciated late afternoon rest.

That evening, they decided to stroll the neighborhood near the hotel, hoping to find an interesting restaurant where they could have dinner. As they were leaving the hotel, Walter stopped suddenly. "Susan, I just realized that I left my wallet on the dresser in our room. We need to go back."

"You go, Walter. It's such a lovely evening. I'll wait here and enjoy watching the pedestrians while you retrieve your wallet."

"Okay, Susan. I'll be right back."

The doorman held the door for Walter, and then followed him into the hotel. As soon as the doorman disappeared, a middle-aged man with a shaggy haircut and peppered beard, wearing a plaid, short-sleeved shirt, khaki trousers, and Birkenstock sandals approached Susan.

"How much, lady?"

Susan turned toward him. "I beg your pardon? What did you say?"

"How much?"

Puzzled, Susan frowned. "What are you talking about?"

"Don't play games," he replied. "You know what I want. Don't play coy and try to up the price."

"Mister, I think you have the wrong person. I'm just waiting for my friend to return."

"Sure you are," he sneered. "Maybe you just don't like my looks. In your profession you don't have the right to be picky." He grabbed her arm and pulled her toward the hotel. Susan struggled to free her arm.

"Let go of me!"

The doorman returned and saw Susan struggling. He approached the pair. "Mister, unhand that woman instantly. She is a guest of this hotel. What do you think you're doing? Move away or I'll be forced to call the police."

Walter emerged from the hotel and noted the trio. He moved toward them.

"What's going on here? What are you doing with my fiancé? Let go of her or I'll let you have it where it will hurt!" Walter raised his fists as if he were going to strike the man. Susan snatched her arm away and ran to Walter who wrapped his arms around her. Realizing he had been mistaken about Susan, the man turned and walked away, muttering under his breath.

"What was that all about?" demanded Walter of the doorman.

Susan responded to his question. "I was standing here watching the pedestrians after you left. That man approached me and demanded to know 'the price'. I didn't realize what he was talking about."

"It's my fault", said the doorman. "I wasn't at my post. When I held the door for you to enter the hotel, Sir, the front desk clerk indicated that he wanted a word. I went into the hotel to talk with him. After the conversation, I took advantage of the moment to use the restroom, leaving the front door unattended. That man assumed that your lady friend was a prostitute. Your energetic approach with fists raised gave him a good scare."

"Why would he assume that? Does she look like a prostitute to you?"

"Certainly not, sir! I suspect that the man is a visitor to the city. He may have picked up a prostitute here at the hotel in the past. You see, our company just recently bought the hotel and refurbished it. After the 2008 recession, the economy was very bad. Not only the hotel, but much of downtown Portland felt the effects. Many businesses failed and remained empty for years. This part of town became somewhat seedy.

"We learned after we bought the hotel that a group of prostitutes had rented a suite of rooms during the recession. I was told that they would stand outside the hotel and wait for customers. Presumably, the man who approached your wife visited during that prior time. If I had been at my post, he wouldn't have dared approach. I apologize to you both for my dereliction of duty."

"Thank you for your apology and for intervening. I hate to think what might have happened if not for your timely intervention," said Walter, shaking the doorman's hand. "I must admit that this episode has diminished my appetite for adventure tonight. We had intended to stroll around looking for a romantic restaurant. At this point, if you could suggest a good place to eat nearby, I'd be grateful."

"Does Chinese food appeal to the two of you?" Susan and Walter nodded. "Then I suggest the *Peking Moon*. It has excellent food at a reasonable price and is only two blocks north on the other side of the street."

They soon found the small Chinese restaurant. After they ordered, Walter looked at Susan with concern. "Are you sure you are alright? That must have been a terrible shock! I'll never again leave you standing alone outside a hotel."

"I'm fine, Walter. I'll admit I was scared when it happened. I had no idea that standing alone on a busy city street could be so dangerous! I've spent so much time in the suburbs in recent years that my city antennae are out of order. I'll feel quite safe as long as you're with me. I was impressed by how you came charging to my rescue. Would you really have hit him? You could have been hurt if he hit back!"

"When I first worked for the FBI, I was trained in self-defense techniques. I haven't used them in years, but could still probably put up a passable defense. I'd rather it weren't necessary. You and I need to be more alert to risk when we're in an urban environment."

"I agree. But, do you know, in retrospect, it's a compliment that he thought I looked good enough that he would pay for sex—at my age!"

"You look great, for any age. But, I'm not willing to share

your good looks or anything else about you, now that I've finally gotten you. Call me selfish, if you wish."

"I like it that way. I don't want to share you, either. Oh look, here comes our dinner. I could eat a horse."

An excellent dinner restored their good spirits. Back in their room, they discussed their day and their plans for the next one. Since coming to Portland, they had heard much about Washington Park and its hiking trails, the International Rose Test Garden, and Portland's famous Japanese Garden. It seemed a pity to leave without seeing them. They decided to spend one more day in Portland before visiting the Columbia River Gorge.

— CHAPTER 9 —

Sunday, July 31

Susan and Walter arose early. They lingered over a leisurely breakfast, then drove to Washington Park. The day was warm and sunny, with a cooling breeze. They parked near the *International Rose Test Garden* and strolled toward the garden entrance. As they approached, they stopped and stared in amazement. Spread over many acres below them were roses in vivid shades of pink, orange, red, yellow, white, and more. Never had they seen so many different varieties—tea roses, floribundas, old English roses, miniatures, climbing roses. The edges of the garden flowed onto park grounds filled with rhododendrons, azaleas, and tall trees. On the horizon beyond the park was the Portland skyline with snow-covered Mount Hood looming above the city.

"What a breathtaking view!" Susan exclaimed. "It's even more beautiful than Seattle."

Holding hands, they wandered into the garden, strolling among the explosion of color and scent. "I've never seen such healthy roses before. The fragrances are heavenly."

"The man at the front desk told me that Portland has the perfect climate for growing roses. That's why they have the

International Test Garden here. It's an incredible setting for growing roses, with Mount Hood in the distance and the rhododendrons and beautiful trees of the park surrounding them. How wonderful it must be to live nearby and be able to visit this whenever you please. It doesn't even have an entrance fee."

"It is special, Walter. Washington Park is beautiful. I read that, in addition to the rose garden, it contains a Japanese garden, a zoo, an arboretum, and a forestry center. Portland has over 100 miles of hiking trails within city limits, many of them in this park!"

"I didn't know that, Susan. Truly impressive. I wonder how many Portlanders take advantage of all this. Are these residents we see, or are they tourists like us? I suspect that the tourists outnumber the locals. If I lived here, I'd visit often. Shall we spend another half-hour here? Afterwards, we can catch the tram to the Japanese garden. Since we plan to hike later, riding up the long hill to the garden sounds like a better plan than walking."

"I agree. Yes, another half-hour here sounds perfect."

Three hours later, Susan and Walter settled on the benches of a picnic table under some trees near the rose garden with sandwiches and ice cream they purchased from a nearby pushcart vendor.

"I really enjoyed visiting the Japanese garden, Walter. No wonder it's reputed to be one of the best examples of a Japanese garden outside of Japan. The designer cleverly incorporated natural features of the landscape. That cliff behind the koi pond, with the waterfall dropping down its face into the pond is awesome. The streams and ponds throughout the varied elevations of the garden, together with the paths, arched bridges, flowering shrubs and trees, and large swaths of greenery create a vibrant landscape, dotted with islands of peace and tranquility. The Japanese-style buildings, the raked gravel gardens, the mimosa arbor, and shaping of the trees all contribute to the ambiance. It's easy to imagine you are in Japan."

"Best of all, from my point of view," commented Walter, "is that even with so many visitors roaming the garden, there are private spaces to sit and contemplate the beauty. It felt so private when we sat on that bench in the lower garden, drinking in the scents of flowers, sounds of running water, and movement of the birds. I was almost unaware of other people wandering by. It is one amazing place, an oasis tucked away from the world!"

"I've always thought I'd like to have a Japanese-style garden around my house. One could certainly obtain some useful ideas on how to create one by observing what's been done here."

"Well, my dear, let's keep that in mind. Once we've decided where we want to live, I'll help you create our own small Japanese garden. I'm assuming, of course, that you have no desire to live in a city apartment."

"I think I'd wither and die in a city apartment! I'm grateful that you love nature as much as I do. Speaking of which, we had planned to go hiking this afternoon. I'm tired. We've been walking all morning. I'd be happy to forgo the hike for some quiet time reading one of the books we bought yesterday. Afterwards, we could have dinner at one of the restaurants overlooking the marina, followed by an after-dinner stroll and some people-watching by the river."

"You're becoming a mind-reader, Susan. Then, we need to get some sleep, so we can start early for our trip to the Columbia River Gorge tomorrow."

They deposited the remnants of lunch in the trash barrel and strolled arm in arm to the car. Walter's cell phone rang. He glanced at the number.

"It's my son, Keith. Do you mind if I take the call?"

"Of course not. Say hello from me."

"Hello Keith. How is everything down there? Everyone is well? Work is fine?"

Susan gazed at the scenery as Walter chatted with his son. She had enjoyed their visit to Portland. Recalling Walter's comments about how he would visit the sights frequently if he lived here, she thought about Seattle. She had always liked Seattle with its mountains, the Puget Sound, numerous parks, and a busy waterfront. But Portland's Washington Park was unique and its waterfront people-friendly. They both loved Hawaii. How were they going to make a decision about where to live? This wasn't going to be easy.

"Okay, son. Say hello to the family for me. Thanks for calling. I love you. Bye."

Walter closed his phone and turned to Susan. "Keith says hello. Everyone is fine. The kids are doing well in school and Jan is busy with all her volunteer work. However, he did say something odd--about things disappearing from their pantry. Jan is sure that food is disappearing on a regular basis. The kids deny eating any of it. Weird, huh?"

"Did he say what kind of food was disappearing?"

"Yes, Jan told him it was staples, whatever that means."

"Walter! Surely you know that staples are necessities like flour, sugar, pasta, canned goods. Certainly, if that sort of thing is disappearing, it's very unlikely to be the kids. Snacks, yes, but not staples. Has much gone missing? Perhaps she just forgot to replenish? That's happened to me on many occasions. What does Jan plan to do?"

"She plans to do an inventory so she can be sure of what goes missing. Apparently, she considered the possibility that she just lost track. She told Keith it had happened several times. She concluded it was more than her being absent-minded, unless she's becoming consistently forgetful. Once Jan investigates, this may turn out to be just a tempest in a teapot! Maybe she did just lose track.

"Keith asked when we're coming to visit. I didn't tell him we're engaged, and I put him off about the visit. You and I need to discuss how to announce our engagement, and select dates for our wedding and for visiting our children. Let's see if we can talk in the next day or so, okay?"

"Yes, we need to do that. It feels overwhelming! Having plans will make it seem more manageable. Maybe we can have that conversation tomorrow evening when we're in Hood River. We should have some quiet time at the end of the day."

"Deal. Now let's get back to the hotel. I'd enjoy an afternoon nap. And maybe a little loving first?"

— CHAPTER 10 —

Monday, August 1

Susan and Walter sat at their window table in the dining room of the historic Columbia River Gorge Hotel. They sipped their wine and watched the windsurfers on the river far below. It had been a full, eventful day since they left Portland at eight that morning.

Traffic was moderate on the interstate highway heading east toward the Columbia River Gorge. Once they passed Troutdale, Oregon, signs of human occupation began to dissipate. Eventually, nature took center stage. The road ran through a narrow plain. Thickly forested, high granite cliffs on their right hosted waterfalls that spilled in thin ribbons from the top and could be glimpsed through gaps in the trees. On their left, the broad Columbia River meandered alongside the road. A chained cluster of four barges pushed by a tugboat moved slowly upriver. The foothills of the Cascade Mountains rose gently on the Washington side of the river.

Their first stop was at Multnomah Falls. They followed a path uphill from the parking lot to a pool. Here they could see the lower level of the double-decker falls spill from above, forming a curtain of water as it fell. After watching the show for a time, they meandered upward along a winding, wooded trail that led to an arched bridge suspended above the upper pool. From here, they watched the water pour over the edge of the cliff above and drop seventy feet into the upper pool before it cascaded over the edge into the lower pool, and then into a stream that carried it off toward the parking lot.

"This is spectacular! I've always thought Hawaii was beautiful, but this surpasses anything I've seen there. Susan, look at the beautiful colors of the leaves, moss, and that pale green lichen growing on the rocks. It's a symphony in green!"

Susan was in her element, taking photographs to record their visit. "I'd love to be able to capture the cool, moist feel of this place in a painting, but I'm afraid I don't have the talent. I'll have to settle for capturing the visual aspects of the setting." She turned to look at the mountains across the Columbia River to the north. Seen from this height, the view was breath-taking. "It doesn't matter which direction you look, there is overwhelming beauty. I'm so glad you thought of doing this side trip, Walter."

After leaving Multnomah Falls, they continued their trip east on an old two-lane highway that edged along the base of the cliff and past a series of waterfalls to the town of Cascade Locks. At the town dock, they boarded a paddle-wheeler that took them up the Columbia River toward the locks above Stevenson, Washington, then down-river, past Cascade Locks, under the Bridge of the Gods, and then back upriver to the dock. Before leaving town, they picked up sandwiches from the local Subway. A few miles east of town, they found a state park with a picnic table that overlooked the river. There, they enjoyed watching the shore birds and river traffic while they ate their lunch.

After passing Hood River, Oregon, they left the interstate and picked up an old country road. It crossed the Hood River, then veered inland as it meandered through farm country and orchards. Further east the road began to climb. On both sides of the river, they saw signs that the climate was becoming dryer.

On the Oregon side of the Columbia River, the trees were getting shorter. On the Washington side, trees were replaced by grasslands, initially green, but eventually golden, and then brown. The road led to an overlook with 360-degree views that included both states. Through the center of the landscape ran the Columbia River.

Susan and Walter could clearly see lush rain forest when they looked back toward the west. To the east, they saw a desert landscape. The hills on both sides of the river gradually lost their rounded tops and became rock escarpments, reminiscent of Idaho. To the north of the river, beyond the foothills, they could see snow-covered mountains--Mount Adams, Mount Saint Helens with its flat top, and, in the far Northwest, the tip of Mount Baker. To the southwest, was Mount Hood, snow cap glistening in the sun as it loomed over the rural landscape of Hood River County with its farms and fruit orchards. Susan and Walter stood transfixed, arms around each other, imprinting the sight in their memories. No words were needed.

When they finally returned to their car, they decided not to continue on to The Dalles, Oregon, as planned. Anything would be an anticlimax after what they had just seen. Instead, they returned to Hood River, where they had a reservation for the night at the historic Columbia River Gorge Hotel.

The hotel had once been a grand place. It was an elegant, three-story Spanish-style building set on a cliff overlooking the Columbia River. A lovely garden surrounded the hotel and provided a path for strolling. A stream meandered through the garden, around the south side of the building, then spilled over the cliff into the Columbia River below.

The hotel interior retained its formal, elegant architecture, with high, arched ceilings supported by marble pillars. The vast spaces were filled with period furniture. The guest rooms, also furnished in period furniture, showed signs of wear. One could imagine what it must have been like in earlier, more prosperous times. The hotel even retained the original elevator, operated by a hotel employee. No modern self-operated conveyance here!

After they checked in, Susan and Walter strolled in the gardens, and then settled on a bench overlooking the river and the waterfall.

"You know, Susan, these last few days have been special. I really like this area of the country. The weather has been perfect. Portland feels like a friendlier city than Seattle. It has such fabulous amenities too, the Chinese and Japanese Gardens, Washington Park, the River Walk Park, Chinatown, The Pearl District, and more. The surrounding areas also have much to offer—the Columbia River Gorge, Hood River with its orchards and vineyards, the high desert, fairly easy access to the Oregon Coast. I understand that Mount Hood has not only excellent hiking, but also great skiing, and only an hour's drive from Portland. Then there is Mount Saint Helens, with its post-eruption regeneration and recreational opportunities to explore. Traffic is heavy around Portland, but once you get outside the city, it quickly dissipates. It seems considerably less congested than Seattle. And, of course, they have their light rail system."

"Are you thinking you'd like to live here?"

"The thought did enter my mind. It's something to think about. We both have children and grandchildren in California, a short flight from Portland. I couldn't live in California. Those freeways with six lanes in each direction are intimidating. To find what I consider manageable traffic there, one must travel far from major cities. Rural areas can be a problem when it comes to medical care and other amenities.

"Portland has a major airport and numerous flights to Hawaii, which we both love. I checked it out last night," said Walter sheepishly as Susan looked at him inquiringly. "From Portland, we could drive to Canada for occasional visits. British Columbia is beautiful. It's not a bad flight to Mexico. I know I'm jumping ahead. We're not ready to make such decisions, but it's something to consider among our options."

"Everything you say is true, Walter. After seeing this area, I think I like it better than Seattle. It also has the advantage that it doesn't hold memories for me of my life with Scott. However, you've never experienced Northwest weather. As you've discovered, summers are beautiful. No other place has such perfect summers. Much of the rest of the year is cloudy, with rain or drizzle. Portland is probably a bit dryer than Seattle, but still is grey much of the year. Although there's not much ice or snow, the greyness and dampness can get depressing, believe me. Spending part of the year here, part in Hawaii would help with that problem. That means maintaining two residences. We must decide if we're going to be up to that as we age. Do I sound like a spoilsport?"

"No, Susan. You sound realistic. Perhaps we should list our criteria for what we want in our place of residence, then generate a list of places that meet most of those criteria. We could even think about living abroad. We have lots of choices. Making a decision is what will be hard."

"I would love to visit Europe again," Susan said, wistfully. "I'm not so sure I'd like to live there. It's so far from our children and grandchildren. As I get older, I'm less and less enthusiastic about flying, especially long flights. Not only is there the issue of my stiff joints which get worse when I sit for any length of time, but flying has become downright uncomfortable. People are getting taller and broader, while seats get narrower and closer together front to back. My claustrophobia is becoming a problem when I fly. There I go, seeing the negatives again."

"You make legitimate points, Susan. Fortunately, we can afford to fly business class, which will help with your issues. Since that is expensive, we would have to be careful about how often we fly. At the moment, we have more urgent decisions to make than one about where to live. Perhaps we should postpone our discussion about that until later.

"When and how do we tell our children about our engagement? Do we send out announcements? Do we call each of them individually? What about our wedding? Do we try to have a wedding with everyone there? If so, where should it be?"

"Decisions, decisions! Lord, but I hate decisions!" exclaimed Susan. "I'm a procrastinator. Because I don't like making decisions, I put them off as long as possible. You're right, of course, Walter. We need to deal with these questions now. I can offer you a list of pros and cons for each option, if that would help.

"Regarding our engagement, it's simplest if we each tell our own children about it. The wedding is another matter. The logistics of trying to get everyone together seems like a nightmare to me. With my daughter on the east coast, your son, Dan, in Chicago, and our other three children in various parts of California, I don't know where we could hold a wedding that wouldn't entail considerable expense for at least some of the children and their families. We could offer to pay their expenses, but having everyone available on the same date seems difficult. I'd rather we just get married quietly before a justice of the peace or, if you prefer, a minister.

"On the other hand, I haven't met two of your children. You haven't met my son. We once talked about visiting all of our children and their families before we made any commitments. That implied that we wanted their approval. Obviously, we aren't asking permission. We've already decided to marry. If we ask them all to attend our wedding, we wouldn't need to visit each family. We could meet each other's children and our respective families could all meet each other as well.

"If we go ahead and get married quietly, we can visit the children after the wedding. While that seems intimidating, it would give them a chance to get to know us as a couple without the pressure of a crowd. All our children and grandchildren together would be some crowd! Getting married before we visit also takes care of Kristin's question about sleeping arrangements. Some of our children might not approve of our sharing a bedroom before we're married. Once we have visited all our children and their families, we'll probably appreciate some time alone. We can take a delayed honeymoon, or skip the honeymoon and concentrate on figuring out where we want to live. What do you think, Walter?"

"You make some excellent points, Susan. Part of me likes the idea of a big celebration and getting everyone together. I'd be happy to pay for a wedding and the expenses to get the children there. I can certainly afford it. But, as you indicated, that could be awkward. Do you think it would be worth asking their opinions on the matter when we call to tell them about the engagement?"

"That's an idea. But what if we get a split opinion, with half wanting the big wedding and half preferring that we visit after we get married? We could end up with some hurt feelings either choice we make."

"Interesting thought, my dear. Maybe we should just get married in Seattle after we meet with the lawyers and get the legal issues settled, then visit the children. If we do that, I'd still want to get our two families together. Perhaps we could invite everyone to Hawaii. They all seem to like it there. We could set a date in the winter, pay their fares, and arrange to put them up for a week. What do you think?"

"That's a lovely idea, Walter. I'm sure Kristin and her family, and Dan, in Chicago would love to have a winter vacation away from the cold. Since Keith and his family, my son Brendon, and your daughter, Celia, all like Hawaii, and as it's an easy trip from California, they'd probably agree to come. Let's do it. But, I want to help pay for the expenses. I can certainly afford to share the cost."

"We'll sort that part out later, Susan. Let's first set a date for our wedding. We'll call the kids after we get back to Seattle to let them know we're engaged. If they ask about attending the wedding, we can give them the date and tell them attendance is optional. I'd be delighted if they decide to attend. We can plan a simple wedding without the fuss, bother, and expense of putting on a show. If any of the family shows up, we'll take them out for a celebration dinner at a restaurant after the ceremony. Does that work for you?"

"That sounds like our best option, Walter. How far out do you think we should set our wedding date? Now that we've decided to get married, I'd like to do it sooner, rather than later."

"It will probably take several weeks after we get back before we can get an appointment with a lawyer to deal with estate planning. It will be a few more weeks until the lawyer has prepared documents for us to sign. Shall we look at dates a month to six weeks from now? Does that sound reasonable?"

"Six weeks allows time for unexpected delays. It would also mean that we start family visits after Labor Day. By then we'll have more choice of flights and lower fares. It also gives our children time to plan for our visits. Depending on where we'd like to spend our honeymoon, we can start our visits on the west coast and work our way east, or vice versa."

"Okay, Susan. Six weeks it is. Meanwhile, let's consider how we want to structure our finances. We'll want control of our funds while we're alive, so we can live the kind of life we want. At the same time, we want to protect our respective children's interests after we're gone. How do you feel about having joint checking and savings accounts, credit cards, and so forth?"

"I prefer joint accounts to separate accounts. It implies a sense of sharing and trust. Scott and I put our paychecks into a joint checking account to cover our recurring living expenses. We also had joint savings and investment accounts. Whenever the balance in the checking account got above a set amount, we transferred the excess into the investment account.

You and I could do something similar, depositing our regular income--Social Security checks, pension checks, and so on into a joint checking account. Are you comfortable with that approach?"

"Yes, Susan, I am. Marge never worked outside the home, yet we had joint checking and savings accounts."

"Scott and I had similar incomes. I don't know anything about your income, Walter, or you about mine. If yours is considerably higher than mine, perhaps you'd prefer that we put equal amounts into our joint account."

"No, Susan. I think that our incomes are ours to enjoy. Let's deposit our income directly into the joint account. What you and Scott did with setting a cap on the account and moving any excess into a joint savings account or investment account is a good way to go."

"What about income from investments, Walter? So far, because I haven't needed it to live on, I've had dividend income automatically reinvested in more stock. For my IRA, I've just transferred my required minimum distribution (RMD) to my brokerage account and then invested it."

"I've done much the same with dividend income. I've been putting my RMD into my savings account. If we don't think we currently need investment and IRA income for living expenses, we can keep reinvesting. That will provide us with a cushion against inflation. If we decide our lifestyle will require that income, we can put the money in the joint account.

"It's our investment principal and the value in property that we need to protect for our children. When we talk to the lawyer, we must assure that, if we need money from some of those sources in the future, we'll have access during our lifetime. You and I have a lot of living yet to do. Decisions about what to do with our various properties can wait until we decide where we want to live. Before we see the lawyer, we need to list our finances in detail so we can develop a budget and identify what needs to be included in any trust or similar vehicle that we create."

"We seem to agree, Walter. I'm glad, because money can be a major source of disagreement. Neither of us is extravagant, although you're more comfortable spending than I am. We should use what we need to have a comfortable life. Like we agreed when we left Neskowin, we'll ask ourselves whether any given expense will make life easier or whether it is an unnecessary, wasteful expenditure. I hate to waste money!"

Water smiled at Susan. "I promise we won't become spend-thrifts, sweetheart. Now, I think we need to end this conversation. It's dinnertime. I'd like to change into something more formal, befitting the elegance of the hotel dining room. Then let's just relax and enjoy a good dinner and a glass of Oregon wine. We can deal with our other decisions later."

Susan leaned toward Walter and gave him a hug. "Great idea. I am hungry. But, I'm pleased with our decisions. Now we can enjoy a romantic dinner in that gorgeous setting with no thought of pending responsibilities."

— CHAPTER 11 —

Irvine, California
Monday, August 8

Juanita had decided that things could not continue as they were. She must speak with Miguel about her needs. Taking a deep breath to fortify her courage, she shuffled into the living room.

Miguel and Henry were sitting on the sofa. Miguel leaned against Henry, his head on Henry's shoulder. Henry's arm was around Miguel's waist, his head resting against Miguel's. They were murmuring quietly to each other, oblivious of the television program playing in the background. Juanita gasped! A wave of dizziness passed over her and she had to grasp the walker tightly to keep from falling.

They're lovers! No wonder Miguel is under Henry's influence! Now I understand why he's reluctant to talk to Henry about moving out. I can't let this stop me from talking to Miguel about my needs.

She took another deep breath. "Miguel, I need to talk to you. Now!"

Miguel sat up abruptly, startled. "Grandmother. What is it?"

Henry also sat upright. He stood and angrily addressed Juanita. "Go to your room, old lady. Can't you see we're talking? I told you to stay out of this room when we're here."

Juanita turned toward Henry. "I must remind you that this is my home. Out of the kindness of my heart I have allowed you to stay here. How dare you address me that way? Now sit down. I wish to speak with my grandson. Miguel, please come into my bedroom."

She turned toward the bedroom. Miguel followed. From behind them, Henry shouted at Miguel. "You don't need to jump when she says jump. You don't owe her anything. This is our time together. Be a man!"

Miguel turned and looked at Henry. "Please Henry. Try to understand. I love my grandmother. I owe her everything. She took me in when I was at the lowest point in my life. You and she are all I have. I need to hear what she wants." He followed Juanita into her room and closed the door. She sat down in her armchair, he sat on the edge of the bed.

Silently, they looked at each other. Juanita gathered her thoughts. "Miguel. Are you and Henry lovers? That's how it looked when I walked into the living room."

"Yes, Grandmother. I'm sorry."

"That's not what you need to be apologizing for. These things happen. I'm not shocked----well maybe a little. Mostly I'm just surprised. I hadn't considered the possibility. What you need to apologize for is neglecting your responsibilities to me. We had an agreement. You were to do errands, and chores around the house, keep the pantry stocked, and prepare food so I could have a nourishing meal every day. Many times recently I've have had nothing to eat but a can of beans or a few crackers that your sister brought me. She misses you. You haven't been around for her visits in several months. Just what is going on?"

Miguel looked sadly at his grandmother. Finally, he registered her pallor and how thin she had become.

"Are you ill, Grandmother? I'm sorry I haven't been looking after you as I promised. I've been working some overtime, painting new works, framing them, and helping Henry at the gallery to prepare for my solo show. By the time I get home, you're usually asleep. Henry convinced me that you are able to prepare your own meals now, and we've been eating our meals out, so I forget that I need to shop for you. I'm afraid I got caught up in my feelings for Henry to the exclusion of everything else. I've been lonely for so long, and he filled an empty place in my soul. I'm afraid of losing him. He's very demanding and threatens to leave me when I don't do as he says. I've been selfish and neglected you. That's inexcusable, and I'm sorry."

"Your neglect of your responsibilities to me is indeed inexcusable, Miguel. I cannot get out to shop, and I'm alone almost all the time. One of the best things about having you live here was your company. Because you've been handling my finances, I have no cash or checkbook, so I can't even give Delia money to shop for me, or try to have something delivered.

"You never told me you were going to have a solo show. Don't you think that after how I've supported your painting classes, bought you art supplies, and provided a studio here in the house so you would have a quiet place to work that I'd be interested? This is not what I'd have expected from the Miguel I knew. You've changed."

Miguel hung his head, but said nothing.

"I'm glad your life is coming together, Miguel. But, I think Henry is a bad influence. He's taken advantage of my kindness and learned how to manipulate you. He has no manners, and is rude and abusive toward me. Frankly, I'm afraid of him. I often cringe when he's around. A few times, I thought he might hit me.

"I intend to issue him with an ultimatum. He has one month to be out of here. I expect you to support me in that decision. Since I can't seem to depend on you, I intend to have my lawyer invalidate your power of attorney. I will take over managing my own finances. Perhaps, I can hire someone to help me with shopping, cooking and cleaning, since you can't seem to manage. It's time you started to pay rent in lieu of the services that were part of our original agreement. Or maybe you prefer to live with Henry after he moves out? Until I can hire help, you will need to shop for me and cook meals that I can reheat. Do you understand?"

Miguel looked at the floor. Juanita waited patiently. Finally, he looked up at his grandmother.

"Yes, Grandmother. I behaved badly. You didn't deserve to be neglected. I abused your trust. After the way I've behaved, you may find it hard to believe I love you. I realize how much I owe you for all you've done for me. I selfishly got caught up in my own life, lost track of time, and forgot my obligations to you. Maybe Dad was right when he refused to allow me to move home. I'll help you find someone to do chores around here and try to do more until then. If Henry moves out, I probably will too. He'll need my help to pay his rent. Apartments really are expensive. Until I move out, would five hundred dollars a month be sufficient for you as my rent?"

"Five hundred dollars a month is acceptable. You can pay on the first of each month. Please understand that I'm not asking for rent because I need the money. It's the principle of it, Miguel. I want to teach you responsibility. Also, I will need some cash and a checkbook. Please bring me one thousand dollars from my bank account in twenties and fifties, and a checkbook. That way, I have some resources here, in case of an emergency.

"I will also offer you some advice, unwelcome, I'm sure. Think carefully before you decide to move in with Henry. He has a controlling personality. You sometimes seem a bit afraid of him. He could become physically abusive, if he's not already. If you always feel like you need to comply with his wishes in order to maintain peace, you will not be happy in the relationship. Eventually you will want out. He will not make it easy for you to leave. It would be better to get your own place, despite the extra expense, or continue to live here, until you have matured and are able to be in the relationship on equal terms, or to find another. If you can't stand up to Henry, you will never be happy. I say that because I love you, Miguel. Now give me a hug, then we'll go give Henry the bad news."

Miguel rose and reached for his grandmother. "You are a wise and caring person, Grandmother. Thank you for forgiving my bad behavior." He hugged her close.

"It may be that looking back, I will thank you, Miguel. This situation has pushed me to rethink my life. I think I will try to sell this house and move into a senior housing facility where I can reliably obtain the services I need, some companionship, and activities to help pass the time. Before I can put the house on the market, however, I must have the exterior painted, get a new roof, and take care of minor repairs inside that you should have done, like the leaking toilet and the latch on the bathroom window. I'm ready to reengage and take action to make my life better. Now find your courage and support me when I tell Henry he must leave."

Juanita opened the door and moved into the living room, Miguel followed behind. Henry looked at them sullenly.

"Henry, my grandson and I had an agreement. Since you have been here, he's neglected his responsibilities under our agreement. I've been patient with both of you. Once Miguel failed to ensure that there is food in the panty, neglect became abuse. The situation is intolerable. I agreed to allow you to stay here for a few months until you could get on your feet. You've been here nearly nine months. It's time to move on. I expect you to move out by the end of next month. If you do not, I shall obtain an eviction notice. Is that clear?"

Henry's face expressed his surprise. "Miguel, do something! I have no place to go!"

Juanita watched as Miguel took a deep breath before saying weakly, "Henry, I need to support my grandmother in her decision. She has been kind to you. I allowed my feelings for you to get in the way of my responsibility to her. I'll try to help you find a place. But she's right, you should not stay here any longer."

Henry grabbed Juanita and shook her hard. She grabbed her walker to avert a fall as he released her. "You're a useless old woman. We are young, in the prime of our life. We have things to do, places to go. Who are you to tell us what we must do? And you!" Henry turned toward Miguel. "I thought you loved me. Instead of standing up for me, you cave when she says jump. If I move out of here, we're through!" He stormed from the room.

Juanita glanced at Miguel. She saw his shoulders sag, his head droop. Then a single tear fell down the left side of his cheek before he turned and left the room.

— CHAPTER 12 —

Monday, August 22

It had been a difficult few weeks for Juanita. She hated being emotionally estranged from Miguel. Since the confrontation, the atmosphere in the house had been tense. Although Miguel had become more attentive, attending to shopping, meal preparation, and cleaning, he crept around sheepishly in her presence, saying little.

A subdued version of Henry came to tell Juanita that he had arranged to share a house with Nathan Stearns, someone he and Miguel knew from the art supply store. The house would be available five weeks from now, when the current housemate moved out. He asked to be allowed to stay until then, and offered to pay Juanita rent. She refused the money, and agreed he could stay. She wasn't expecting an apology for his past behavior, so was surprised when he made an awkward attempt to apologize.

She couldn't tell whether the relationship between Henry and Miguel had been affected by what transpired. She rarely saw them together. When she did, they appeared to be maintaining an emotional arm's length. She would be pleased if the relationship ended. She truly believed that Henry was, and would continue to be, a bad influence on Miguel.

Juanita wished that she knew how to repair her relationship with Miguel. She loved the boy, and regretted that confronting him had created a barrier between them. Miguel had always been unduly sensitive. She believed what he had said about loving her, and suspected that he carried a load of guilt that made interactions with her awkward. She hoped he could eventually accept that she bore him no ill will. She needed to enlist his assistance in obtaining a part-time caregiver, and someone to look after the house. Perhaps, the process of doing that would begin to restore more normal relations between them.

The following Saturday afternoon, Juanita found Miguel in the kitchen. The fragrance of cumin, coriander, and garlic permeated the air. "Something smells good in here, Miguelito," commented Juanita as she struggled onto one of the counter stools. He turned.

"Hello, Grandmother. I went to the grocery store, and replenished the pantry. Now I'm cooking a selection of dishes for your meals this week. I'll freeze some in meal-size portions you can reheat in the microwave. There are fresh vegetables for making salads in the refrigerator.

"I put the thousand dollars in cash you requested in the blue ginger jar on your dresser and two checkbooks next to the jar. I really am sorry I neglected you for so long!"

"Learn from your mistakes and you'll be a better person, Miguel. You're making amends, and I appreciate it. I'll enjoy eating some of your excellent cooking again. Thank you.

"Have you made a decision about what you want to do from here on? You're welcome to stay here until I sell the house. I meant what I said about the situation forcing me to make decisions about my future. I was being selfish, relying on you for companionship. Just as it's important for you to have friendships, develop your talents, and build a future, I need to move on. I became content to wither and die in this house. I'm only 73, I still have a life to live. Will you help me find someone who can come several days a week to clean, shop, and cook? That would take pressure off your schedule and provide me with what I need. I hadn't realized how busy you are. Between overtime and preparing for a solo show of your art, I'm surprised you have any free time! When is your show?"

"The opening is Friday, the twenty-first of next month, from five-thirty to nine in the evening. The show runs for a month. I'll pick you up and take you to see it earlier that week. I'll let you know which day, once I see how the preparations are going and most of the paintings are hung. I'm sorry I can't take you that night; I'll be tied to the gallery most of that day and all night too."

"Thank you, Miguel. I'm really looking forward to seeing your recent work. I'm so proud that you're to have your own show. You must be excited!"

"I think I got too excited, Grandmother. It's like I was wearing blinders and couldn't see anything but the show for a while. You brought me down to earth. I've asked around about people who do cleaning. Agencies that specialize in cleaning services are very expensive and don't do shopping or other chores, like cooking. The home health service agencies that supply aides to shop or cook, don't do major cleaning, and require a doctor's referral. A friend at the art cooperative says his aunt, Bessie Jones, does cleaning. She could also shop and cook for you. That might be a good solution. I can set up an interview with her, if you like."

"Thank you, Miguel. I'd like that. Can we interview her together?" Miguel nodded. "The sooner the better. Once she starts, you'll have more time available for what you need to do. Have you and Henry sorted things out? I'm sorry if I made things difficult for you with him."

"He was very angry with me for not challenging you. He wasn't physically abusive, but he dragged me over the coals emotionally. Then, he announced he found a place to live with Nathan. I suspect they may have had a relationship already. I was very hurt. I thought about what you said about long-term happiness being unlikely with someone so controlling. I'm sure you're right, so I'm relieved it's over. He filled an emptiness in my life, but I was never truly happy in the relationship. I always felt like I was walking on eggshells. Since he's leaving me, rather than me leaving him, we can probably be civil and continue to work together at the gallery. Had it been the other way around, he would have made it impossible. His ego couldn't have tolerated the situation."

"I am sorry, Miguel. I really do think it is for the best. You will meet someone else. Meanwhile, your professional success may compensate to some degree. Now, please give me a hug and let's be friends again."

— CHAPTER 13 —

Seattle, Washington
Tuesday, August 23

Susan and Walter chose September 15 as the date for their wedding. They called their children to share the news. Reactions ranged from surprise, to cautious endorsement, to enthusiastic congratulations. Questions about whether family was expected to attend the wedding led to sighs of relief when told it was optional; their lives were busy. Nonetheless, their children were pleased to hear that the newlyweds wanted to visit and become acquainted. A few questions about financial arrangements were raised and quickly put to rest once Susan and Walter disclosed their intention to meet with a lawyer and draw up documents creating trusts to protect their children's interests.

Later, Walter referred to those conversations with their children. "They need to understand that it's our money to use as we choose while we are alive. We earned it, saved it, and invested it carefully. It's not their entitlement!"

"I know, my dear. I agree. Please understand that our children have expected to inherit when we die. From their perspective, the possibility of a new spouse inheriting most everything threatens that expectation. They need reassurance that our union will not undermine their inheritance. They've probably heard horror stories about greedy people who set out to marry for money. By putting legal protections in place we give them peace of mind."

"I know you're right, Susan. But, when I remember Keith's reaction that day he unexpectedly arrived at my house in Hawaii, and his assumption that you were a gold-digger, I still get angry! He jumped to conclusions before even trying to get to know you. Besides, no one ever left me anything."

"Did you have any expectation that you would receive an inheritance?" Walter shook his head. "I thought not. That does make a difference. By the way, any mention from Keith about the pantry burglar?"

"Just before we ended our conversation, he brought that up. Jan did her inventory and has been monitoring the pantry contents closely. She updates the inventory as she uses or purchases new items. She didn't mention the inventory to the kids. For several weeks after she began monitoring use, the only things she noticed disappearing were some snacks, like packs of peanut butter crackers, and a few individual cups of fruit cocktail or applesauce. When asked, the children readily confessed to eating those or sharing some with visiting friends. Jan did think that the children seemed to be snacking more than usual. Since their snacks don't seem to be interfering with eating their meals, she decided to ignore it. She had bought the snacks so they could help themselves when hungry. At least they were eating the healthier snacks like fruit cups, peanut butter and cheese crackers, and fresh fruit from the fruit bowl and the refrigerator. Recently, two boxes of pasta and two jars of spaghetti sauce seem to be missing. Also, a can of baked beans and a pound package of rice."

"Has there been a food drive lately? Could a family member have taken something to donate? Those sound like the kind of items one would give to a food drive."

"Apparently she asked, and the answer was no."

"An interesting mystery. Perhaps we can look into it when we visit. After all, we did discover that we have some talents in that regard while we were looking into the mysterious blood stains on the carpet pad in my condo in Hawaii."

"I thought you had given up playing detective!"

"Well, I did too. But when a mystery comes your way....."

Walter grabbed Susan by the shoulders and pulled her close, kissing her soundly. "Enough with the mysteries. We have more important things to attend to."

"Kiss me like that again and we aren't going to finish our lists of financial resources for the lawyer. Our appointment is in two days, or have you forgotten?"

"No, I haven't forgotten. But doing lists can't compete with making love."

"Let's get on with them. Making love can be our reward for our diligence."

"Okay, boss. You do know how to motivate a man." Walter grinned.

They returned to sorting through piles of records for relevant information and recorded the pertinent data on a form Susan had prepared. An hour later, Walter pushed back from the table. I need a snack. I've finished my list, I think. Can I bring you anything?"

"A glass of iced coffee would be welcome. I left this morning's coffee in the pot to cool after I turned off the warmer. Pour some in a glass with some ice and a little milk, please. I'm almost finished here. Another ten minutes should do it."

Walter returned and handed Susan her iced coffee. "When you're finished, please look at my list. You should know about my finances. That list will give you a complete picture."

"Thank you, Walter. You should review mine as well. We can draw up a budget based on our projected joint income. It may change, but we'll have some idea of our resources versus expenditures."

Susan handed Walter the copy of her list, then glanced at his. "Unless we're really extravagant, we shouldn't need to touch our dividends or minimum distributions. Our income will easily support anything I'd like to do in this life! Of course, inflation could change that. For now, we've plenty to do most anything we want!"

Walter looked through Susan's list. "You've done well financially, Susan. We have more than enough to meet both our needs and our wants. We are fortunate indeed! One day soon, we should talk about which charities we'd like to include in our budget."

"Good point. We ought to share our good fortune with others. Right now, it's time for that reward I promised you," said Susan, setting her glass on the table and taking Walter by the hand.

— CHAPTER 14 —

Thursday, September 15

Susan and Walter shook the hand of the Justice of the Peace. He had performed their wedding ceremony in his living room. His wife and eldest daughter served as witnesses.

"Best of luck to you both," he said as they turned to go. "We wish you many happy years together."

"Our thanks to all of you."

Nodding to the family, Walter led Susan down the front steps of the cottage, then paused in front of the car. He hugged her, then kissed her tenderly.

"I know I kissed the bride inside. I'm just so happy that we are man and wife! I needed to do it again. Pinch me so I'm sure this is real."

Susan pinched him on the arm.

"Ouch! You don't need to pinch with such enthusiasm. I'm convinced."

"Maybe you should think twice before you ask me to do something." Susan grinned impishly. "You know I always put my full efforts into any task I attempt."

"I'll keep that in mind in the future, Mrs. Conway."

"Mrs. Conway. I like the sound of that. Oh, Walter. I can't

believe we are really married. I'm so happy! Not so long ago, I thought I'd never be truly happy again. Now I look forward to each and every day."

"I share your sentiments, my love. On a more practical note, shall we stop to grab a bite on our way back to the house? That way, we can relax this afternoon. We want to feel fresh for our celebratory dinner tonight. I remember passing a funky little roadside restaurant on our way here. They probably have something simple like a salad, a hamburger, or fish and chips."

While you were still asleep this morning, Walter, I made a curried chicken salad for us to have when we get back. We have some of that lovely whole grain bread from the bakery to go with it."

"Thank you, my dear. That was most thoughtful. It's probably tastier than what we would get at that restaurant. Healthier too."

Susan and Walter found several parcels by the front door when they arrived at the house. The answering machine light was blinking; several of their children had called to wish them well on their wedding day.

The parcels were from their daughters. The one from Kristin and her family contained a framed picture of the two of them that Kristin had taken in Hawaii and then enlarged. Beneath was inscribed a poem about love the second time around.

Walter's daughter, Celia, and her family, sent a card and a beautiful photo album. Celia had hand-lettered the top of each page in calligraphy. The first page, left empty, was labeled Walter and Susan Conway, with space to put a picture of the two of them. Each page in the next section was labeled with the name of one of Walter's children or grandchildren, and contained one or more pictures of each on their page. Pages in the subsequent section were labeled with the names of Susan's children and grandchildren. A note attached to the first of these pages said, 'Dear Dad and Susan, I didn't have pictures of Susan's family, but I suspect Susan has plenty. There is room here for pictures of each one of her children and grandchildren, already labeled. This way, you have the start of a family album. In the back section, the two of you can put pictures of your evolving life together. Congratulations on your wedding. Love Celia, Dave, and Sandra.'

"What lovely, thoughtful gifts!" Walter exclaimed. "Both feel like an endorsement of our marriage."

"The girls put considerable thought and effort into them. These gifts are unique. How long has Celia done calligraphy? How did she get the names of my children and grandchildren?"

"She took a calligraphy course shortly after college. She loved doing it. When her children were small, she had a calligraphy business. Initially, she swapped doing calligraphy on invitations and other documents for babysitting or services she needed. Later, she worked for several companies doing invitations, certificates, or other documents in calligraphy. As for the names of your children and grandchildren, I'm sure you've guessed that she asked me for those. She wouldn't tell me why she wanted them.

"Since we're opening gifts, Susan, this may be a good time to give you my wedding gift. I had intended to present it when we returned from dinner."

Walter left the room. He returned with a large, rectangular, fairly flat package wrapped in silver and gold paper with a huge white bow. He handed the package to Susan. "I hope you like it, Mrs. Conway."

"It's heavy." Susan carefully removed the bow and wrapping, folding the paper neatly after she removed it. Then she unwrapped the inner padding and gasped as she saw the painting inside. "Walter, it's beautiful—Proposal Rock with Neskowin Beach and the cliffs in the background. It's by Jason Hall! How did you ever get this? He doesn't paint Neskowin, he specializes in painting Cannon Beach." Susan gazed intently at the painting. "This is so special! Thank you so much." She carefully set the painting on the sofa and enveloped Walter in a hug.

"When we visited his gallery in Cannon Beach, you mentioned how much you've always admired his work. Once we became engaged, I tried to think of an appropriate wedding gift. I remembered that, though the vast majority of paintings displayed in his gallery were of Cannon Beach, two were of other places along the coast. I called the gallery and asked if he takes commissions. They said he usually did not, but sales were slow right now and gallery expenses constantly increasing, so he might consider it. They gave me his private phone number. I called and talked with him. He's got a romantic streak, as it turns out. When I told him our story, he agreed to do it. I gave him a general sense of the view I wanted and agreed to leave final decisions about the perspective up to him. This is the result. I think he captured the sense of South Beach very well. Proposal Rock, where I proposed is the element that draws one's eye. He must have been standing on the North Beach by the water line at low tide to get this perspective."

"Walter, you are so good to me. I can't believe you remembered that comment I made about Jason Hall's work. And then to commission this painting of where you proposed to me.... I'm overwhelmed! And so grateful to have you as my husband." Susan hugged him again.

"I'm delighted to have pleased you. That is my mission in life."

"Since this has turned out to be the gift hour, let me get my wedding present to you." Susan disappeared into the study and returned with a package the same general shape as the one Walter had given her, but smaller in size. She handed it to him. "Happy Wedding Day, darling. I'm afraid this pales in comparison to your gift to me."

"This is not a contest, my love. I'm sure I will like it."

Walter removed the card from the front of the package. "Happy Wedding Day," he read. "I thought that this might remind you of your happy past and the start of what I pray will be a happy future. All my love, Susan."

Walter tore off the wrappings, balling up the paper, and then turned the frame to reveal the painting. He sat there quietly, gazing at his house in Hawaii where he had lived with his wife, Marge, for nearly 30 years prior to her death. It was also where he first got to know Susan after she had sprained her ankle on the golf course and he drove her to his home on his golf cart so he could treat the sprain. Susan's painting included his house in the foreground, with glimpses of the ocean, golf course, and mountains beyond. A tear ran down his cheek. He turned to Susan and reached for her hand.

"Oh, Susan! How clever of you. You've captured not just my house, but the feel of the Hawaiian setting where Marge and I were so happy, and where you and I began my second life. By encouraging me to retain and revisit memories of my life with Marge, you allow me to fully engage the future. Thank you. The painting is beautiful. You are an accomplished artist. When did you manage to paint it?"

"I took pictures with my cell phone one day when I visited you. I started the painting during that month in Hawaii when we didn't see each other because we were hiding from the mob. I finished it during the weeks we were apart, after I returned to Seattle. Painting helped me pass the lonely days and gave me a sense of connection to you, even though you were thousands of miles away."

"Thank you, my darling." He hugged Susan. "I shall treasure the painting as I shall treasure you. I think we are going to be very happy! Now, I hate to break the emotion of the moment, but before I pass out from hunger, do you think I could have some of that chicken salad you so thoughtfully prepared? I'll prepare some fruit and slice the bread while you set the table and pour some iced tea. After we eat, let's relax a bit. Then we can return calls to those of our children who left messages on the answering machine, and thank Kristin and Celia for the wedding gifts."

"Aye, aye, Captain. I must admit I'm hungry as well. Thanks for offering to help get lunch on the table."

Following a brief nap, Walter and Susan felt refreshed and ready to enjoy their celebratory dinner that evening in downtown Seattle. They were enjoying a beer and the sunshine on the deck when the telephone rang. Water picked up the phone when he recognized the number as that of his son in Chicago. "Hello, Dan. Thanks for calling."

"Hello, Dad. Congratulations on your wedding."

"Thank you, son. I'm going to put the phone on conference mode, so Susan can say hello."

"Hello, Dan, this is Susan. Thank you for calling us on our special day. I'm looking forward to meeting you and your family."

"I hope you and Dad will be very happy, Susan. As happy as he was with my mom. I have some news for you two. My company asked me to attend a conference in Seattle next week. The person who was to represent the company is seriously ill. My wife is from Washington State and misses it very much, so I'm bringing Alexa and our son, George, with me. This gives us a perfect chance to meet Susan. We'll arrive on Wednesday evening. My conference is Thursday and Friday. I've arranged for us to stay through late Sunday afternoon.

"Don't worry about putting us up; we'll just stay at the conference hotel. Alexa and George, will spend Thursday and Friday visiting with relatives who live south of Seattle, near Olympia. They probably won't get back to town until late Friday. I thought if it's not too much trouble to come into town, you two could join me for dinner at my hotel Friday night. Then, we could spend Saturday with you. On Sunday, Alexa wants us to play tourist in Seattle with George and take him to Pike Street Market and the Space Needle."

"That sounds great! It will be wonderful to meet all of

you. Your father and I have a flexible life. We can arrange to meet you for dinner in town on Friday night, can't we Walter? Would you like to come here on Saturday, Dan? We live on Lake Washington. You, your wife, and son could do some fishing, and canoeing or kayaking. Come for an early lunch, say around eleven o'clock. We'll do a cookout. If you'd like to stay for dinner, we can have dinner early so you can get back to your hotel and be rested for your long day on Sunday."

"Thanks for the invitation, Susan. That sounds wonderful. I'll call Dad on Thursday to give him the information on our hotel and set a time to meet for dinner on Friday. I'll know the conference schedule by then. Bye to both of you. Again, congratulations."

When they hung up the phone, Susan turned to Walter. "I hope you didn't mind my jumping in with the invitation. I acted on impulse without consulting you."

"Given the circumstances, I'm fine with it. And, I'm pleased that it occurred to you that I might want to be consulted. This invitation was in our best interest. We want to get to know each other's families. Soon, we should talk about when to consult each other and when we can act unilaterally. By agreeing in advance, we'll avoid hurt feelings. We're both used to functioning as individuals. Becoming a couple will take some effort. I'm sure that when either of us does something without consultation, it will be with good intentions, like your invitation to Dan and his family. We're still feeling our way and have a lot of history to overcome."

"Indeed, my love. Getting used to being Mr. and Mrs. Conway instead of just Susan and Walter will take some getting used to."

"Should we return phone calls before we dress for dinner, Susan? We can probably reach Celia and Kristin to thank them for their lovely gifts. Keith and Brendon are probably still at work; let's text to thank them for calling and say we'll try to call tomorrow."

"It's a plan. Let's start with Kristin."

Later that evening Susan and Walter sat snuggled close together on the living room sofa, each holding a snifter of brandy.

"I feel good about the children's response to our wedding, Susan. They all seem to be accepting our marriage. Our worries were for naught. The girls' gifts definitely indicate approval. Dan's plan to visit us with the family is also good news. Not only does it indicate acceptance of our marriage, but it will save us a trip to Chicago!"

"I agree completely. It's been a lovely day, Walter, one I'll remember for a long time. Our dinner this evening was so romantic. Having that private corner all to ourselves with candles on the table, champagne, and that delicious lobster dinner, followed by the wedding cake was a special way to celebrate our wedding. Thank you for arranging it."

"You are most welcome, my dear. I thought that since we didn't have a formal wedding, we should at least have something formal and symbolic to mark the occasion. Now we also have the photographs of the two of us that the waiter took. We can put them on the front page of Celia's album. You looked absolutely stunning, by the way. I have a beautiful wife."

"Thank you for the compliment, my handsome husband. You look very elegant in that suit. Do you realize that today is the first time I've ever seen you wearing a suit? You're usually Hawaii-casual."

"A suit will continue to be a rarity. I hope you don't mind. And now that you've finished your brandy, Mrs. Conway, may I escort you to the bedroom?"

— CHAPTER 15 —

Saturday, September 24

The visit with Dan and his family was delightful. The weather cooperated, a beautiful fall day, warm and sunny during the afternoon, then a crispness in the air after sunset. Walter basked in the pleasure of being with his son and his family. Susan and Dan established an immediate rapport. After several hours, Dan's wife, Alexa, had relaxed and actively joined in both the activities and the conversation. George, their nine-year old son was a delight! He had been thrilled to learn to how to kayak and fish, but was disappointed when the six inch bass he caught was too small to keep. After Susan snapped his picture with his catch, he released it, expressing a hope that he could catch it again another time when it was bigger. George helped Walter build a bonfire so they could roast marshmallows and make s'mores. By the time the family left, he was already asking when they could come again.

Walter talked to Dan and his family about getting the Conway and Brooks' families together in Hawaii during the late winter. Dan remarked that he had not seen both of his siblings and their families together for several years, and that it would be fun for George to see his cousins again. He would also enjoy meeting Susan's family. Even Alexa had seemed enthusiastic at the prospect; she said she had always wanted to visit Hawaii, but never had the opportunity.

Saturday evening after the family departed, Susan confided to Walter, "I really like your son, Dan. The way he thinks, and his mannerisms remind me so much of you. But, he doesn't look much like you, does he? He must take after Marge's family."

When Walter didn't respond, she glanced at him. He sat there with a stunned look on his face.

"Walter, are you alright? What is it?"

It was a few minutes more before Walter responded.

"Dan isn't my biological son, Susan. He is my son in every way that matters. I changed his diapers, bandaged his scraped knees, read him bedtime stories, and consoled him when he encountered bullies or didn't make the soccer team. I celebrated with him when he won the award for best essay or was elected captain of the debate team. It's the day-to-day engagements with a child that make them your own."

"So he's adopted."

"No. He's Marge's son with another man. She had an affair."

"Oh, Walter, I'm so sorry. That must have been awful for you!"

"It was painful. But, largely my own fault."

"I don't understand."

"It happened when Celia and Keith were small. The FBI was investigating the mob in New York City. I had to work long hours, often successive days for weeks in a row. Many nights I didn't even get to go home. We were closing in, so I couldn't get time off. That was in the days before cell phones. It was difficult to reach Marge by telephone. When I had a minute free and had access to a telephone, it was usually when she was out running the children to school, shopping, doing other errands, or sleeping.

"Marge was left alone with two small children. Since I wasn't there, she couldn't talk to me about her problems. She told me later that she had started getting telephone calls threatening to harm the family if I didn't stop the investigation. She was terrified!

"She said that one evening she put the children to bed, then sat on the porch, sobbing. She didn't want the children to hear her crying. She was lonely and frightened. The widowed man who lived next door heard her crying and came to investigate. He consoled her until she had calmed. After that, he would drop by occasionally in the evening to be sure she was alright. One thing led to another and one night they had sex. She said it was only that one time. She was unlucky enough to get pregnant.

"When she told me, I was crushed. I couldn't breathe. I loved Marge with all my heart and soul. It was love at first sight that autumn day when I first saw her, standing in a shaft of sunlight on the porch of an old country store in North Carolina. After that day, I couldn't imagine loving anyone else.

"It never occurred to me to leave her. She seemed so fragile and frightened when she told me about the pregnancy. She insisted that she hadn't meant for it to happen, that she loved only me and always would. When she told me about her loneliness and the threatening phone calls, I could understand how much she must have needed someone to reassure her, to care for her.

"We discussed abortion. Neither of us could accept that as a solution. We decided she would have the child. I would be its father in every way but genetically. He would be our child, like our other two. He would never be told. To this day, nobody knows. We never told a soul.

"I couldn't leave her there alone next to that man. Marge found another house to rent in the same school district and moved the family to the new house. We installed a phone with an unlisted number. We never told him about her pregnancy. Since I had to stay involved in the investigation for the duration, we arranged for Marge's parents to come stay with the family until things returned to normal.

"I love Dan as much as I love my other two children. I am his father, he is my son. His son is my grandson. We never told Dan. Beginning and end of story."

"Oh, Walter! I've caused you pain with my questions. I'm so sorry. I hadn't meant to pry."

"Susan, you weren't prying. You asked an innocent question, following an innocent observation. You are my wife, and I love you. You have a right to know."

Susan reached for him and held him tightly. "It's our secret, I promise you."

— CHAPTER 16 —

Irvine, California
Thursday, September 29

Juanita woke from her afternoon nap to the sound of pots rattling and water running in the kitchen. She sat on the edge of the bed for a few minutes before standing; she often got dizzy if she stood too rapidly. Grabbing her walker for stability, she followed the heavenly scents of Latin American cooking that wafted from the direction of the kitchen.

"Whatever you are cooking smells awfully good, Miguel!" Her grandson turned at the sound of her voice.

"Grandmother. I'm sorry if I woke you. I tried to be quiet as a mouse, but I guess I didn't succeed."

"It was time for me to get up anyway. I had a long, restful nap. What are you preparing?"

"I'm making your recipe for chicken mole'. I thought you would enjoy some for dinner. It was always one of your favorite meals. Even after we've both eaten, there should be enough left to freeze for several future meals. I was able to get the afternoon off, so did some grocery shopping on my way home. I'm also making beef stew and some tortilla soup you can use for lunches and dinners later this week. Please accept it as partial amends for my recent neglect."

99

"Miguel, stop berating yourself! What happened is in the past. I love you. I'll enjoy eating your excellent cooking, and having your company for dinner. It's been some time since we had the leisure to sit and chat. I want to catch up with your life. Have you made any decisions about whether you want to stay on here until I sell? That's likely to be at least a year."

Miguel shook his head. "I'm too busy getting ready for the show to have given it much thought, Grandmother. But, it probably makes sense to do so. With Henry gone from my personal life, your companionship will be welcome. You know that I've always enjoyed spending time with you. By the way, I'd like to take you to see my paintings at the gallery on Tuesday evening of the week after next. I'll take you out to dinner after we visit the gallery."

"I shall look forward to that. It will be my first outing in years, a real treat! And I'm eager to see your work. I'll be delighted if you decide to stay on here at the house. Truly, what happened forced me start thinking about my future, something I should have done long ago. After your grandfather's death, then the stroke, I didn't want to go on living. You encouraged me to get better and reengage with life. But loneliness is debilitating and leads to inertia. Finally, I recognize that selling the house and finding a place in an adult community will improve my life. I'll have a safe, secure environment, with meals, cleaning, and maintenance provided, and also lots of opportunity for companionship. I'm actually beginning to get excited at the prospect."

"That does sound like a good solution for you, Grandmother. Meanwhile, I've arranged to have my friend's aunt, Bessie Jones, come by the house on Saturday morning so we can interview her. I need to give her a time. Is ten o'clock good for you?"

"That should work just fine. Thank you for arranging it."

"You're welcome. Now, let's get you situated at the table, and I'll serve dinner. While we eat, I'll tell you about the show preparations and we can talk about arrangements for taking you to see the exhibit."

— CHAPTER 17 —

Tuesday, October 4

Juanita had help! She and Miguel had jointly interviewed Bessie Jones, his friend's aunt. Bessie was personable, perky, and came with excellent references. Bessie and Juanita liked each other instantly. Best of all, Bessie could start work at once, since Juanita could offer her the flexibility to work around her present schedule. She would come for six hours on Tuesday and Thursday of the first and third weeks of the month, and three hours on Monday, Wednesday, and Friday of the second and fourth weeks.

On Tuesday, her first day of work, Bessie arrived with her husband.

"Ms. Juanita, I'd like you to meet my husband, Micah. I don't have a car this week. Mine is in the shop for repair; we're waiting on some parts. Until I get it back, Micah will drive me here, then pick me up at the end of my shift. He's a handyman, so if you need anything done around the house, Micah's your man. He does good work, Ma'am."

"I'm sure he does, Bessie. I'm pleased to meet you, Micah," said Juanita, shaking his hand and appraising the six-foot, well-muscled, black man who stood in her entry hall. His smile lit up the room. "I will most likely be calling on your services one of these days soon, Micah. This house needs some attention."

"I'll be happy for the work, Ma'am. I promise you'll be pleased with what I do. And my charges are reasonable."

"Can't ask for more than that. I'll let Bessie know when I'm ready for you to start. Thank you for dropping her off." Juanita closed the door behind him.

"I'll list what you need from the grocery store before I leave and shop on my way here on Thursday. If it's okay with you, Micah can help bring in the groceries when he drops me."

"That should work, Bessie. Now, how about we sit down with a cup of tea while we review what needs to be done and work out a schedule?"

"Yes, Ma'am. I'll heat the water. You sit down there in that comfortable chair and I'll bring the teapot and cups in here. You'll just need to tell me where to find things in the kitchen until I learn my way around."

Bessie brought the tea. As they sipped, they scheduled the chores to be done on a regular basis. Bessie inquired about the availability of equipment—vacuum, brooms, her preferred cleaning products. Juanita agreed to purchase those she did not have on hand and told Bessie to put them on the shopping list. When they had finished the lists, Bessie stood to take the tea tray to the kitchen. Juanita interrupted her.

"Please sit with me, Bessie, and have another cup of tea. I need companionship as much as I need a clean house. Let's enjoy a second cup before you get started. Tell me about your family. Do you have children?"

Bessie looked at Juanita with surprise as she sat down. "Chile, this be de first time I ever done got paid to chat. Tis a real treat for des old bones. I do love to brag on my husband and my daughter."

Juanita burst out laughing. Bessie, pretending to look affronted said, "Is you laughing at me, the way I done talked?"

Juanita smiled at Bessie. "I am indeed. That didn't sound like you at all. It tickled my funny bone. I haven't laughed in ages. You're going to be good for me, Bessie. Thank you. Now tell me about your family, please."

"It's nice to see you smile, Ms. Juanita. Now, about my family. I've been blessed. Been married to Micah for 25 years. We met in high school. Our daughter, Joanna, will be graduating from the local junior college this year with an associate degree in nursing. After she works a few years and saves enough money, she wants to get her bachelor's degree in nursing. Micah said he'd pay for her education, but she has an independent streak. Wants to make her own way. She's done it right well so far."

Half an hour later, Bessie picked up the empty teapot and smiled at Juanita. "I think I better get to work or you'll still have a dirty house when I leave. I'll clean the downstairs, then fix you lunch." She disappeared into the kitchen, leaving Juanita alone with her thoughts.

Juanita smiled contentedly. She and Bessie came from very different backgrounds, but they appeared to share the same basic values. Bessie had been as interested in hearing about her family as she had been to hear about Bessie's. It would be lovely to have someone closer to her own age to talk with. It gave her something to look forward to.

I must call the lawyer's office for an appointment, she thought. *I need to cancel the power of attorney that Miguel currently holds, and revisit my will. I also need to meet with someone at the bank to review my accounts and investments. If I'm going to move into a senior housing facility, I need to know just how much I can afford to pay. I've heard they can be quite expensive! I'm so grateful that Bessie has agreed to drive me to appointments and to visit some of those senior complexes. I'm beginning to feel as if life is worth living after all.*

Juanita was awakened by Bessie's voice calling her. "Ms. Juanita, I have some lunch ready for you. Can you come to the table in the kitchen to eat, or would you like me to bring your tray table in there?"

"Oh my! I fell asleep! I'll try the kitchen table today, Bessie. Just be patient. It takes me a while to get there. Please have lunch with me."

"No hurry, missus. I'll have a quick bite with you, then finish cleaning the upstairs before Micah comes to pick me up."

"Okay, Bessie. It will be pleasant to have your company, even for a little while. I've been alone too long."

They lingered over lunch longer than Bessie had intended, so she was still working on the upstairs cleaning when the doorbell rang.

"Goodness, it's already two o'clock. That must be Micah. I'll get the door and tell him to wait in the car until I'm finished."

"No, ask him to come in, Bessie. He can have a cup of tea with me while he waits. We can talk about the kind of work he can do for me."

Bessie answered the door and issued Juanita's invitation to Micah. He entered the living room, cap in hand. "Thank you for the invitation, Ma'am, but I'm dirty from working my last job."

"Oh, please do sit down. Bessie, would you put a towel on that chair, so Micah doesn't have to worry about making it dusty? Micah, I want to talk with you about the work that needs doing around here. Would you prefer something other than tea? There is probably a beer in the refrigerator. I know that my grandson and his friends enjoy drinking beer."

"A glass of cold water would be appreciated, Ma'am. One does get thirsty in this hot weather. I don't drink alcohol anymore. It tends to get the best of me."

"I'll have a glass of cold water, too, Bessie—no ice. Thank you."

Bessie covered the chair and brought two glasses of water. "I need about twenty minutes to finish here, Micah," she commented before leaving them to return to her cleaning.

"Now, Micah. Tell me what kinds of skills you have, so I can assess which of my many chores might fit your skills."

"Well, Ma'am, I'm a licensed electrician. I used to do that exclusively. But, over the many years I worked on construction projects, I began to help out with other aspects of the work when they were short-handed. I learned new skills in the process. During the recession, construction projects were few and far between. Since people were staying in their homes, rather than moving up, demand for handyman services increased. Folks these days don't seem to know how to do many of the fix-ups around the house that were routine once upon a time. The elderly may have the skills, but are reluctant to climb ladders, or find that doing things with their hands is difficult because of arthritis or other problems that come with aging. So, I've expanded my scope of work. These days, I have my own handyman business, *Micah's Handyman Services.* Two assistants help me. We do house painting, plumbing, electrical and dry-wall repairs. We fix screens, refinish wood floors, clean and re-grout tile, fix door latches, and many more things that need attention around a house. Our website has a complete list of the services we offer. I can give you some references from folks I've done work for, if you like."

"I'm afraid that I haven't learned to use the computer, so I can't look at your website. I'll just have to ask you if you can do the repairs I need, Micah."

"That's fine, Ma'am. Or, I can print the list and bring it to-morrow. But then, I may be able to do something that's not on the list, so maybe just asking me works as well."

"I like the way you've adapted what you do to the changing times. That shows initiative. Why don't we start with a few small things that need fixing here, then move on to the bigger things? For starters, I'll feel much more secure once the lock on my bathroom window is repaired. There is a toilet leak in the powder room that is only going to get worse with time. Can we start with those? Then, perhaps you can go through the house and make a list of things you notice that need attention. I haven't been able to get to the second story in several years; I have no idea what might need attention up there. Here, on the first floor where I spend my time, I use mostly the bedroom suite, living room, and kitchen, so you may wish to survey the other rooms. Once you've done that, let's see how much you've identified that needs attention. I'll worry about the outside once we've completed the inside work. Does that sound like a plan?"

"I'll take a look at the window lock and leaky toilet now, while Bessie's still working, if that's okay with you. I should be able to fix those for you when I drop Bessie off later this week. That should give you some peace of mind. I didn't much like the look of some of those young men hanging around in the street! I think they may be using drugs."

"Thank you, Micah. That would indeed give me an easier mind. You can have a look around at the other rooms after you finish those two jobs. Then we'll figure out how to proceed."

Bessie returned. "I've finished the cleaning, Ms. Juanita. I'll do the grocery shopping Thursday morning. I left some dinner on plates in the refrigerator for you to warm for tonight and tomorrow night. Have a good evening."

"Thank you, Bessie. I'm so glad we found each other. Micah and I have made our plans. He will do some fixing for me when he brings you later in the week. Enjoy your evening."

— CHAPTER 18 —

Raleigh-Durham, North Carolina
Thursday, October 13

Susan sat in her first-class window seat waiting for the San Francisco flight to finish boarding. Walter dozed in the seat next to her. She took another sip of her tonic water over ice. *So much has happened since our wedding. I can't believe it's been nearly four weeks! If someone had told me a year ago that by now I'd be engaged in living life to the fullest, I wouldn't have believed it.*

First, there had been the visit from Walter's son, Dan, and his family the week following their wedding. Two weeks after Dan's visit, Susan and Walter flew to North Carolina to visit Susan's daughter, Kristin, and her family. Kristin and Walter had been delighted to see each other again and reminisced about the times when they were getting acquainted in Hawaii. Kristin's husband, Jim, had not previously met Walter and had been shy at the start of their visit. He and Walter soon discovered things they had in common—a love of fishing, golfing, and classical music.

Susan's grandchildren, Jack and Alex, quickly engaged with Walter, who had an easy way with children. He treated them with respect and showed interest in their activities and thoughts. The boys soon found themselves discussing Hawaii, computer security issues, and sports with him. To Susan's surprise, Walter held his own in an impromptu basketball-shooting match with the boys. Susan had enjoyed reconnecting with her grandsons. They were growing up so fast! Their lives were packed with school, sports, scouts, friends, and family outings. She only got to see them once or twice a year and felt like their life was passing her by.

Kristin and her family enthusiastically endorsed Walter's suggestion of a Brooks-Conway family event in Hawaii so the two families could get acquainted. Susan shuddered whenever she thought about the logistics. Walter assured her that it was not an insurmountable obstacle and promised he would take care of the arrangements. She was happy to leave it in Walter's hands.

It has been a lovely visit, but entirely too short. I'm sorry to be leaving. I look forward to seeing them this winter in Hawaii.

Now, they were on their way to Oakland to visit Walter's daughter, Celia, and her family. Susan had been touched by the girl's thoughtful wedding gift and enjoyed chatting with her when she and Walter called to thank her. According to Walter, Celia's husband, Dave, was outgoing, funny, and always looking to be helpful and accommodating. Susan especially looked forward to getting to know their five-year old daughter, Sandra, Walter's favorite grandchild.

After visiting Walter's daughter, they would drive from Oakland to Thousand Oaks to visit Susan's son, Brendan, and his family. The round of family visits would conclude in Laguna Hills, where Walter's son Keith and his family lived. Although Susan had met Keith during his surprise visit to his father in Hawaii, she had yet to meet his family. The drive from Thousand Oaks to Laguna Hills would give Susan and Walter a short break from family to enjoy sightseeing and quiet time together, a brief delayed honeymoon.

"Ladies and Gentlemen. We are loaded and about to push back from the gate. Please make sure your seat back is upright, and your tray table is stowed. Place any carry-on baggage that is not in the overhead bin under the seat in front of you, and check that your seat belt is securely fastened. Thank you."

Susan checked her seatbelt, then Walter's; he was still snoozing, oblivious to the commotion around him. Susan smiled fondly at him. Even though he was only five years older than her, Susan had noticed that when he wasn't actively engaged in activity or conversation he had a tendency to catnap, perhaps because he frequently didn't sleep soundly at night. These short naps seemed to energize him. He was always ready to go once he awakened. After take-off Susan settled in with a book. Eventually the drone of the engines lulled her to sleep. Both of them awoke when lunch was served. By the time they had eaten, and then sipped an after-lunch glass of wine and chatted, the pilot announced that they were beginning their decent and would soon be landing in San Francisco.

"I can't believe we're already here! Flying first-class really does enable one to arrive with enough energy to finish the journey. When I fly coach, I arrive feeling grubby, irritable, achy, and tired. I almost enjoyed this trip. The flight attendants were attentive, the food was decent, I could visit the restroom when I needed to, and I had room to move around, so I'm not too stiff. I even slept for close to an hour, something I can never do in coach. Since we can afford this, I think the extra expense is well worth it!"

Walter smiled indulgently. "You worked hard to earn your money and invested it carefully. Now, you deserve to treat yourself well. I'm here to help you move past your frugality and occasionally splurge on yourself."

Their bags were already there when they arrived at the baggage carousel, so they had been among the first in-line at the car rental counter. Now they were on the interstate, headed toward Oakland. Their timing had been good; traffic wasn't yet too heavy. They had beat the rush-hour traffic.

"Thank God for GPS," said Walter when they finally exited the freeway and were driving on local streets. "Much as I enjoy maps, they have limitations when driving. Even passengers have difficulty following progress on a paper map while looking for street signs. Traffic moves so fast! It's nice to have a voice telling you when to turn. With the visual display of the local area, your passenger can alert you to change lanes when a turn is coming up."

"GPS certainly reduces my anxiety when I drive in unfamiliar locations. Walter, it looks as if you will need to turn right in about half a mile."

"Thanks for the advance notice. Things are starting to look familiar. Once we've turned into Celia's neighborhood. I can find her house without the gadget."

Several blocks, and several turns later, Walter alerted Susan. "Celia's house is on the right toward the end of this block. It's white with blue shutters."

As they neared the end of the block, Susan asked, "What is the house number? I don't see any white house with blue shutters. Are you sure this is the right block?"

"I'd have to look it up on my phone. I've always relied on spotting the house." Walter pulled the car to the curb and perused the houses on the right side of the street. A few minutes later, he frowned, pulled out his phone, and then looked up the number. "Its 785. We're sitting in front of 773." He continued slowly down the street.

"There it is, 785" said Susan pointing at a light grey house with white shutters and a bright yellow front door. Fronting a manicured hedge of azaleas that ran across the front of the house was a bed filled with low growing marigolds, and a profusion of cosmos, coneflowers, and coreopsis in shades of white, yellow and orange.

Walter parked at the curb and stared at the house in astonishment. "Amazing that a coat of paint and change in landscaping can alter the appearance so much! Even knowing that we're at the right place, I'm having trouble imagining the house I remember from my visit last year. Celia never mentioned that they had painted the house. Well, let's go in."

Their knock was answered almost immediately. Celia opened the door and enveloped her father in a big hug. "Dad, it's wonderful to see you! It has been too long."

Releasing her father, she turned to Susan. Without giving her father a chance for introductions, she extended her hand. "You must be Susan. I'm pleased to meet you."

Susan took her hand. "Celia, I'm delighted to meet you. I've heard so much about you from your father. I was touched by the lovely and thoughtful wedding album you sent. We've already added our wedding pictures and pictures of my family. We think of you every time we add photos.

"Your house is so pretty. As one approaches, those yellow and orange flowers fronting the azalea hedge emphasize your bright, cheerful front door. It announces that someone happy and creative lives here. The inside has the same upbeat, happy feel," Susan commented as she followed Celia into the house and glanced around.

"Thanks, Susan. That's the impression I wanted to create." Just then, Sandra, Celia's five-year old daughter entered the room.

"Sandra, come give me a hug!" commanded Walter. She ran to her grandfather who hugged her, then picked her up and swung her around three times before setting her down. "How's my big girl?"

"Fine, Granddad." She glanced shyly at Susan, and moved back to lean against her mother's leg.

"Sandra, this is Susan, your grandfather's new wife. I told you about her. She's your new grandmother. Say hello."

Sandra moved closer to her mother. Susan stepped forward and squatted down in front of the child.

"Hello, Sandra. I'm happy to meet you. Your grandfather told me that you like to paint, and that you have a kitty you like to play with. Perhaps later you could show me some of your paintings, and introduce me to your kitty?" Sandra nodded shyly. "Good. I look forward to that. Maybe we can paint together? I love to paint." Sandra nodded again.

Celia grinned at Susan as she stood up. "I think you and Sandra will get along famously. She takes time to warm up to new people, but you've zeroed in on her two favorite things." Susan smiled at Sandra who smiled back.

"Let's get you two settled in the guest room." Celia picked up a suitcase and led the way. "I'll prepare some tea and appetizers. We can chat on the back deck until Dave gets home. Commuter traffic is so uncertain, I'm never sure when he'll arrive home for dinner. Sandra, please help me carry plates out to the deck."

Susan and Walter changed into clean clothes, unpacked, and collected their gifts. Finding Celia in the kitchen, they gave her the set of calligraphy pens, inks, and paper they had brought for her, and a bottle of wine. Sandra looked expectantly at her grandfather. "Didn't you bring me a present, Granddad? You always do."

"Sandra! You're not supposed to ask. Its bad manners." exclaimed her mother.

"It's to be expected, Celia. She knows I never come without something for her." Walter brought out the package he had been holding behind his back. He looked at it carefully. "I do believe this says Sandra on it." He handed it to the child, who ripped off the paper. It was a large plush cat, the same color as the household cat that Sandra loved.

"Oh, Granddad, it looks just like Christy, our cat! Sleeping with it will be like sleeping with Christy at night. I asked Mom if I could sleep with her, but she said that Christy must sleep in her basket. Thank you!" Sandra gave her grandfather a big hug.

"Give Grandma Susan a hug too. She picked it out for you after she saw a picture of you with Christy."

Sandra shyly hugged Susan. "Thank you, Grandma Susan. I love the present."

"I'm glad that you do. It really does look like Christy."

"I think it's time for some sustenance. You must be hungry after your long trip." Celia led them out to the deck. They settled into their chairs. Sandra offered Susan tea sandwiches from the tray she carried. "I helped Mom make these."

"I'll bet they are yummy. I hope your mother appreciates her helper."

Celia took the tray from Sandra after she had served her grandfather and then set it on the table. She gave her daughter a brief hug. "I don't know what I'd do without you, sweetheart."

The sound of a car door sent Sandra running toward the garage. "Daddy's home! He can have some sandwiches with us." She flung herself at him as he entered the house.

"Whoa, Peanut. I love your enthusiastic greetings, but this time, you almost knocked me over!" He bent and hugged Sandra, who took his hand and dragged him toward the back deck.

"Granddad is here! He brought Grandmother Susan with him."

Dave hugged Celia, then shook Walter's hand. "Nice to see you again, Walter. It's been too long." He turned to Susan, "You must be Susan, the beautiful bride. I'm Dave. I'm pleased to finally meet you. Walter's been talking about you for some time. You've brought a smile back to his face and purpose to his life. Welcome to the family."

"Thanks, Dave. I'm happy to meet you. Your wife and daughter were preparing to feed us, in anticipation that you might encounter heavy traffic."

"I often do. Since you are visiting, I left early today."

"We're glad you did," said Celia, giving her husband a smile. "Before you make yourself comfortable, would you take drink orders? Then we can enjoy drinks with our tea sandwiches while we catch up with Dad and Susan's lives. Afterwards, perhaps Susan and Sandra will give me a hand in the kitchen while I prepare dinner? That will give you and Dad a chance to converse."

———

The days with Dave, Celia, and Sandra passed quickly. Susan and Walter arrived on Thursday. Dave took Friday off, so they had three full days with the entire family before he had to return to work early on Monday. On Friday, a warm day in the mid-seventies, they visited a local park. They chose a picnic table located under the canopy of a sizable maple tree. Celia unpacked a virtual feast—sandwiches, deviled eggs, a mixed green salad, potato salad, chips, fruit, and chocolate chip cookies—something to appeal to everyone. Lemonade, water, and beer were the beverage choices. After a leisurely lunch, they watched Sandra joyously feed the ducks that came begging in swarms. Later, they rented canoes and rowed on the large lake. When they returned from their day's excursions, Susan and Sandra spent time playing with the kitten, then talking while they painted.

That night, a neighbor had Sandra over for a play date with her daughter. Celia and Dave took Walter and Susan to one of their favorite local restaurants, a bistro on a tree-lined street, for some good food and adult conversation.

Saturday was spent locally. They lingered over breakfast before taking Sandra to the zoo. It was hard to know who enjoyed that excursion more, Sandra or the adults. Following a late lunch, Walter and Dave watched a golf match. While Sandra took a nap, Susan and Celia got better acquainted. They discovered that they had much in common. Both women had grandparents who retired to Florida, and had fond memories of visiting there when they were children. They also shared a love of gardening and reading.

That evening, Dave cooked burgers and corn on the grill for dinner, ending with grilled peaches with whipped cream, Sandra's favorite dessert. While Susan and Celia did the dishes, Walter and Dave played a game of croquet with Sandra, who kept trying to move her ball when the adults weren't looking. Sandra was ready for bed by the time they finished their game. Susan read Sandra her bedtime story, allowing Celia to have some time alone with her Dad and Dave.

The family spent Sunday in San Francisco. They began their day with a visit to Golden Gate Park. While Sandra ran off some of her excess energy chasing pigeons, Susan and Celia sat in the shade of a large tree, chatting and enjoying the views. Walter and Dave sat on a park bench, engaged in conversation. Afterwards, the family lunched at a seafood restaurant on Fisherman's Wharf that overlooked the bay. To compensate for a calorie-filled lunch, they strolled on the wharf, watching the mimes, itinerant painters, and the crowds. One mime coaxed Sandra to join him in his act, pretending to lift a heavy weight. When she got the giggles and 'dropped' her end of the weight, it caused him to drop his; it landed on his foot. The mime's portrayal of a broken foot was so convincing that Sandra ran to console him, to the delight of the crowd. Poking around the shops in Chinatown occupied the remainder of the afternoon, leaving them just enough time for a Chinese dinner before heading back to Oakland. Walter was surprised to learn that Chinese food was his granddaughter's favorite these days.

On Monday morning, Susan and Walter spent an hour over breakfast talking with Celia and Sandra before reluctantly heading out for the next leg of their trip. Sandra grabbed Susan's hands as she started toward the car. "Please stay, Grandma Susan!"

Susan squatted down in front of the child. "I'm sorry, Sandra. We must leave. I promise Granddad and I will see you soon. We'll call you on the telephone to talk. Maybe you and Mommy can call us sometimes too!"

Sandra hugged Susan, holding on to her, reluctant to let her leave. Celia finally had to pull Sandra away. "Granddad needs a hug too," said Walter, distracting Sandra as he squatted to give her a hug, then whisper in her ear. Sandra giggled. "You're funny, Granddad." Then she waved as Susan and Walter got into the car and drove away.

— CHAPTER 19 —

Irvine, California
Tuesday Evening, October 18

Juanita patted her hair into place and sprayed it with hair spray. She touched up her lipstick and blotted it. Then she looked one last time in the mirror and smiled.

I haven't looked so good in a long time. I've put on some weight, so my clothing almost fit again. I'm not so pale; there's some color in my cheeks. I hope Miguel will be proud of me. I'm so excited that he's taking me out to dinner after we go to the gallery. This is my first excursion outside the house since I had my stroke, except of course, for visits to the doctor. I wish I didn't need to use that walker. Too late to do anything for tonight, but I intend to work on improving my walking so I can manage with a cane one of these days.

Juanita heard the sound of a car door closing, then the front door opening and closing.

"Grandmother. It's Miguel. Are you ready to go?"

"I am," said Juanita, coming into the living room. "What do you think? Will I do?"

"You look very pretty and elegant in that navy dress! Your jewelry makes it look festive. Tonight, I'm escorting the best looking lady in town. Shall we go?"

Miguel helped his grandmother navigate the front steps, then settled her in the passenger seat of the car, and put her walker into the trunk. As he got into the driver's seat, he said, "I'll show you my paintings at the gallery first. That way, we can have a leisurely dinner. The gallery is located in an old building on the road through the canyon to Laguna Beach. I thought we'd go from there to a lovely Mexican Restaurant with an ocean view for our dinner. It has its own parking lot, so we can pull up in front of the door. Do you think you could manage to walk into the restaurant and to our table holding my arm, rather than using the walker? I worry that it will be difficult for you to maneuver the walker among the tables."

"That's very thoughtful of you, Miguel. I was concerned about how I'd manage the walker in a crowded restaurant. I'm sure I can manage by holding your arm. I've been trying to stand and walk more at home of late. I'm stronger than I was. And I'll be delighted to be escorted in on your arm. I'm proud of my grandson."

When they pulled up in front of the gallery, Miguel turned to his grandmother. "Well, this is it, *Galeria de el Renacimiento*."

"I like the name of the Gallery, Miguel. *Gallery of Rebirth*. Every artist feels reborn when he discovers and develops his talent."

The name of the gallery hung on the side of the building facing the road. A bright yellow banner with the words, ART SHOW, October 21-November 19 was draped between two poles in the yard. The entrance to the building appeared to be on the wall perpendicular to the road.

"I know it doesn't look like much from the outside. Like many of the buildings around here, it's old and has seen better days. The inside has been spruced up and I think the paintings show well. If you'll wait here for a moment, I'll go in and turn on the lights, then come back for you. There's plenty of space inside to maneuver your walker and there are also some benches to sit on while you view the paintings."

When Juanita entered the gallery, she couldn't believe the number of paintings hanging on the walls surrounding her. "Are all these your paintings?"

"Yes, Grandmother. For the past year, every hour that I'm not at work, I've been painting and framing to get ready for this show."

Juanita walked slowly, absorbing the intense colors and abstract forms in the paintings. Occasionally, she sat to rest and study a painting that she especially liked. Miguel remained silent as she studied his work. Finally, she turned to him with tears in her eyes.

"Miguelito, your work is powerful---the colors, the brushstrokes, the feelings evoked by the entirety of each work. While the images sometimes lean toward the modern and abstract, one instinctively knows that the work is based on the landscapes of the California coastline and plains, which you have always loved. Your style is unique. I like your paintings very much! I'm proud of what you have achieved. I think you have a future as an artist."

"Thank you, Grandmother. I'm so happy you like them. Thank you for your faith in me. It was that which enabled me to evolve as a painter and to express my feelings through my paintbrush and canvas. Now, let's just hope that I can sell some of them. No matter how much people may say they admire my work, I can't feel successful unless people are willing to part with hard, cold cash in order to own them."

"I understand why you feel that way. Artists in all fields, whether painting, music, writing, or production arts must find it a struggle to create when they must also work a full-time job to pay the bills. I will be interested to see how your work sells. Have you publicized your show widely?"

"We've put ads in the local papers, sent announcements to people who bought art from artists in the cooperative, and posted flyers in various businesses that might have customers interested in art. We also put up notices on the bulletin boards at local businesses, like grocery stores. I put announcements on social media. Hopefully, it will be enough to draw good attendance for the opening. A reporter from the local newspaper will be attending with his photographer. He will write an article for the art column. He hopes to get at least one photograph on the front page."

"It sounds like you've covered all the bases. I'll add a prayer that all goes well."

"Thank you, Grandmother. You realize that none of this would have been possible without you. I can never repay you for your support. I only wish my family could attend. But, I'll not waste time on idle dreams. Have you finished looking at the paintings or would you like to stay a bit longer?"

"I could stay and look all night. I wish I had thought to bring a camera so I could have photographs to remember my grandson's great accomplishment."

"I can take some pictures for you tomorrow after everyone goes home and the gallery is empty. I'll also ask Henry to take some pictures on the night of the opening."

"Thank you, Miguel. Then I'm ready to go. I can't tell you how much tonight means to me. Thank you for bringing me. I'll never forget what I've seen."

Miguel assisted his grandmother to get settled in the car, put the walker in the trunk, and closed up the gallery.

"Now for a good dinner. I hope you're hungry, Grandmother."

"I think I can do justice to my dinner. It will be a treat to eat again in a restaurant and to spend an evening with you."

— CHAPTER 20 —

Wednesday, October 19

Juanita slept late the next morning, an unusual occurrence for her. Sleep was often a problem. The excitement of seeing Miguel's paintings, enjoying a dinner out at a restaurant, and the physical challenges of getting out and about had conspired to tire her. Now, she sat in the kitchen reminiscing about the evening over tea and toast. It had been wonderful in so many respects.

Getting out of her house had made her feel like a bird released from a cage. Seeing the splendor of Miguel's paintings, full of color exploding like a California sunrise, had filled her with awe and reverence for his talent. Her emotions had been touched deeply by his work. . She had felt as if she were on an emotional roller coaster as she had perused the paintings. Something indefinable about them evoked strong feelings. Miguel's love of his subject flowed from the canvas.

Their dinner at *Las Brisas,* the Mexican Restaurant overlooking the bay in Laguna Beach, had been special. Not only was the food excellent, but the interior of the restaurant was quietly elegant and the service personal and attentive. Miguel and Juanita had arrived around five-thirty, so the interior rooms were not yet packed and noisy. Most of the diners already present were sitting on the outdoor patio. She remembered from when she had dined there in years past with Manuel, that it usually got very busy later in the evening.

Juanita and Miguel were given a table by the windows in a quiet corner. Juanita was able to walk to her seat by supporting herself on Miguel's arm. She was sure that Miguel had talked to the management in advance about her disability. She hadn't seen the sea in a long time, so she feasted on the beautiful sea view.

They had shared a dish of assorted Mexican appetizers. For her entrée, Juanita had *Snapper Vera Cruz*. Miguel had a steak. Juanita couldn't manage to eat dessert, but had indulged in a bite of Miguel's mango cheesecake.

During dinner, they discussed Miguel's paintings, how his style had evolved, and how he managed to juggle his restaurant job with his participation in the art cooperative and the gallery. Miguel had glowed in her praise of his paintings. She suspected that he missed the emotional support and approval of his family more than he was willing to admit. He had seemed strangely uneasy when she had asked him about his relationship with the gallery and how that had developed. Because of that seeming discomfort, she had changed the subject. She talked to him instead about Bessie and Micah, and how happy she was that they had come into her life.

Last night, before Juanita went to bed, Miguel had dug out an old pack of photographs that included some of his paintings. He gave them to her and promised to take more of those hanging in the gallery. Juanita was eager to show them to Bessie when she arrived later today.

She glanced at the clock on the kitchen wall. It was eight-twenty. Bessie was due in ten minutes. Micah would be with her to do some repairs. She left her dishes on the table and hurried to her room to dress. She would skip her shower until after they were gone; she had lost track of the time reminiscing about her evening with Miguel. The doorbell rang just as she finished buttoning the last button on her dress.

Juanita hurried toward the door, feeling insecure in her slippers. There had been no time to put on her shoes. She reached the door as the bell rang for the third time and opened it.

"Hello, Bessie, Micah. I'm sorry I kept you waiting. I lost track of the time. I was dressing when you rang. Come in."

"We may be a bit early," said Micah.

"No. You're on time. I lingered over my cup of tea thinking about my night out with my grandson. He took me to see his paintings at the gallery last night. His solo show opens on Friday night. It was a wonderful evening! I have some pictures to show you of my grandson's paintings. I'm bursting with pride, I have to share it!

"Bessie, if you'll make a fresh pot of tea and set out some scones and plates, I'll tell the two of you all about it while we enjoy our tea. I'll go and put on some shoes while you make the tea. While I'm in the bedroom, I'll get my extra key for you, Bessie. If you have a key, I won't have to worry about rushing to open the door and falling."

"Ms. Juanita. Please don't be offended if I don't join you and Bessie for tea. I want to do those two repairs for you, then I must meet my men at a job. And I need to carry in the groceries we picked up on our way here."

"I understand, Micah. I'm afraid I get carried away with my pride in my grandson's accomplishments."

"I'll enjoy hearing all about it," commented Bessie. "I'll just put the groceries away and wash up your breakfast plates while the tea water heats. Then you can share your story and the pictures."

Juanita put on her shoes and put her nightclothes in her dresser. She retrieved the extra key and headed for the kitchen. Bessie was busily putting away groceries. Micah came in with the last bag, then headed to his truck for tools to do her repairs. She soon heard him flushing the toilet in the bathroom.

Bessie thanked her for the key, and placed it securely in the zipper compartment of her purse. She prepared the tea, set the pot on the table, put scones on a plate, set the table, and then joined Juanita who was already seated.

"All set, Miss Juanita. Tell me all about it. I can see you are bursting to let it out!"

Juanita smiled at Bessie, then began to talk. Twenty minutes later, as Bessie was looking at the pictures, Micah came in.

All fixed, Miss Juanita. The latch is secure and I put a new seal on the toilet. I need to go meet my men now. I'll check the rest of the house for needed repairs early next week. The charge for today's repairs is sixty-five dollars, including the parts. I'll give you an invoice and you can pay me when I come back. Maybe you can show me your grandson's paintings then. I'm sorry I don't have time now."

"Thank you, Micah. I'd be happy to show you his paintings then, if you are really interested. I'm afraid I'm so filled with pride that I assume everyone is interested."

"You have every right to be proud. How many artists ever have a solo show? I look forward to seeing the photographs of his paintings."

Micah left and Bessie closed the door behind him. "Before I forget, Miss Juanita, we are picking up my car tonight from the shop. You can go ahead and schedule those appointments you told me about for one of my scheduled days, and I can drive you there."

"Thanks, Bessie. I'll go and make some calls now before I forget."

Juanita went into her bedroom and located the telephone numbers she needed, a pen, and some paper. She settled into her comfortable chair and made her calls. A short time later, she returned to the kitchen.

"I've scheduled an appointment with my lawyer for ten on Friday morning, and one with my bank manager at eleven-thirty that day. They're near each other. I should be finished shortly after noon. Perhaps I can take you to lunch?"

"Are you sure you don't want me to bring you back here. I can prepare lunch for you."

"I'm sure. I had such a good time the other night that I want to enjoy another meal out in the world. I've been cooped up in this house for too long. As long as we're going to be out anyway, I may as well take advantage of it."

"As you wish. I'll be pleased to accept your offer. Now, I'd better get some work done."

After Bessie started her work, Juanita went into her room, sat down in her chair, and picked up the telephone. She dialed her daughter-in-law, Dolores.

"Hello. Juanita? How nice to hear from you! It's been such a long time. I've wanted to call, but you know how Sergio is when he gets stubborn. The family has been forbidden to contact you since the two of you had your argument. I was afraid to make waves."

"That son of mine has no right to decide that you and the children must be cut off from Miguel and myself. I'm sure he has his reasons, but it's a selfish thing to do. I, too, didn't resist his decision before now. I was still too depressed from my stroke, and angry at his cutting ties with his son.

"Lately, Dolores, I've become more assertive. I recently threw Miguel's friend out of my house. At Miguel's request, I had allowed him to move in so he could save enough for a deposit on an apartment. Eight months later, he was still here. He's an aggressive man and generally not very nice. He consumed Miguel's time and attention to the point where Miguel didn't follow through on our agreement that he would help me out. The positive aspect is that I was becoming desperate. That desperation drove me to act and to rethink my life.

"The reason I'm calling is to tell you that Miguel has become an accomplished painter. He is going to have a solo show of his paintings at the *Galeria de el Renacimiento* on Canyon Road in Laguna Beach. He took me to see his paintings and I was astounded at the number of paintings and their quality. He has a unique style. Miguel accomplished all this while working as a cook at a restaurant. You should be proud of your son.

"The show opens on Friday evening, beginning at seven o'clock. I think that you and Sergio should attend. I hope that when Sergio sees what Miguel has accomplished, he will be proud of him and change his mind about ostracizing him from his family. I know that Miguel misses you all very much. If you can't make the opening, then drop by with Sergio during the run of the show, which is October twenty-first through November nineteenth. I know it will be hard for you to cross Sergio, but please do this for your son. If Sergio will soften his position, you, Delia, and Fernando will benefit as well."

"You've brought me such good news, Juanita! Thank you. I promise that I'll find a way to get Sergio to the gallery, preferably on the night that the show opens. Pray for success in my efforts! I'll let you know what happens. Good-by, Juanita. I can't thank you enough. You have made my day."

"Good-by, Delores, and buenas fuerte!"

— CHAPTER 21 —

Friday, October 21

Juanita's appointment with her lawyer proceeded smoothly. He had prepared documents she needed to sign to rescind the power of attorney she had given Miguel after her stroke, and a revised version of her will. She asked to take the will home with her. She wanted to review it carefully before signing. She signed the other document and set an appointment for the following week to finalize the will.

Bessie next drove her to the bank. She settled into a chair in the waiting area outside the manager's office while Juanita went in for her meeting. It was almost an hour before Juanita emerged from the room. She looked shaken.

"Miss Juanita, are you alright? You look pale!"

"No, Bessie, I am not alright. I had a shock. I'll tell you about it over lunch. I could use some advice. Perhaps you can help me with my problem."

"I'd be happy to help, if I can. You look really shaken. Let's get you in the car. Do you still want to go to a restaurant, or would you prefer to go home?"

"I think I had better go home. I may break into tears when I tell you what's happened. I'll take you to lunch next week when we return to the lawyer's office."

Bessie drove Juanita home and settled her at the kitchen table with a cup of tea.

"I'm going to fix lunch now. After you've eaten something, we'll talk. Some nourishment will help steady your nerves."

"I'm not very hungry, but I'll try to eat something. Make something simple like a bowl of soup."

Twenty minutes later, Bessie set their soup bowls in the sink and assisted Juanita to settle in the living room. She sat down next to her.

"Now, tell me what has happened?"

"Oh, Bessie. My world had fallen apart!"

"Tell me about it. I'll see what I can do to help you."

"Well, you know how proud I was of my Miguel after he took me to see his paintings. I think I told you once that he's always been my favorite grandchild. When he was little, he was shy and vulnerable, constantly being criticized by his father for not being macho and engaging in sports. We were always close. He moved in here when his father refused to allow him to live at home after he served a year in prison for drug use. He did some of my heavier chores and simple maintenance in exchange for a place to live. After my stroke, he looked after me. I was very depressed at the time. When we decided it would be good to create a bedroom suite on this level, so I could have a private space, I gave Miguel my power of attorney. That way, he could manage the project, and my finances in general. I had no interest. He gave me the invoices for the remodel, so I could see what it cost, but I refused to discuss them with him because of my mental outlook at the time.

"Today, when I reviewed the accounts with the bank manager, it was clear that a considerable amount of money had been taken out during the last year. We looked over deposits and withdrawals for the past five years, and could see the regular monthly debits for things like utilities and groceries, insurance, semi-annual deductions for property taxes, and the quarterly estimated federal income tax payments. Those have been on-going since before Miguel took over. We could also identify withdrawals that occurred during the time when the house was being remodeled.

"About ten months ago, a single payment was made of forty-five hundred dollars, followed by regular monthly payments of fifteen hundred dollars. Nine months ago, monthly payments of eighteen hundred dollars began. Other unidentified payments of varying amounts were made during the past year, totaling around twenty thousand dollars. That's about fifty-five thousand, seven hundred dollars that I can't account for, a significant amount of money!"

"So you think Miguel was stealing from you?"

"It certainly looks that way. He seemed very uncomfortable and changed the subject last evening over dinner when I asked about how he had negotiated to have his show at the gallery. I think he is renting the gallery space so he will have a place to show his work and is paying his friend Henry to manage it for him. I believe that he remodeled the property to make it suitable for his needs. The timing of the unexplained payments certainly fits that scenario. The forty-five hundred dollars could have been a deposit, and the first and last month's month rent usually required when you rent. That would fit, if the monthly fifteen hundred dollar payments are rent. The eighteen hundred dollar payments started just around the time that Miguel told me his friend Henry got a job managing a gallery. Other individual payments probably are for remodeling. The bank manager is going to look into the recipients of the payments and get back to me."

"I assume you plan to talk to Miguel about this."

"I must. Some of the blame is mine. He was probably too young to manage my affairs. I was ill, depressed, and had no interest in the world when I asked him to take over. I never showed any further interest, and flatly refused to discuss expenses with him. Knowing I wasn't interested, that I had supported his painting efforts in the past, and that he was my major heir, he may have assumed I'd be alright with this. But, it is theft. I'm very disappointed in him!

"Learning about this now, at the moment of his greatest triumph is painful. Yesterday, I talked to his mother and urged her to persuade his father to attend the opening tonight. I thought that Sergio would be proud of Miguel, and hoped that once Sergio saw what Miguel has accomplished, he would relent and allow Miguel to spend time with his family. If Sergio learns of this, he'll never reestablish ties with Miguel. Being ostracized from his family has been extremely hard on him."

"Would he be able to pay you back?"

"Certainly not until his paintings start to sell. Expenses for rent, and Henry's salary will be ongoing. I don't know how he can manage even that unless he sells a lot of his work. His salary as a cook at the restaurant certainly won't cover it."

"He must have given that some thought. Have you told him that you were going to revoke the power of attorney?"

"Yes, when I gave his friend Henry a month to leave the house. I didn't set a date by which I would take back the power of attorney, and I haven't told him I made an appointment to see the lawyer."

"Do you want the money back?"

"I don't care about the money. I can get an apartment or condo in a senior living facility with what I get from the sale of this house. My income is adequate to live comfortably. That money was a cushion against inflation. But, Miguel has to learn that what he did was wrong! Had he told me his hopes and asked for the money, I'd probably have given or loaned it to him. If there are no negative consequences to what he has done, he won't learn anything about responsibility and what is right. The question is, what should those consequences be? I could demand that he repay it all. Or I could demand that he set a repayment plan for half of the money and deduct the remainder from what he will inherit.

"Currently, I'm the only person in Miguel's life willing to offer him guidance. However I handle this, I can't do it in a way that destroys my relationship with him. I also don't want to end his dreams of being an artist. And, I don't want the law involved."

"Can you wait a bit to deal with it? Once the art show is over, you'll know whether his work is commercially viable."

"Yes, that would be useful to know. But, I need to tell him soon that I rescinded his power of attorney. He won't be able to continue writing checks on my account. His rent and Henry's salary are due at the end of the month. That's the latest I can deal with this."

"I wonder if he made a long-term business plan for the gallery. It would be totally irresponsible not to have thought ahead. His show can't be the endpoint of his plans."

"That's a good thought, Bessie. I think I'll put this aside until next week when I know how he did from the opening, and a few additional days of the show. By then, I'll also know how his father responds after seeing his work. Thanks for listening and helping me think it through."

— CHAPTER 22 —

Thousand Oaks, California
Friday, October 21

Susan and Walter planned to take four days for their trip from Oakland to Thousand Oaks. That would give them some much needed time alone. They would arrive at Brendon's home on Friday afternoon, around the time Brendon returned from work.

They followed the coastal route down the California coast to Carmel, where they spent two nights. The peaceful setting and views of the sea from their hotel room suited them both. Leisurely breakfasts, walks on the beach, and a quiet hour or two in their room after lunch soon restored the intimacy to which they had become accustomed before beginning their family visits. They filled the afternoons with visits to galleries and shops in the town, then ended their days with quiet dinners in elegant courtyards filled with lush greenery and bright flowers.

During their last dinner, Susan said sadly, "I'm sorry we must leave here, Walter. These two days in Carmel felt like a honeymoon. It's a beautiful place! I could easily enjoy another week of this. Still, I feel refreshed for the next leg of our journey."

"I share those sentiments. However, duty calls. We'll plan

our delayed honeymoon when we get back to Seattle. Remember, this trip is in the interest of forging good family relationships."

They spent the next day on the road. During the early part of the journey there were few towns. After San Simeon, municipalities were situated closer together, and traffic became heavier. Views of the sea compensated for the traffic. Late Thursday afternoon they arrived in Santa Barbara, where they would spend the night.

"The tension of driving all day in heavy traffic has left me a bit tired, Susan. How about a short nap, then a walk on the pier before dinner?"

"Yes to both those suggestions."

They fell asleep almost immediately after cuddling in the soft bed in a cool, quiet room. Light seeping in around the curtains as the sun moved lower in the west woke Susan half an hour later. She got up, showered, and then sat quietly by the window to read the information book about Santa Barbara provided by the hotel. She found an Italian restaurant near the pier and decided to suggest having dinner there.

Soon, she shook Walter gently. "Wake up, Sleeping Beauty. If you don't become functional, you won't be able to sleep tonight."

"What? Oh, Susan. It's good you decided to wake me. I'll shower, then we can take our walk on the pier. Have you been up long?"

"About half an hour. I showered, then checked out the restaurant scene in town. I found this Italian Restaurant not far from the pier. It has excellent reviews. Shall I make us a reservation?"

"Sounds good to me. You know I'm fond of good Italian food."

The sight and sounds of the sea soothed their souls as they strolled on the pier and drank in the fresh sea air. Afterwards, they enjoyed a delicious dinner at *Due Lune Cucina*. Over an after-dinner cordial on their hotel balcony, they listened to the sea and watched the stars as they discussed plans for the next day.

"It's only a short drive from Santa Barbara to Thousand Oaks. Shall we enjoy a leisurely morning here in Santa Barbara before starting our drive, Walter? We don't want to arrive much before four o'clock, when Brendon gets home from work. We also need to pick up some gifts for the family."

"Sleeping in always appeals to me, Susan. And I would enjoy a chance to explore Santa Barbara while we're here. Maybe we can do our shopping in the old town."

The next morning they arose at eight, enjoyed a swim, and then sat by the pool for half an hour, soaking up the morning sunshine. After they showered, they enjoyed a late breakfast in the hotel's patio garden before they packed and checked out. In the charming old section of town, Susan found a hand-blown glass vase for Brendon's wife, Maria. They purchased a bottle of wine, and a bottle of Brendon's favorite scotch. For Susan's two-year-old granddaughter, Anita, they found a stuffed pelican. An outdoor café with bright orange and yellow umbrellas, and planters overflowing with flowers, enticed them to stop for lunch. They ordered a garden salad and a plate of shrimp scampi over angel hair pasta.

"You look pensive, Susan," commented Walter as they waited for their food.

"I was thinking about how long it has been since I last saw Brendon and his family. I've only seen Anita, my granddaughter, twice! Then, my thoughts drifted to when Brendon was a child. He's always been such a contrast to his sister. Kristin's a bundle of life and humor, engaged with everyone around her, usually leading the way. Brendon was an introvert. He lived in a world of his own, lost in his thoughts. Science captivated him in high school. I suppose that's why he chose to become a cell biologist. As an adult, his thoughts were usually absorbed by the current project at his lab.

"Six years ago, shortly before Scott died, he met and married Maria, a woman who had emigrated from Mexico with her family when she was three. They seemed like such an unlikely couple. They say that opposites attract. Brendon is quiet and introspective, Maria outgoing, full of life and laughter, comfortable with who she is, and not needing to present a front to the world. I sometimes feel that she's Brendon's missing half. They grew up in different worlds, and there is a wide gap in their educations; Brendon has his Ph.D., Maria a high school diploma. But they seem happy together."

"How did they meet?"

"Maria was working as a secretary at the company where Brendon works. I was amazed that he connected with her. His job was always his life, absorbing him day and night. Maria worked to pay her bills; when she left the office at the end of the day, her life began. She lived life to the fullest with her many friends and large family.

"Since they married, her family has drawn Brendon into their circle and out of himself. They diverted Brendon's attention away from his job, and showed him a broader vision of life. They believe that life should be fun.

"When their daughter, Anita, was born, Brendon changed. He loves the role of father and dotes on his daughter. He reduced the hours he spends at work, and doesn't allow thoughts of his job to constantly intrude when he's at home. Most of the transformation occurred when I was mourning Scott, so it was a bit of a shock the first time I visited them after Scott's death. I've not seen them often since then and need to get to know this new Brendon of mine."

"I look forward to meeting him. He sounds like an interesting person. Ah! Here comes our food. It looks wonderful and I'm hungry. Let's enjoy our meal."

Walter and Susan pulled into the driveway of the 1960's ranch in the foothills of the Santa Anita Mountains at 3:55 p.m.

"We're here, Walter. I'm so excited to see my son! Are you ready to meet Brendon and his family?"

"It will be a pleasure to finally meet him. He lives in an interesting neighborhood. These contemporary ranches were very popular in the nineteen-sixties. Looks like a few of the owners have modernized their houses, adding floor-to-ceiling windows. I bet they have some fabulous views!"

As they got out of the car, the front door opened. Walter looked up to see a tall, slender man with wavy light brown hair, dressed in khaki slacks, a short-sleeved tan dress shirt, and brown loafers striding energetically down the front walk toward their car.

"Mom! I'm so glad to see you!" Brendon gave his mother a big hug, then turned to Walter, hand extended. "Walter, I'm Brendon. Welcome to our home."

"Thank you, Brendon. I'm pleased to meet you. Susan has talked so much about you and your family that I feel as if I already know you. We're delighted to be here."

"I thought you'd still be at work, Brendon. How nice that you're home already!"

"I went in early today, Mom. I had to finish a project that was due by noon. Early in, early to leave. Let me help you with the luggage, Walter. Mom, why don't you go in and say hello to Maria while we collect the bags. She's in the kitchen giving Anita an afternoon snack. When she's finished, we can all settle on the back patio with some wine and cheese."

Susan headed for the house. Walter and Brendon unloaded the luggage. "You don't have much luggage for such an extended trip, Walter. How did you ever get my mother to pack so lightly?"

"We planned in advance. Fortunately, California temperatures vary little from place to place. We simply add layers when it's cooler. The casual way people dress these days also helps limit wardrobe requirements. Susan was able to do laundry at Kristin's, and again at my daughter, Celia's. At our age, we're grateful not to have to lug heavy cases."

"Makes sense. But, I do think that I see some of your influence on Mom's thinking. In the past, she always took several times more than she needed."

"Well, I've encouraged Susan to be more relaxed about things in general. She tends to become anxious, to see obstacles rather than opportunities. I'm sure you know that about your mother. Recently, she's been trying hard to consider the opportunities, rather than the difficulties. Hopefully, one of these days that approach will become second nature for her."

"I fear that I take after her in that regard. I applaud your efforts and hope they succeed. I'm sure life is easier with that approach. Perhaps you can give me some pointers as well."

Walter and Brendon set the luggage in the guest room. Walter opened the case containing their gifts for the family. He presented Brendon with the bottles of Scotch and wine, then picked up the gifts for Maria and Anita, and followed Brendon toward the patio. Maria and Susan were chatting as they set the table. On the way, Brendon set the brandy and wine Walter had given him on the kitchen counter, and grabbed a bottle of white wine, which he set in the ice bucket Maria had waiting. On the table was a platter of nachos, and a bowl of cubed mango. Wine glasses and the wine opener were on the table.

Maria turned to Walter as they came through the patio door. "Hello, Walter. I'm Maria, Brendon's wife. This young lady is our daughter Anita. We've been looking forward to meeting you. It is such a pleasure to meet the person who has put a smile back on my mother-in-law's face! She hasn't looked so good in years!"

"I'm happy to meet you, Maria. Susan has also put a smile back on my face. We're good for each other." Walter handed Maria a wrapped package. "We brought you a small gift. I hope you will like it."

"Thank you, Walter, and Susan," said Maria turning toward Susan. May I open it now? I just love opening presents!"

"Certainly, as you like," said Susan, smiling at Maria's child-like response.

Maria ripped off the wrapping. She opened the box. "Oh, Mother Susan, Walter. It's beautiful. What lovely colors! The shape is exquisite! Thank you so much!"

"You are most welcome. I know you love flowers, and one can never have too many vases. I fell in love with this piece when I saw it in the shop. It seemed perfect for you. There's some information about the artist on the small card in the box."

Walter turned to the child sitting in her high chair. "I'm your new grandfather, Anita. Your Grandma has told me so much about you. I'm happy to meet you. And so is this guy." He handed the stuffed penguin to the child. "His name is Puffy, the penguin. He has come with us all the way from Santa Barbara to meet you."

Anita hugged the penguin close to her. "Thank you," she said shyly. "Mama, can I sleep with Puffy?"

"Of course you may. You have lots of room left in your bed. We'll make room for him among your other stuffed animals."

"Please, make yourselves comfortable," said Brendon. He pulled out a chair for Susan, then one for Maria. "May I pour you some Riesling? Or would you prefer a beer, a soft drink, lemonade, or water? Anita likes lemonade."

Susan and Maria chose Riesling. Walter requested a beer, so Brendon brought two *Dos Equis*. Maria passed the nachos and mangos, placing a few chips and several mango chunks on Anita's plate.

"Here's to the bride and groom and to a good visit," toasted Brendon. "To a long and happy marriage! We have a lot of catching up to do! Maria and I want to hear all about how you met."

Susan and Walter began their tale. Brendon and Maria listened with rapt attention. That story led Brendon to reminisce about times he spent in Hawaii. When he had finished, Walter told them about the plans to hold a Conway/Brooks family event in Hawaii during the winter. Maria, who had never been to Hawaii was intrigued and excited by the idea. Brendon also liked the prospect, not the least because he would get to see his sister and her family again.

Soon afterwards, Maria stood up. "It's time for me to organize dinner. Brendon, please start warming the grill." Walter went to help Brendon, while Susan went inside to assist Maria.

The visit passed quickly. Maria facilitated opportunities for Susan to be alone with Brendon, sending them on errands, while she took Walter with her and Anita to show him the town. She also facilitated opportunities for Walter to get to know Brendon. Surprisingly, despite their differences in age and background, Walter and Brendon enjoyed each other's company. They would sit over a glass of beer and talk at length. Walter, always curious about the world asked Brendon endless questions about his work. Brendon loved teaching him about how things were done and telling him about the importance of his work in developing treatments for rare diseases. Brendon enjoyed listening to Walter talk about his own family and his life as an FBI agent. He was surprised by how comfortable he felt with Walter. During one of their discussions, he turned to Walter. "May I ask you for some advice? I need to make a decision that affects my professional future and don't know what to do."

"I'm not sure that I should be giving you advice about something so important. But, I'd be glad to listen to your concerns and what you think about the situation. Sometimes just talking about a dilemma can help clarify one's thinking. What is this decision you must make?"

"My company has a facility in San Diego. It has more

sophisticated equipment than the lab where I currently work and can do more advanced technical analyses. They've asked me to move to San Diego and work with the team there to extend the work I've been doing beyond what is possible without the advanced equipment. It's a promotion and means a substantial increase in salary, as well as exciting work."

"It sounds like a great opportunity."

"It is. I've reached a dead end with my work here. It's an area I'm very excited about and the opportunity to continue pursuing this line of research is huge."

"So what's the problem? Professionally, it sounds like a no-brainer to say yes."

"Professionally, it is. The problem is personal. I worry about the impact on my family. Maria is very close to her family. She spends at least several mornings a week with her mother. Also, her mother frequently babysits Anita, so Maria can run her errands and spend some time with her friends. We have dinner with them at least once a week. Also, we often do things with her siblings. I worry that Maria will be unhappy so far from her family."

"That's a legitimate concern. Have you discussed this opportunity with Maria?"

"No. I know that I need to, but I'm so worried that it will make her upset. I don't want to make her unhappy."

"What will happen to your career if you say no to this offer?"

"I imagine they will just give me something else to work on here. We're pretty busy and looking to hire, so I don't suppose I'd lose my job. I should clarify that, I suppose."

"I think you should. You also need to think about what it will do to you if you have to work on things in which you have little interest. You're young and have most of your career ahead of you. There's nothing worse than hating to go to work in the morning!

"You should tell Maria about the offer without delay. Let

her tell you how she feels about a move. Think about ways you can provide her support away from her family, for example, day care for Anita a few days a week, driving Maria up here for periodic weekend visits to her family. You might also offer her the opportunity to fly up with Anita and spend a few days alone with her family every few months. With the extra income from the promotion, you can afford to do things like that. She may surprise you. Women are stronger than we think. Definitely talk to her soon, Brendon. I wouldn't be surprised if she already senses that something is bothering you."

"I will, Walter. You've given me something to think about. Thanks for listening."

"I'm grateful if my thoughts are helpful to you."

Since Maria preferred eating at home to eating out at restaurants, Susan and Maria bonded as they prepared meals and played with Anita. Susan mentioned to Maria that she had always loved Mexican food. Maria happily taught her how to prepare some of her favorite Mexican dishes, chicken enchiladas verde, burritos, and chicken mole. While they were waiting for the mole sauce to finish simmering, Maria said to Susan. "Mother Susan, does Brendon seem preoccupied to you?"

Susan thought for a minute before replying. "Not that I've noticed, Maria. But then, I've seen so little of him recently that I might not detect it. Why?"

"I think he has something on his mind that he isn't sharing. Before you came, he seemed more withdrawn than usual, lost in thought. He was often like that before we were married. I feel shut out."

"How long has he been like that? Have you said anything to him?"

"It's been several weeks. I haven't said anything because I

didn't want to upset him. He gets irritable when I ask if anything is wrong."

"Maria, if you are feeling shut out, you need to press him to tell you what he is thinking. He may get upset with you briefly, but it isn't good for your marriage if he doesn't discuss what's on his mind. Tell him you're concerned because he has been remote lately and that you miss being close to him. Remind him that you love him and you want to help if he has a problem. Don't put it off."

"Thank you for the advice. That's what I've been wanting to do, but wasn't sure it was the right thing."

Their one excursion during the visit had been a picnic lunch in the park by a nearby lake. After lunch, they sat near the sandy shore, where Anita built sand castles with her father and Walter and watched the turtles sunning on the rocks. When the four adults began to mind the afternoon heat, they went for a stroll in the adjacent forested area. Anita was constantly running ahead, then back to check on the adults. Finally, exhausted from the exertions, she was happy to ride in her stroller.

On Sunday, Maria's family invited Walter and Susan over for traditional Mexican fare. The entire Alverez family was there. Maria's parents welcomed Susan and Walter with hugs, then introduced them to the other members of their large extended family. To make the evening particularly memorable, a mariachi group played authentic Mexican folk music while they enjoyed before-dinner drinks. Anita, naturally, wanted to dance. Her grandfather Guido, and all her uncles were happy to join her on the dance floor. Soon all her cousins had joined in the fun. Anita loved the music and dancing.

Susan enjoyed the convivial evening with Maria's family. The food was plentiful and delicious, representing a variety of Mexican cuisines. She had met Maria's siblings briefly on a previous visit. They were all interesting and talented people who had established successful lives in California. Susan welcomed this opportunity to get to know them better and was sorry when the evening drew to a close. Although Walter enjoyed the evening, he had been content to sit on the fringes of the gathering and be an observer, unusual for him. He later commented to Susan that he was not used to so much chatter, activity, and exuberance.

— (HAPTER 23 —

Laguna Beach, California
Friday Night, October 21

Miguel stood among the crowd of visitors attending the opening of his solo show. The turnout exceeded his expectations. Comments about his work were affirming, both those he overheard as he strolled among the guests, and those from people who approached him to converse. He glanced around. Seven paintings had red dots by their title signs, an indication that they had been sold. That meant that four paintings had already sold tonight, three large canvases and one of the smaller ones. Henry had tagged three paintings to give the impression that there was demand for his work. Miguel had been reluctant to agree to the strategy when Henry proposed it. He felt it wasn't cricket. But, Henry had been persuasive. "It's psychological, Miguel. People always want what they think others want. If folks see that someone's buying your paintings, they too will want to buy."

Once Miguel reluctantly agreed to the ploy, they argued over which paintings to falsely label as sold. Henry had wanted to label at least five paintings. Miguel finally agreed to three. Now, whether because of Henry's strategy or because people truly liked his work, four paintings had sold.

The reporter from the local paper approached Miguel with his photographer. He asked to take a picture of him with the crowd of attendees in the background. Earlier in the evening, he had interviewed Miguel, and the photographer had taken pictures of Miguel standing by some of his paintings. As the photographer moved away after taking the shot, Miguel froze. Standing just inside the gallery door, looking uncertain, were his mother and father. Miguel wanted to go to them, but was uncertain of his reception. As he stood there, trying to make a decision, Henry approached them and welcomed them, waving his arm toward a wall of paintings. As Henry moved away, his father turned toward the paintings. His mother looked directly at him. He started to move toward her, but she held up her hand. She seemed to be indicating that he should remain where he was. Then she pointed to his father and made motions that seemed to indicate that she would bring his father to him later.

Emotions overwhelmed Miguel. The pain of the past years during which he had no contact with his family cut yet again. Warring with that pain was hope that perhaps things could change. A guest approached him with a question about a painting. He walked with the man toward the painting, wanting to turn and watch his father, but needing to focus his full attention on the man who was talking with him. Soon Miguel was again surrounded by guests eager to chat. When finally he was able to free himself from the crowd, he looked for his parents. His father was talking animatedly with Henry in front of one of Miguel's favorite paintings. His mother stood quietly at his side, a fond smile on her face. Miguel was distracted by a guest who wanted to tell him how exciting she found his work. As he finished the conversation, he felt someone touch his arm. He turned and was face-to-face with his father, who reached for him and gave him a long hug. His mother, tears in her eyes followed with a hug that felt as if she never wished to let go. Miguel wanted to stand there all night in his mother's arms.

"Miguel, my son!" said his father, choking on his emotion. "You are a talented painter. I'm so sorry that I never recognized your potential, and ridiculed your interest in art as sissy. You've developed an impressive body of work these past few years. Your paintings have a power to move the viewer. I'm proud of you, son. I'm so proud that I bought your mother one of your paintings to hang in our home."

"Dad," said Miguel, fighting to hold back the tears of joy that threatened to overwhelm him. "I'm so happy to see you again. I've missed you, Mom, and the family so much! It has been this huge hole in my life. If it weren't for Grandmother, I would have given up long ago. I'm pleased that you like my paintings. You don't need to buy one for Mom. I'm happy to give you the pick of my canvases."

"No, Miguel. You are a man, and painting is your profession. You deserve to be paid for your work. The painting I bought is worth every penny I paid. I only regret that I have been so hard on you. Can you forgive me?"

"I love you, Dad. How could I not forgive you?" Miguel felt a tear run down his cheek.

"I owe your grandmother an apology as well. She is a kind and wise woman. I was too pigheaded to listen to her. All these years, my wrongheadedness has kept her from the family she loves. The family has felt the loss of her involvement. I truly regret what I did. Your mother will tell me that I must find a way to make it up to you both." He looked at his wife, who nodded and smiled, and then beckoned toward the door. "I don't know how I'll do that, but I will find a way."

As Sergio took a step backward, he realized that their family reunion was causing a stir. There was a silence in the gallery as attendees stopped to watch the drama.

"I'm sorry we are monopolizing our son," said Sergio to the surrounding crowd. "We're just so proud of him, we got carried away. We're leaving, so you can enjoy his company. Miguel, can we expect you for dinner on Sunday at one o'clock?"

"Can we make it five-thirty? I need to man the gallery until five."

"Five-thirty is fine, Miguel," said his mother, giving Sergio a glance that said clearly, *Not a word from you!* "That will give me more time to prepare some of your favorite dishes."

She took Sergio's arm and led him toward the gallery exit.

Miguel stood, rooted to the spot by emotion at the events that had just unfolded. Henry approached and handed him a glass of champagne. He touched his own glass to Miguel's, and then turned toward their guests. "To our new artist, destined to become great! We wish him all the best." The guests raised their own glasses, which Henry had distributed while the family drama had played out. "To our new artist!" they toasted.

Finally, remembering where he was, Miguel grinned happily. "Thank you all for coming to support me." He focused his mind on his guests. They stopped to wish him well as they prepared to depart. When finally the last guest exited the gallery and Henry turned the key in the lock, Miguel dropped into a chair. "I'm exhausted. I don't think I've ever been so tired in my life!"

"You did well. You were charming. Several ladies who couldn't resist your charm said they are coming back to buy one of your paintings later this week. The art critic from Los Angeles had good things to say about your work. And we sold five paintings tonight, not counting the one your father bought!"

"For real?"

"Yes, for real."

"Thank you, Henry for your hard work in getting this event organized. You did a superb job! I was amazed by the way you circulated, kept things moving, and persuaded people to part with their money. You're good at what you do. The way you distracted everyone from my family drama was inspired!"

"The toast was planned anyway. But, when I saw the reunion playing out, I decided to just move up the timing a bit. The distribution of the glasses of champagne distracted the attendees from gawking at you and your parents. It was a good way to bring the evening to an end. I was afraid that you'd be useless at small talk after your Dad came to you."

"You were right about that! Thank you, friend," said Miguel, giving Henry a hug.

— CHAPTER 24 —

Irvine, California
Sunday Morning, October 23

Juanita sat over a second cup of tea, pondering her problem. So much had happened these past few days. First, the discovery that Miguel apparently used her money to fund his gallery. That was still to be confirmed, but she couldn't think of an alternative explanation that fit the pattern of withdrawals. On Friday, she had been so upset that she found it difficult to be sincere in wishing Miguel luck when he departed for the opening. She was still tense and upset at bedtime, so she took a sleeping pill. As a result, she was sleeping soundly when Miguel returned from the opening.

On Saturday morning, Miguel made them breakfast. As they ate, he excitedly told her about the events of the evening before. She couldn't help feeling pride at his success. He told her that not only did attendance exceed expectations, but he had sold six paintings, taking in more than nine thousand, six hundred dollars! She was astounded at the amount! Clearly he did have commercial potential. Furthermore, he told her that the art critic from the Los Angeles Times had good things to say about his work. On Monday, the opening would be written up in the local newspaper.

The most exciting news he had to share, however, was not about his successful opening. It was that his parents had attended. His father liked his work and bought one of Miguel's paintings for his mother. More importantly, he told Miguel he was proud of him, and admitted he had been wrong in cutting Miguel off from the family. Finally, he invited him to come to dinner at the house on Sunday.

To Juanita, Miguel seemed like a new person. The man who had been an empty shell was now was filled with life and hope. She was happy for him, and relieved that he would finally have the love and support of his family. The last thing she wanted to do was to jeopardize that relationship, a major consideration in how to deal with his unauthorized use of her money. Juanita also worried what would happen if Sergio ever found out about Miguel being gay. Sergio would not take that well; he might again refuse to have anything to do with his son. Dolores and Delia would probably accept the news with regret. She feared that Sergio would again expect them to obey his wishes and break ties with Miguel. Another break with his family would devastate him.

Now that she was past the initial shock of the missing money, she could justify what Miguel had done. Was she just making excuses for him because she loved him so much? How much did her disinterest in her financial affairs and refusal to discuss them after her stroke contribute to Miguel's decision to act on his own? She had supported his efforts to become a painter when she suggested turning the upper room into a studio and paid for his painting classes. Maybe he assumed she would approve of what he was doing. Still, it was wrong to make that assumption.

What action could she take that would teach Miguel that what he had done was wrong, without wrecking his career or his life? There must be a penalty if he was to learn a lesson, but not so severe that it would derail his success in getting his life back on track. Juanita decided to give the problem more thought. She would try out some ideas on Bessie when she arrived on Monday.

Yesterday afternoon, Sergio had called her. He apologized profusely for the way he had treated her. She knew it was hard for him to admit that he had been wrong and accepted his apology without comment. He invited her to join the family at noon on Sunday for their mid-day meal, and to stay on for their dinner with Miguel. Sergio said he would pick her up at her home around eleven o'clock Sunday morning, and drive her to their house.

Juanita happily accepted the invitation to join the family for their noon meal. It had been years since they had been together. She looked forward to seeing them, but wondered if getting reacquainted might be awkward. Fernando had been a child the last time she was with him. Now, he was a pre-teen. Dolores would probably feel guilty that she hadn't reached out to Juanita during all those years. Juanita bore Dolores no hard feelings. Defying your husband's wishes was not acceptable in the Latino culture. She must remember not to let anything slip about Delia's visits to her.

Juanita wondered whether she could move past her anger with Sergio for his long years of obstinacy. She would have to, she told herself. Forget the past. Work on building relationships with the family for the future.

Juanita did tell Sergio that she would not stay for dinner. She still tired easily. Further, since it was the first time in several years that the family would be with Miguel, she thought they needed time alone with him. Sergio protested at first, then agreed, reluctantly. Juanita felt sure that she was correct in insisting. She didn't want Miguel worrying that she might make some comment during dinner that would give away his secrets.

Juanita glanced at her watch. She realized it was time to stop thinking and begin dressing for lunch. She had planned carefully what to wear. She wanted to look her best.

— CHAPTER 25 —

Monday, October 24

Juanita was waiting for Bessie to arrive, eager to tell her about all that had transpired over the weekend. She needed her as a sounding board for her ideas on how to deal with Miguel's unauthorized use of her money. While she waited, her thoughts returned to yesterday's visit to Sergio's family. Being with his family for the first time in years, had been wonderful! After nearly four years without them, being together felt like finding an oasis in the desert after a long trek.

When Sergio arrived at her house to pick her up, he hugged her so long and so tightly that she thought she would faint from loss of breath. Juanita was equally glad to see him. Despite her anger with him over his behavior toward Miguel, she had missed him terribly. Sergio suggested they stop at Starbucks and converse over lattes; he wanted time alone with her to apologize properly for his behavior.

"Mom, I feel like an ass. I have no excuse for the way I behaved. I can only try to share what I was thinking at the time. When Miguel was released from prison, I was still angry that he had gotten involved with drugs. I feared he would fall in with the same bad characters that led him into trouble in the first place. I didn't want Monica and Fernando exposed to druggies. I also felt that Miguel was not macho. His interests were inconsistent with my expectations of male behavior. I'm sure you realize that I was trying to mold him into my view of an ideal son. When he was arrested and convicted for drug possession, I felt like a failure as a father. Maybe that's another reason I didn't want him at home. I was afraid I'd fail again.

"Seeing Miguel's paintings at his show made me realize that he has a unique talent. It deserves to be nourished. Looking back, I remember what you said to me when I refused to let him live at home and he asked to live with you. You said that he needed love and guidance to protect him from the risks of life inherent in the challenges that awaited him. Having family support would give him the confidence and freedom to evolve as his own person. I wasn't willing to risk that he would make mistakes, concerned they would reflect on me. That attitude was not only short-sighted, but also selfish.

"Delores told me last Friday night how painful it has been for her, not seeing her son. She told me in no uncertain terms how painful it has been for our other children. I'm sure you have also suffered, being kept from your grandchildren. Our estrangement also meant that you've not had the help and emotional support from your family that you needed and deserved after your stroke. I'm grateful to Miguel for being there to assist you. I plan to thank him. Can you ever forgive me for what I've done?"

It was clear that Sergio's remorse was deeply felt. How could Juanita not forgive him?

"Sergio, mi hijo," said Juanita, reaching for his hand. "I've been very angry with you for the past several years. At first, because of how you treated Miguel. Subsequently, I was hurt and angry that you prohibited me from seeing you and your family. You punished me for helping my grandson. I've always loved Miguel with a special love, because he was so shy and vulnerable. The estrangement made a difficult time in my life even more difficult. Despite my anger, I never stopped loving you. No mother could ever stop loving her child, no matter what that child has done. I do forgive you. I pray that we can return to the type of relationship we had before all this happened."

Juanita watched as Sergio wiped away a tear. Then she continued.

"We've all changed these past few years, Sergio. After listening to you today, I think you've become a more humane individual, less self-centered, and also more aware of the impact of your behavior on those around you. When I talked with Delores earlier in the week, I had the impression that she has become more confident as a woman. I don't believe she could have managed to drag you to Miguel's show two or three years ago. Nor could she have expressed to you her feelings about how difficult these years have been for her and your children.

"Miguel became a man as he worked hard to make a living, looked after me, and developed his painting talent. Although he is still not macho in your sense of the word, by forging his way through the isolation and adversity of the past few years, he has found himself and his calling. A father's guidance could have made it easier.

"I've changed too. I spent too much time wallowing in self-pity, an invalid, existing from day to day. I allowed myself to become dependent on Miguel for company, as well as for physical care. Recently, I began to realize how pathetic that was, and how unfair to Miguel. I've begun to re-engage with life. Miguel recently helped me to find household help. Bessie, the housekeeper I hired offers me companionship. Now that my home situation is more stable, I am preparing to find a suitable over-fifty-five community in which to live. I'm going to fix up this house and put it on the market. With the money from the sale, I'll purchase a condo in a setting where I'll have company, activities, and services that I need. Let's hope we can all move forward by building on what we've learned from these past few years, leaving our negative feelings from that time behind us."

"Amen to that, Mother."

———

From the moment Juanita entered the house with Sergio, her grandchildren monopolized her. Sergio allowed them uninterrupted time with his mother, while he relaxed in a chair and watched with a smile on his face. Delores joined them in the living room shortly after Juanita's arrival. Like Sergio, she remained in the background, enjoying the sight of her children with their grandmother.

Lunch, served on the shaded patio that overlooked the spacious, neatly maintained backyard was delicious. Lively conversation flowed as the family caught up on each other's lives. Delores had prepared tacos, stuffed with mildly spiced shrimp and pineapple coleslaw, accompanied by sweet potato fries, lightly seasoned with cumin, salt, and pepper. Mango iced tea was the beverage. For dessert, there was a choice of fresh fruit and *tres leches* cake.

Juanita, exhilarated from the pleasure of being with her family, was tired. She wasn't used to so much stimulation. At two o'clock, she announced that she needed to go home for an afternoon nap. Delores pressed her to stay.

Juanita replied firmly, "Darling Delores, I really am tired. I live a quiet life without much interaction with other people. I won't be good company if I stay. Being with my family means everything to me. This afternoon, I'm happier than I've been in years. Besides, my dear Delores, you need to rest before it's time to begin cooking dinner for Miguel's visit. I'm sure you've planned to make many of his favorite dishes--a lot of work. You want enough energy to enjoy his visit. It's best if you and the family have him all to yourselves after so long without him. We'll see each other again soon. Thank you so much for today."

"I thank you, Mother. If you hadn't called to tell me about Miguel's gallery opening and insisted that I find a way to make my stubborn husband attend, we'd still be estranged." She gave Juanita's hand a squeeze and kissed her on the cheek. "I promise you, I consider it my primary responsibility to keep you in our lives. I'll be in touch soon."

Juanita hugged each of her grandchildren before joining Sergio, who was waiting to drive her home. As they drove, he said, "Mother, this family get-together made me realize how much we've all been missing you. I promise you'll be an important part of our lives in the future. I was glad to hear about your plans for moving to an adult community. When I came by to pick you up this morning, I didn't like all those young men hanging out down the street from your house. They were smoking, drinking, and probably using drugs. Are they always around there?"

"There are often young men hanging around on the street. They seem to congregate by that empty house three doors down. I do wish the bank would sell or rent it. There are more at night and on weekends than during weekdays. They sometimes get quite boisterous when they're drunk or stoned, and their noise keeps me awake. Miguel told me last week that he heard there were several break-ins in the neighborhood during the past few months."

"I'm concerned for your safety, Mother. I think you should put a deadbolt on your front door. I suppose Miguel uses the garage for his car?" Juanita nodded. "In that case, it would be a good idea to have him lock the door from the house to the garage behind him when he leaves. I've been reading that burglars troll neighborhoods with garage door openers until they find a door they can open. Locking the connecting door would make it harder to get into the house. In fact it would be a good idea to have a deadbolt on that door too. Perhaps you should also think about installing grilles on the first-floor windows."

"Thank you for your concern, Sergio. The deadbolts are a good idea. I have a handyman, the husband of my housekeeper, who recently fixed a few things for me. I'll have him install them. If I were planning to stay in the house, I'd agree that window grilles are a good idea. Since I'm planning to move as soon as I can find a place I like, I think I'll concentrate on getting a new roof and doing other necessary maintenance, like painting the exterior, a necessary step to make it saleable at a fair price."

"I'll be relieved when you get settled somewhere safe and secure, Mother. I hadn't realized how much this neighborhood had changed. I should have been looking after you all these years. Where will Miguel go when you leave?"

"We haven't discussed it, since my move isn't imminent. I should probably raise the issue with him soon, so he can make plans."

"Do you think I should ask him if he'd like to move back home?"

"No, Sergio, I don't. Miguel has been making his own way now for nearly five years. Moving back home would be a step backward. He will welcome frequent contact with the family, I'm sure. But, even if he would consider an offer to live at home, I don't think it would be the best thing for him."

"I suppose you're right. It's probably my guilt talking. I wouldn't want to give Delia and Fernando the idea that I'm willing to support them all their adult life. Having Miguel move back home might contribute to that idea."

Sergio stopped the car in front of Juanita's house. "I'll help you get inside. Then I'd better go see if Delores needs any help getting ready for tonight."

"Thank you for today, Sergio. I'm so happy that we're friends again. I've missed you, my son. Please don't be a stranger. Once the deadbolts are installed, I'll give you keys for the house so you can let yourself in when you come to visit, rather than waiting for me to get to the door. I'm still slow, and I'd rather not rush to answer the door. When I hurry, I tend to lose my balance."

"Thanks, Mother. I'll try to visit often. I love you."

"And I love you, Sergio." Juanita smiled as she remembered the long hug she had given her son before he turned to go. It had felt so good to hold him again.

Miguel arrived home from the dinner at Sergio's house around nine o'clock. Juanita was waiting for him in the living room. She took a long nap after lunch. She wanted to stay up to hear Miguel's account of his visit with the family.

Miguel was positively glowing! When she stood up to greet him, he had wrapped his arms around her and lifted her off her feet as he hugged her.

"Abuela, I haven't been so happy in years. It's wonderful to be part of my family again. I knew I missed them, but didn't realize the size of the hole in my soul without them in my life. Mother says it's all because of you! She told me how you called her and demanded that she bring Dad to the opening. How can I ever thank you? Ever since I was released from prison, you've been there for me."

"We've been there for each other, Miguelito. Tell me about your evening."

"From the time I entered the house, Mom, Delia, and Fernando treated me as if I'd never been away. We had so much to catch up on! Initially, talking to Dad was like walking on eggshells. Just before dinner, he sent Delia and Fernando into the kitchen to help Mom. Once we were alone, he apologized for cutting me out of their life. He asked for my forgiveness. Of course, I gave it to him. I also apologized for getting involved in the drug scene as a teen. Then I described for him how lonely and painful it had been to be without family all this time. I told him I've worked very hard to build a successful life so I could demonstrate to him that I am a worthy son. I told him that his approval means everything to me.

"He couldn't speak for a time. Then, he said that when I was young, he had tried to make me into his vision of a man, rather than letting me develop as my own person. He blamed himself for my involvement with drugs. He hugged me and told me that he is proud of what I have accomplished. He said he is proud that I am his son. While he was hugging me, I was so overcome that I sobbed like a small child.

"There was a time Dad would have admonished me for being a sissy and told me to behave like a man. This time, he didn't say a word. When he released me from the hug, I saw tears on his own cheeks. He said, 'I love you, Son.' I replied, 'I love you too, Dad.' We took a few moments to compose ourselves, then went in to join the rest of the family at the dinner table. Mom made many of my favorite dishes to welcome me home. I have the best mother in the world. Conversation at dinner was relaxed, like old times. There was so much to learn about my family's life. They were full of questions about my life these past five years. Delia never let on that she had visited you and spent some time with me here. I kept her secret."

Juanita's reveries were interrupted by the sound of Bessie's voice. "Hello, Ms. Juanita. It's me. Didn't want to startle you. How are you today?"

"I'm good Bessie. I had such a wonderful weekend! Get us a pot of tea and I'll tell you all about it."

"You look and sound better than you did after the visit to the bank last Friday. I'm glad of it."

Bessie bustled about the kitchen. She boiled water, set the table, and brewed a pot of tea. After she set the pot on a trivet on the table, she drew up a chair to join Juanita, who poured the tea into their cups. They added sugar and milk to their tea, and then Juanita began to talk. She excitedly told Bessie about Sergio's visit to Miguel's opening, his apologies for his behavior of the past few years, and her visit to Sergio's family.

"No wonder you're looking so much better! I'm so happy for you. It's a wonderful thing for your family to be reunited. I assume you didn't tell Sergio about what Miguel has done."

"No, and I have no intention of telling him in the future. If I did, it would end any likelihood that their relationship can be repaired. Miguel needs his father in his life; he needs his advice and guidance. This will be between me and Miguel. I've been thinking a lot about what to do. Here's what I'm thinking. Tell me what you think, please."

"I'll be happy to listen and share my thoughts about what you propose. Ultimately, the decision has to be yours. I can help mostly by telling you what I see as positives and negatives of your plan. Is that satisfactory?"

"Of course, Bessie. I know I must make a decision on my own, but you may think of things I haven't considered. That would be very helpful to me."

Bessie refilled their teacups.

"As I've already told you, I had refused to discuss my affairs with Miguel because I was so depressed after my stroke. When I signed over my power of attorney, I told him it was totally in his hands to manage my affairs. He may have felt I had given him leave to use my funds as he saw fit. I understand how he might have thought I'd have agreed to support his efforts to start a gallery by giving or loaning him the money to do so. After all, I had earlier paid for art lessons and remodeling the room over the garage for an art studio. He also knew that he was my primary heir, so he may have felt this was money that would come to him anyway. Maybe he planned to replace the money once he started selling his paintings."

"It sounds to me like you're excusing his behavior."

"I may be. Before I can hold him to account, I need to hear

from him what he was thinking, why he did what he did. If he was thinking what I just described, then the action I take ought to be different than if he just saw this as an opportunity to further his own ends because the means were available to him."

"Why didn't he come to you once you were functioning better?"

"I need to ask him that also. I can rationalize that he was busy with his work and his painting, I was usually asleep by the time he got home at night, he was caught up in his relationship with Henry, and so forth. But, of course, he should have done so."

"Are you going to demand that he return the money?"

"I don't want him to think that what he did was okay. It's not. There must be consequences, but not so severe they would ruin his life. I love him. He worked hard these past few years to rebuild his life and create a viable future. Except for that short, disastrous relationship with Henry, he has been alone. Since I withdrew, Miguel has had no responsible adult to whom he could turn for help or advice.

"If his thinking when he accessed the money was what I described, I thought I'd give him the benefit of the doubt. I'll treat the missing money as a loan. I'll ask him to sign a paper that states I gave him an interest-free loan for the purpose of developing an art gallery. That will protect him against repercussions at some future time.

"The document will include a repayment schedule. If he does not repay according to the schedule, the loan would become subject to interest. I recognize that the gallery may not become self-sustaining for some time. So, I'd ask Miguel's input on when he can feasibly begin repayment. I certainly will not allow him to use any additional money from my account. I will ask for a business plan that outlines how he plans to make the gallery sustainable. He cannot expect to continue with the current level of expenses and break even. I don't see how he can afford to keep his friend Henry as a full-time gallery manager. Henry may totally desert Miguel if he loses his job. That would be another blow.

"To serve as his own manager, Miguel would need to find a different job that gives him flexible hours, or lets him work hours when the gallery is closed. He will need to work day and night, because he must continue painting. That would be a stretch and put a lot of pressure on him. But, if it's important to him, it will be worth it. He may need to think about limiting the hours that the gallery is open. Perhaps he could paint while he is manning the gallery and no customers are present. Those are problems for him to solve."

"You're certainly bending over backwards to accommodate him. But, I can understand why. What will you do if he didn't go through the thought process you described?"

"I haven't figured that out yet. Probably because I don't believe he would have cold-bloodedly stolen from me. I guess I'd have to demand a repayment schedule that disregards his desire to keep the gallery open as an outlet for selling his work, and ask him to pay interest. That would probably be the end of his painting career, just when it looks like he could be a commercial success. That would hurt me as much as it would hurt him. I hope it doesn't come to that."

"When will you approach him about this?"

"Well, his show runs for a month. I don't want to do it until that is over. Let him enjoy his success. It's not as if confronting him is urgent. I don't need the money for anything right now. On the other hand, I should let him know early next week that I've revoked the power of attorney before he tries to draw out another rent payment or salary for Henry. I also need to obtain those documents the bank manager is getting for me. Those will confirm where the payments have gone, in case he should deny that he did this, which I can't imagine. But, best to be prepared."

"How will you raise this issue with him?"

"Since I'm never sure when he will be here, I thought I'd try to set up a time in advance. I'll invite him to have dinner with me, and tell him that there are some things I need to discuss with him. Perhaps you would cook something for us that I can reheat for our dinner?"

"Is that a good idea? Won't that make him defensive? Isn't he likely to guess what you want to talk about?"

"There are a number of issues we previously left unresolved—whether and how long he will continue living here, when I might be ready to put the house on the market and move to a senior community, and so on. So, it's natural that we should continue that discussion. Naturally, I also want to hear about how the show went this week."

"Okay, Ms. Juanita. I'll be happy to cook something for your dinner. Just let me know what night you schedule with Miguel."

"Thank you, Bessie. Wish me luck."

"I'll pray for you. This is going to be hard."

"Oh! Another thing. Sergio advised me to have deadbolts installed on both my front door and the door to the garage. Would you ask Micah when he would be able to do that?"

"I'll tell him to do it this week. When he comes to do that, he can also do that assessment of needed repairs in the rest of the house that he promised to do."

"Thank you, Bessie. You're a treasure."

— CHAPTER 26 —

Laguna Hills, California
Tuesday, October 25

Susan and Walter were on their way to Laguna Hills, to the home of Walter's son, Keith. They had left Brendon's home in Thousand Oaks this morning, after a late breakfast with Maria and Anita. Brendon had to leave early for work, so they had said their good-byes the previous evening.

Susan was excited about seeing Keith again and meeting his family. She smiled, remembering Keith's shock when he had walked, unannounced, through the back door of his father's home in Hawaii last spring, and found Susan and Walter in the kitchen, chatting while washing dishes. He had wanted to surprise his father, so hadn't told Walter he was going to visit. Instead, Keith had gotten the surprise! He jumped to the conclusion that Susan was living with Walter, and was shocked and upset that his father had never mentioned Susan to him. He had envisioned his father as he had last seem him, still distraught over his mother's death, showing little interest in anything. Following a long discussion with his father, and spending time with Susan, Keith had come to accept their relationship.

"Walter, we have ample time before we're due at Keith's and

we need to pick up some gifts. Laguna Hills is only a short drive from Laguna Beach. Could we detour to Laguna Beach and have lunch at *Las Brisas?* It's a Mexican Restaurant Scott and I went to many years ago. We enjoyed the food and the atmosphere so much we returned several times during our stay in town. With today's beautiful weather, it would be delightful to sit outside on the patio and enjoy the views of the bay. After lunch, we can go downtown to find gifts for Keith and his family."

"I know that restaurant! Keith took Marge and me there once when we visited him. I'd enjoy going for lunch, if it's still open. It's another way to connect our past with our new lives."

Over lunch, they discussed gift ideas for Keith and his family. Walter suggested books for the two children; both were fond of reading. Jan had mentioned to Walter that James, age ten, had developed an interest in photography, and his parents had given him a camera for his birthday. A book on photography might be of interest. Monica, age thirteen, was interested in fashion, but buying clothes or accessories for a teenage girl could be risky. Teens tended to have such definite tastes. She was also interested in oceanography and ecology, so a book relating to one of those subjects might work. As for Jan, he didn't know what to suggest.

"What are her interests?" asked Susan.

"That's the problem. I don't really know. She's a practical, down-to-earth girl, very bright, a good conversationalist, but doesn't talk much about herself. She's very wrapped up in her family. She volunteers as a nurse several mornings a week at a free clinic."

"Is she interested in clothing, jewelry, things for the house or yard?"

"I don't know. She limits her wardrobe to basic colors and classic styles. When an occasion demands that she be dressy, she uses a piece of jewelry, a scarf, or sweater to spice up her basic pieces. The house is fully furnished. There may be something she'd like to have for the house, but I have no idea what that might be. She has an extensive garden with trees, shrubs, vegetables, and flowers. I have no clue what, if anything she might like for the yard."

"Does she like to read? If so, what kind of books?"

"I know she reads the newspaper daily. I've not seen her reading anything else. I suspect she's too busy."

"Buying for her is a challenge! I suppose that if she's too busy to read, she doesn't spend time on crafts or other hobbies either. Her garden must be her creative outlet. An accessory like a hand-painted silk scarf might be worth considering."

"That might work. We could give her the receipt from the shop, so if she doesn't like what we pick, she can return it and pick something that suits her better."

"Let's do that. What about Keith?"

Keith is a history buff, so history books are good. He also appreciates good wines, so that's also a possibility."

Let's try to find a history book or DVD. We can also take some good wine as a host gift."

"Done. With those decisions made, we've simplified our shopping. Now let's relax and enjoy our lunch. Are you interested in a stroll along the cliff path before we start shopping?"

"Yes, Walter, I am. We've been sitting too much again."

Three hours later, they were ready to leave Laguna Beach. They had a successful shopping excursion, and enjoyed a leisurely walk along the bay. Susan was intrigued by the many languages she heard from people they passed on their walk. English speakers seemed to be a minority! From Laguna Beach, it was only about six miles to Keith's home. As they drove along the canyon road, before the turnoff for Laguna Woods and Laguna Hills, Susan spotted a banner advertising an art show.

"Oh, look! There's an art show at that gallery. Can we just stop and take a quick peek?"

Walter smiled indulgently. "Susan, you're acting on impulse!

How nice that you are overcoming the tendency always to plan things down to their finest detail. Of course we'll stop. I want to encourage this new behavior!"

"Thank you, Walter. Your influence on me is showing."

Walter pulled into the gallery's parking lot. When they entered the gallery, a man was busily sweeping the floor. He looked up.

"Hello, welcome. My name if Henry Jenkins. I'm the gallery manager. I was cleaning up in preparation for closing. But, feel free to look around, if my activities won't bother you."

"Thank you. We're from out of state, so I don't know if we could come back. We're in town to visit family. You know how that can be. Your life is often planned for you."

"I have about fifteen minutes before I'll need to leave. I hope that will give you time to see the show."

Susan glanced quickly over the paintings hanging on the wall. "These are fascinating works. Who is the artist? Is he local?"

"His name is Miguel Sanchez. He is local and this is his first solo show. His opening was last Friday evening. It was well attended, and there was considerable praise for his work. His style is unique. There's was article in yesterday's local paper about it. We actually sold half a dozen of his paintings on opening night!"

"I wouldn't mind owning one of these myself," said Walter. "I love the colors, and have always had an affinity for the spectacular Californian scenery. But, even though I immediately recognize the locations in the paintings as California, there's something abstract and modern about how he portrays them. Landscapes are so often just beautiful pictures, painted replicas, like a photograph. These paintings evoke strong feelings and engage the viewer in the painting. He must love the places he paints."

"I would love for us to own one of these, Walter. Not only are they beautiful and unique, but one would be a wonderful souvenir of our trip. However, I want time to study them before I make a decision. We need to find a way to return to the gallery when we have more time. Perhaps one day over the weekend the children will have some activities and we could come with Keith and Jan."

Susan turned to Henry. "I assume you can ship a painting for us, if we buy one?"

"Yes, Ma'am. That's no problem. I am sorry that I can't stay longer now, but I have an engagement. Let me give you my card and a brochure. I do hope you can return. I truly believe that one of these paintings will not only give you pleasure when it hangs in your home, but it will also prove to be a sound investment. I believe that Miguel has a bright future."

Susan and Walter took the materials and thanked Henry. As they drove on toward Laguna Hills, Walter commented, "I agree with what you said, Susan. One of those paintings would indeed be a great souvenir of our trip. We haven't bought anything for ourselves. The painting would be a reminder of these six weeks of visiting our children. Of course, until we figure out where we're going to live, we have no place to hang it. Henry is probably correct; the painting could be a worthwhile investment. It might appreciate significantly. Let's make sure we revisit the gallery."

Fifteen minutes later, Walter turned right, off the busy main road and into a neighborhood called Laguna Gardens. The road passed between two stone walls fronted with clumps of dwarf Robolio Palms behind flowering red impatiens. The street running through the neighborhood was broad and lined with stately fifteen foot tall palm trees. The houses were elegant, two story stucco buildings with tile roofs, many with columns and porticos. Front lawns were deep and broad, and immaculately landscaped with palms, shrubs, and colorful flowers. Susan caught glimpses of pools behind several of the houses they passed.

"Quite a classy neighborhood your son lives in!" ventured Susan.

"This neighborhood does exude a feeling of prosperity, doesn't it? Keith has done well for himself. I'm proud of him. That's his house just ahead on the right, the tan one with the portico, capped with a balcony. They've lived here about eight years. They moved in shortly before Marge got her cancer diagnosis. They chose the neighborhood because of the excellent school system. Monica was in elementary school at the time, James in preschool. It was a stretch for them financially, but they wanted someplace suitable for the family until after the children went off to college."

"That sort of stability is wonderful for the children. The attractive environment is a nice place to come home to at the end of the day. It's quiet, away from the hustle and bustle of heavily populated Southern California. I like it."

Walter turned into the driveway of Keith's home. He got out of the car and walked around to open Susan's door.

"I heard a car door," said Jan, coming down the front walk. "How are you, Dad?" She gave her father-in-law a hug.

Susan looked up as she got out of the car. Jan was an attractive brunette with straight hair cut to just above her shoulders. She was at least five foot ten, and slender as a bean pole. She wore khaki-colored jeans and a pale green tank top, simple, but elegant. Her necklace was unique, multi-sized metal rings fastened onto the chain at randomly spaced intervals. It was informal, yet somehow made the entire outfit appear unique and classy.

"Jan, this is my wife, Susan. She has been looking forward to meeting you."

Jan hugged Susan. "Welcome to the family. I'm so pleased to meet you. Let me help you with the luggage, then we can settle in with a drink and get acquainted while we wait for Keith to get home from work. James is at soccer practice. Monica is doing homework with a friend at her house. She wanted to finish it today so she can enjoy spending time with you this weekend."

"Thank you, Jan. I'm so happy to meet you. After talking to you on the telephone, listening to Walter, and seeing your picture, I feel as if I already know you. I'm happy to be here."

"We've all been looking forward to your visit. Keith's been talking about nothing else all week. Here, give me that suitcase, Dad. You can take the other one. Susan can carry the overnight bag. Is that all you two have brought? You do travel light!"

"Believe me, Jan. When you get to our age, you'll learn to do the same. Lifting heavy suitcases isn't good for either of us."

"I'm sure that's so. I know when we travel as a family, Keith, who does most of the lifting, ends up feeling stiff and sore. I don't know how people managed before the invention of rolling cases."

"I remember being stiff and sore a lot back in those days. Marge never learned to pack a light case. I once told her that if she didn't pack less, I'd let her carry her own cases. But, of course I never carried through on the threat."

Jan showed them to their room, a spacious suite overlooking the street. "We'll hang out on the patio until everyone is home. I'll get some nibbles and drinks ready while you unpack. Will margaritas do for both of you?"

"I love margaritas," said Susan. "But, they can put me to sleep in a hurry. Please don't make them too strong, Jan."

"I promise. You'll need to be awake to cope with my gang once they're all here. It's such a beautiful day. The kids will probably swim when they get home. Would you like to swim?"

Both Walter and Susan shook their heads no. "I prefer to swim in the morning to get the blood circulating. By this hour of the day, I'm too lazy, just content to sit," said Susan. "Thanks for the offer."

While Walter changed to a clean shirt, Susan splashed her face with cool water. Then they headed downstairs to join Jan on the patio. Jan poured them each a margarita, then passed a plate of asparagus spears wrapped in prosciutto, one of sliced papaya, and a bowl of taco chips. Walter heaped his plate with asparagus spears and chips. Jan and Susan each settled for a small serving of papaya slices.

Susan smiled indulgently as she looked at Walter's plate.

"I know, I know. I'm developing a pot belly on this trip," he conceded. "Permit me to blame it on the lack of exercise, rather than the amount and type of food I've been eating. Everyone has been serving my favorite things. You can put me on a diet and crack the whip to get me moving again when we get home, Susan!"

"Did I say a word?"

"You didn't have to. The look you gave me said it all. Or maybe my conscience is prodding me." Susan smiled.

Jan said, "Well, Dad. Don't let the conscience get in the way of enjoying dinner tonight. I've ordered some of your favorite things from *La Bella Luna*. I didn't want to spend the time you're here cooking. Keith and I thought we could converse better here than in a noisy restaurant and that seemed like a good solution. They are to deliver at seven o'clock."

"Thank you, my dear. I promise to do it justice."

"May I join this shindig? I could use a drink."

Keith was standing in the doorway. "I didn't hear you come in, dear," said Jan getting up to give him a hug. "Please, have a seat. Will a margarita suit, or would you prefer something stronger?"

"A margarita and a plateful of those asparagus spears, with a few taco chips on the side should do just fine. Dad, nice to see you again. You look great!" Walter rose and hugged his son. Keith then turned to Susan and hugged her. "Susan, welcome to our family. I've been looking forward to seeing you again."

"And I to seeing you, Keith, and to meeting your family."

"I know the kids are looking forward to this visit. Will they be home soon, Jan?"

"James will be here directly from soccer practice, probably close to six o'clock. Helena is bringing him home when she picks up her son. Monica promised to be home by six. She's doing her homework at Ashley's house."

"They're good kids. You'll like them, Susan."

"I'm sure I will, Keith."

The adults settled around the table. Keith was soon regaling them with a story about an incident that occurred at work that day. They were all engrossed in the story when Jan looked up at the sound of the front door closing. James limped across the living room and onto the patio.

"James! What happened to you? You're limping!" exclaimed Jan, with concern.

"I'm okay, Mom. Nothing serious. I think I sprained my ankle. I'll ice it and then, if you have an ace bandage, I'll wrap it. I probably should stay off it for a day or so.

"Hi Dad. Hello Grandpa," he said to Walter, who came around the table to hug him. Turning to Susan, "You must be Grandma Susan. I'm happy to meet you."

"And I to meet you, James. Did you injure your ankle at soccer practice?"

"No. I was walking with Sam toward his mother's car when someone called my name. As I turned to see who was calling me, my foot slid off the edge of the sidewalk, and I twisted my ankle. I had forgotten my jersey. I removed it after practice to put on a clean shirt, and my friend, George, was running to give it to me. It was a freak accident. I don't think it's serious. It's only a little swollen, and the pain isn't too bad. I hear that you're experienced at treating an ankle sprain, Grandma Susan. Dad told us the story about how you and Grandpa met in Hawaii."

"Actually, it was your Grandpa who knew what to do. He

took charge. I simply followed orders. What you've proposed to treat your sprain sounds about right. You might want to add a dose of aspirin or acetaminophen to keep the pain from getting worse, and keep your shoe off until the swelling goes down."

"Have a seat, James," said Walter, pulling out a chair at the end of the table and turning it so he could place an ottoman in front of it. He removed James's shoe. "Put your leg up on the cushion of the ottoman to keep it from swelling further. You can ice it while you keep it elevated. Once we're sure it isn't swelling anymore, you can put on the ace bandage. If you can, keep it elevated until dinner."

"Will do. Thanks, Grandpa."

"Can I get you a plate of chips and something to drink?" asked Susan.

"Chips, some papaya, a couple of asparagus spears, and a diet coke on ice would be welcome. Thanks."

While they were getting James settled, Monica entered the room, unnoticed.

"What did James do to deserve all the attention around here?"

"Monica! We didn't hear you come in sweetheart," said Keith. "James sprained his ankle. Come give your Grandpa a hug and he'll introduce you to his wife, Susan."

"Hi Grandpa. Sorry I wasn't here when you arrived." She hugged her grandfather.

"Your mother told us you were doing your homework, so your time would be free while we're here. That is commendable. We appreciate it."

Walter turned toward Susan. "Monica, this is your Grandmother Susan, my wife," said Walter. "Susan, this is my granddaughter, Monica."

"I'm delighted to meet you, Monica. Your grandfather's very proud of you. I was just about to go to the kitchen to get your brother a coke. Can I bring you something to drink?"

"A large glass of ice water with a slice of lemon would be wonderful. Thank you."

Monica found a seat at the table. Susan returned with drinks for the young people and Jan brought James some ice and acetaminophen. Soon they had all filled their plates and began to catch up on each other's lives.

Sometime later, they were interrupted by the sound of the doorbell.

"That must be the delivery man with our dinner," said Jan. "I'll take care of that. Keith, please put several serving platters and bowls in the oven on the warm setting, then open two bottles of wine, one red, one white. Susan, perhaps you'll help Monica clear away the evidence of our appetizers, then set the table for dinner. Dad, you can keep James company while we get organized." She headed for the door.

"Is your mother always so bossy?" Walter asked James with a grin.

James smiled. "She's well organized and efficient. She's good at getting people to do what she wants them to do. But in a way that they aren't offended."

"Well stated, James. You defended your Mom with a lot of tact!"

By the time Jan had paid for the delivery and gotten it into the warm serving dishes, everything was ready. The table was set, wine ready to pour, and the family in their seats at the table.

"This looks wonderful, Jan," said Walter. "You remembered that the *Shrimp Scampi* and *Veal Piccatta* are two of my favorite dishes! Thank you. And, I'm impressed with how well you organized the transition from appetizers to dinner."

"This place can be chaos with four people leading busy, independent lives. I've become the person who assumes responsibility for keeping some order in the chaos. I guess it's become second nature after all these years."

Keith poured the wine as serving dishes were passed around

the table and the family selected their portions of the delicious entrees. "Bon Appetit!" he said, raising his glass. "Bon Appetit!" responded the others.

As the meal neared its end, Keith announced, "I'm taking time off work while you're visiting. I thought it would be nice to have some adult time with Dad and Susan while Monica and James are in school tomorrow and Thursday. Friday there is no school; it's a teacher's day. Is there anything special you would like to do while you're here? Jan and the kids suggested an excursion to Dana Point on the weekend. We could rent a sailboat and go out for a sail while we're there. Other options include fishing, a day in Los Angeles, attending a baseball game, or hiking, although the last is now an option only when James is in school, because of his injury."

"I'd love to go sailing," said Susan. "I haven't sailed in years."

"You and I haven't gone fishing together for quite some time," said Walter looking at Keith. "I'd love to do that. Also, Susan and I have a request. We stopped at a gallery on Canyon Road on our way from Laguna Beach. We want to go back and purchase a painting. The painter, Miguel Sanchez is incredibly talented! He does the most amazing, vibrant, abstract paintings of California landscapes!"

Monica looked up excitedly. "That's my friend Delia's brother!" she blurted. "Can I come along to the gallery with you? I'd love to see his work."

"Of course. We'd be delighted to have you along. Jan, Keith, James, have you any interest in going with us?"

"I'd enjoy that. I haven't been to a gallery in ages. In fact, I can't remember the last time," said Jan. "Keith, would you like to come?"

"I'm not really a fan of art galleries, but Dad did make this artist sound interesting. Tell you what. Why don't we make a day of it on Friday? We can first visit the art gallery, then continue on to Laguna Beach. We haven't spent time at the beach in ages. Last time I checked the weather, it's supposed to be warm and sunny all week. If we go to the gallery mid to late morning, we can go from there to *Sundried Tomato* for lunch. Monica and James both like that place. From there we can go to the beach for a couple of hours, then come back here and order in some Chinese food from the *Jade Moon* so Jan doesn't have to worry about cooking dinner. By Friday, James's foot will have had time to heal a bit. What do you think? Is the gallery open in the morning?"

"I think that sounds like a lovely way to spend Friday," said Susan. "As I recall, the sign said the gallery is open from open from ten a.m. until eight p.m. on Friday and Saturday. We can call to check. Now that I think of it, we arrived at around three in the afternoon and the gallery manager was getting ready to close.

"James, do you mind visiting the gallery with us? I know it probably sounds boring to you."

"Actually, Grandma Susan, since I became interested in photography, I've become interested in all forms of art. The principles of composing a good photograph are similar to those for composing a painting. Also, Monica's friend Delia often talks about her brother, Miguel, and his painting. It will be cool to see his work."

"James, what you just said reminded me. Susan and I have some gifts for all of you and I completely forgot to bring them downstairs. Excuse me while I go get them."

Walter returned with his arms full of packages. "I feel a bit like Santa Claus at the moment."

"You'd look like him too, if you had a beard," commented Susan with smile and a look at his growing waistline.

"You'll notice that I'm ignoring you," said Walter to Susan. He began to distribute the gifts. "Knowing that you all enjoy reading, we went shopping at the local bookstore. Since Jan never seems to have much time for reading, we got her something else."

He handed Jan her gift and the wine they had brought as a host/hostess gift. She opened her package and smiled as she held it up for inspection by the family. "What a beautiful scarf! These are my favorite colors. The tropical flowers are spectacular. It's exquisite. Thank you so much."

"Wow! That's gorgeous. Can I borrow it on a special occasion, Mom?" asked Monica.

"It will have to be a very special occasion, Monica. This scarf is a hand-painted work of art."

"I'm so pleased that you like it. Walter and I were impressed by the work of this artist. I've done some silk painting in my time, and know how difficult it is to retain both the framework of the design and the free flow of paint to achieve the watercolor effect. I only wish I could do it so well."

Keith seemed pleased with the book on Leonardo Di Vinci, which dealt with his life and times, as well as his influence on technological developments in the years since his death. "I usually read books on American or European History. This will be a welcome change. Reading it will help me prepare for the exhibit on Leonardo that is coming to Los Angeles later this year. I thought I'd take the family to see it. Thank you both."

And I thank you for the book of Ansell Adams photographs," said James. "He's a master of landscape photography. I'll learn a lot from studying his photographs. One can revisit his photos over and over again and see something new every time. Thank you, Grandpa, and Grandma Susan."

"You are most welcome, James. Susan and I thought about getting you a book on techniques of photography, since we've been told you're fairly new to the field. Based on your comments, it sounds like you've already done considerable reading about technique. It appears we made the better choice." James nodded.

"I like the book on climate change you gave me," said Monica. "Thank you. My friends and I often discuss global warming. Some of my friends think it isn't real. I do. Our discussions get quite heated sometimes. This book describes the forces under-lying the changes in climate, provides scientific evidence that documents change, and describes efforts to control its impact on the environment. Having facts available for our discussions will be helpful. Also, I'm taking a course next year on environmental ecology. The information from this book may be good preparation for that course. I look forward to reading it."

"I'm glad we made some good choices. Monica, is there a chance we'll meet your friend, the artist's sister?"

"I'll ask her to come home with me after school one day. Mom, would you mind driving her home afterwards?"

"I'd be happy to, Monica, or Dad can drive if I'm tied up."

As the evening drew to a close, Jan and Susan retired to the kitchen to chat while they washed the dishes. Monica and James went to get ready for bed, since they had school the following day. Keith and Walter settled in Keith's study to enjoy an after dinner drink and conversation.

— CHAPTER 27 —

Friday, October 28

Keith pulled the van into a parking space in front of *Galleria de el Renaciamiento.* Monica excitedly led the way to the gallery entrance. As she walked in the front door, she shrieked, "Miguel! I don't believe you're here!"

Miguel frowned a moment concentrating. "You're Delia's friend, Monica," he said finally, with a smile. "For a moment, I couldn't place you. I don't associate you with the gallery and had to remember where I knew you from."

"Hey, everybody! This is Miguel, my friend's brother that I told you about. Miguel, this is my family, my Mom and Dad, Jan and Keith Conway, my brother, James, and my Grandpa and Grandma, Walter and Susan Conway."

"I'm pleased to meet all of you. My sister is very fond of Monica."

"Susan and I stopped by the gallery around three o'clock last Tuesday. We saw the banner about the show as we were passing and decided to pop in. Your manager was sweeping up, said he would be open only for another 15 minutes. We really liked your work. But we need more time to study the paintings in order to decide which one we'd like to buy. We're delighted to meet you. We didn't expect to see you here."

"Henry usually opens the gallery on Friday morning. I arrive around two. This morning, he called and asked me to cover for him. You said he was closing when you came by in the mid-afternoon? That's odd. We're open until five-thirty on weekdays. I'll have to ask him about that. Anyway, I'm delighted that you've come. Please, look around at your leisure. Feel free to ask me questions about the paintings. Like most artists, I love to talk about my work."

The family scattered to look at the paintings. Murmurs of appreciation could be heard. Even Keith, who had admitted to not particularly caring for art had positive comments about what he saw.

Susan and Walter finally settled on a painting that they both particularly liked. It reminded them of the view from the top of the cliffs at the north end of Laguna Beach, looking south at the bay with its crescent beach.

"Susan, how can you see that location in an abstract painting?" asked Keith.

"I don't know. That's just what it reminds me of." Susan motioned to Miguel, indicating that she had a question. "I assume your paintings represent your impression of real locations?"

"Yes. They are of actual sites. The one you are looking at is of the shoreline of the beach park in Laguna Beach, looking south from the cliff walk. The red represents the bougainvillea along the edge of the cliff. The colors and shapes of the sea, sand, surf, and sky are all there. But, I put in only a few impressions of trees and single flowers, rather than a lot of detail, because I want to present the feeling of the place, rather than a photographic reproduction."

"So, I was right about the location. It seemed familiar. You've captured the exact feeling I get when I stand on the cliff looking at this view, a feeling of grandeur and awe, color and movement. I really like your depiction. We'd like to buy this painting and have it sent to our home in Seattle. We're planning to do more traveling before returning to Seattle. Can we pay for it now, then call about a shipping date?"

"Of course. Actually, it helps me to keep it hanging here with a sold tag until time to ship. It's good for business when visitors see that someone bought one of the paintings."

"We'll keep looking while you wrap up the sale," said Keith. Jan really likes the paintings and I told her I'd buy one for her birthday, which is next month. She needs to decide which one she'll choose."

Fifteen minutes later, Jan settled on a small painting. Once Keith paid for it, Miguel wrapped it carefully in bubble wrap and brown paper. "Thank you for your purchases," he said to Keith and Walter. "I do hope you will enjoy the paintings. Please fill out the information on my mailing list, so I can keep you informed of my future shows, new works, and upcoming shows by other artists here at the gallery." Turning to James and Monica, he said, "I hope you guys also enjoyed looking at my paintings."

"We did. Your paintings are amazing!" they assured him as the family departed for their lunch at *Sundried Tomato*.

Gathered around the table on the outdoor patio of the restaurant, the family discussed the art they had so admired. James had been struck by how Miguel's paintings had elements of impressionism and abstraction, so different from photography. Monica shared with her family what she knew of Miguel's history. She told how he had spent a year in prison because he had drugs in his possession when he and several friends were arrested at a party just after he completed high school. She explained that he lives with his grandmother, because his father refused to allow him to return home after his release. She said that he and his grandmother were very close, and that he had looked after her following her stroke two years ago. Recently, after his friend, Henry, moved into his grandmother's house, and since he became more involved in the art world, he spent little time at home.

"For a while, it was as if he forgot that his grandmother needed his help! She can't get out to shop, has difficulty cooking because she uses a walker to get around, and is unable to do any major housecleaning or other heavy jobs. Several times when Delia and I visited her there was hardly any food in the house. Since Miguel controls her finances and she doesn't keep cash in the house, so she couldn't even give us money to shop for her. She has been losing weight and said she often felt weak and dizzy. Delia worries about her. She can't go to her parents for help, because her father has forbidden contact with Miguel and her grandmother. Recently, Miguel's grandmother confronted him about his neglect. Since then, he has helped her find someone who comes in to cook, shop, and clean for her."

"Is that where my missing food went, Monica? Did you and Delia take it to give to Miguel's grandmother? Why didn't you just tell me and ask for help?" asked Jan.

"I'm sorry, Mom," said Monica, blushing. "I was afraid you wouldn't let me go with Delia on her visits, since her father forbade her to go there. She wanted me with her. That way, if any questions came up, she could say she had been out with me. She missed her grandmother and Miguel so much! I couldn't say no. And when we saw how thin her grandmother was becoming, and the lack of food in the house, I felt I needed to do something. Both my allowance and Delia's allowance are too small to buy much food for her. I didn't think you'd miss an occasional can of beans, some spaghetti or sauce, and a few snack packs. Your pantry is always so full."

"You should have asked, Monica. We could have donated some food, then called in social service to assist Miguel's grandmother."

"No! If you called in social services, Delia's family would have learned about her visits. That's exactly what she didn't want. And her grandmother is proud. She would be ashamed to take outside help; she has money, but couldn't access it. I know I shouldn't have taken the food without asking. I'm sorry. Anyway, I'm glad to say that once his grandmother confronted him, Miguel realized how neglectful he had been. He has become more attentive since then."

"Do you realize what you put your mother through?" demanded Keith. "She was worried about the loss of food and spent considerable time making and keeping an inventory to keep track of what was in the pantry. She wanted to confirm that she wasn't just forgetting that she used up her supplies. She worried that her memory was failing, a frightening thought! When she asked you if you had taken food from the pantry, you denied that you had. We didn't bring you up to be a liar!"

"I am sorry Mom, Dad. When Mom asked about taking food, I was embarrassed to say I had, so I didn't take anything again until things were becoming desperate. I wanted to help, and didn't want to get Delia in trouble. I didn't think anyone would miss the food I took. I never thought I'd cause Mom to worry. Please forgive me."

"Of course we forgive you, Monica," said Jan. "You meant well. Please talk to us when something like this comes up. Trust that we want to help. We wouldn't take action without discussing it with you. We'd listen to your suggestions about what is best, given the circumstances, and work to find a solution that works for all concerned."

Monica nodded, acknowledging her parents' concerns. Moments later the waitress arrived with their orders. Soon their attention turned to their delicious meals. Following lunch, they retrieved their beach supplies from the car, and then strolled the few blocks to the beach park. The adults sat on the sand and chatted while Monica and James took a dip. Because of his recovering ankle, James had opted not to bring his surfboard, as he would normally have done. Before long, everyone was hot and tired, and welcomed a quiet afternoon at home.

─ CHAPTER 28 ─

Friday Afternoon, October 28

When Henry entered the gallery that afternoon at one-thirty, he was met by an irate Miguel.

"Finally! You were scheduled to work today at ten-thirty. When you called this morning, you asked me to cover for you until noon. Where have you been? And why were you closing up shop in the middle of the afternoon last Tuesday?"

"What? Who told you that?"

"I had some folks come in this morning to buy a painting. They said they had stopped by on impulse last Tuesday afternoon, but you were getting ready to close. We've only just opened, for God's sake! My show only runs for a month. What the hell are you doing? If we're not open during our posted hours, we'll lose customers!"

"Stay cool, man. I'm sorry. Things were slow. There was no one around, so I decided to close early, and made an appointment I had to keep. Those folks showed up just as I was sweeping the floor, preparatory to closing. They really liked your work and said they'd try to return."

"And suppose they hadn't? I'd have lost a sale. I can't afford to do that. You know I've got to begin paying back the money I borrowed from my grandmother's account. How can I do that and pay rent, utilities, and your salary if we're not open for business when we're supposed to be? How can you be so casual about your responsibilities?

"You're good with customers, Henry, and you did a great job on the opening. You were also a big help in getting the gallery set up. But, I don't much care for some of your unethical practices, like putting sold signs on paintings that aren't sold. Some of your other ideas were even less acceptable and I didn't go along with them. Today there was a message on the answering machine telling you to back off or the caller would make sure you did. The caller didn't identify himself. I suppose you know what that was about?" Henry shrugged.

"I don't want to have to worry about what you'll do next. Closing when we should be open is not acceptable. If I can't depend on you, I'll have to let you go."

"You can't do that, Miguel. I know too much. If I have to, I'll tell your Dad that you're gay. That should have some interesting consequences. I can also tell your grandma about how you got this gallery in the first place."

"Don't threaten me, Henry! You've helped me a lot, but I've done a lot for you too. You were without a job and living in your car when I got to know you. I loved you, so persuaded my grandmother to give you a place to stay, free of charge until you could get on your feet. I gave you a job. Until recently, you were dependable. I couldn't have gotten the gallery going without you. Unfortunately, I still care for you, even though you threw me over when my grandmother decided you had been freeloading for too long. But that doesn't mean I'm going to let you take advantage of me. I've developed some backbone recently. If you want to keep this job, do what you're supposed to do. Is that understood? I'm not going to look the other way again, despite your threats."

"Yeah, okay Miguel. Sorry man."

"I've got to leave. I have an appointment, and I'm overdue, thanks to you. I expect you to stay until the scheduled closing time. Can I depend on you?"

"I'll be here, Miguel. You know I can't afford to lose this job."

Miguel went to his car and drove off. *I think I'll drive by just before closing time to be sure Henry keeps his word. I wonder what he is up to. Why is he making appointments for the time he's scheduled to work? I think I'd better double-check the accounts. If he's willing to do the unethical things he has suggested to me, he may be willing to cheat me. I've trusted him to deal with handling the money from the sale of the paintings. While I'm at it, I should double-check the records for the time we were remodeling. Some of the charges seemed excessive. I should make sure he didn't cheat me by listing higher charges than we actually paid, and pocketing the difference. Now that I think of it, there were several disgruntled contractors. I wonder if he was demanding kickbacks. I wouldn't put it past him. I should have listened when Grandmother said he's not trustworthy. I shouldn't have given him full control of the gallery finances.*

The question is, how can I manage the gallery without him? I must support myself. And I need to sell paintings to return the money I borrowed from Grandmother's account. My restaurant job doesn't give me time to be at the gallery most days, and leaves me little time or energy to do more painting.

Lawrence Tiller is scheduled to open his solo show when my show closes; that will run for a month. I need to prepare for his show. My commissions on sales of his paintings will be much less than my income from selling my own paintings. Although I can continue to show my paintings in the back room of the gallery, sales won't continue at the same pace as during my show. Maybe Lawrence would cover the gallery part-time during his show. He's a decent guy, and grateful for the chance to show his work. He'll probably agree. Perhaps I can use that as a model in the future. The artists who show here will be looking for exposure.

But, what about Henry's threat to tell Dad about my being gay? Or to tell Grandmother that I used her money for the gallery? I shouldn't have done that without asking, even though she had totally withdrawn from the world and refused to discuss her finances. I need to tell her what I've done before Henry does. She will be very upset and disappointed in me. I had hoped I could pay it all back quickly, so I didn't have to face her disappointment. Her good opinion means a lot to me.

As for Dad, what can I do? If he finds out I'm gay, he'll disown me for good. He may cut off his relationship with Grandmother again. That wouldn't be fair to her. Besides, I need him and my family. I can't face being alienated from them again. What am I to do?

Miguel put aside his concerns when he arrived at the artist's cooperative. He was scheduled to meet with Charlie Downs, another artist interested in showing his work at the gallery. He would figure it all out later.

By the time Miguel concluded his discussion with Charlie, he had agreed to give him a solo show the month after Lawrence's show closed. He suggested to Charlie that he commit to covering the gallery for 20 hours a week during his show. Charlie seemed to like the idea of being there to see customers' reactions to his work. *Maybe that model will work. It would help a lot!*

After leaving the artist's cooperative, Miguel stopped for a late lunch, then walked around downtown to settle his nerves. He drove back to the gallery just before the scheduled closing time. Henry was still there. He was surprised to see Miguel.

"Are you checking up on me?"

"Would it be inappropriate if I were?"

"No. After my bad behavior, it would be entirely appropriate."

"I wanted to review with you where we are with sales. We haven't done that for several days. I need to look at our income since we opened and figure out how much I can afford to repay my grandmother's account."

"You've done well with sales. Henry glanced at the account book. Six paintings sold at the Friday night opening. One sold on Thursday, then you sold two on Friday. I sold a small one this afternoon. That makes ten paintings. Pretty good, I'd say."

Henry handed the account book to Miguel who glanced at it briefly.

"That's more than I had hoped for. I worry that our income is likely to drop once we're dependent on commissions. With my paintings, I benefit from the total amount of the sale; sixty percent comes to me, the other forty percent is commission that supports the gallery's expenses. I can use my share for reimbursing my grandmother."

"You may still sell some of your paintings. We planned to continue showing them in the back room. We'll include your works in the advertising for the new show. I think you worry too much."

"You may be right. But, I feel responsible for the success of this enterprise. It's closing time. Go ahead and leave. I want to review which paintings have sold. Then, I need to figure out whether to replace some of those hanging so the paintings on display reflect a balance of subjects and sizes. I also need to check our inventory. It's time to begin painting again."

"Good-night, Miguel." Henry headed for the door. "Don't worry too much. It will all work out."

"I'll focus on positive thoughts. Have a good evening."

Once Henry had driven away, Miguel located his personal list of his paintings with suggested prices appended. He had checked the posted prices against this list the afternoon of the opening to confirm that pricing was correct. Now, he checked his suggested prices against the sales prices reflected in the account book.

Compared with his suggested prices, those listed in the account book reflected a systematic deduction of fifty dollars from the smaller paintings, one hundred and fifty dollars from the midsize paintings, and three hundred dollars from the large paintings. He personally had sold two paintings; those were also listed at the reduced price in the accounts. He knew that he had sold them for the full price. What Henry had entered did not reflect the actual sale price. That meant that one thousand, nine hundred and fifty dollars had been deducted from the income on the ten paintings that sold!

Miguel looked for the credit card slips and sales slips, but couldn't find them. He would have to ask Henry where he kept them. Those slips had to reflect the actual price at the time of sale or customers would notice. Would Henry have made up a second set with the reduced prices listed in the account book? This was serious. Clearly he needed some advice. This stealing from the gallery had to be stopped! Miguel longed to discuss it with his father, who ran a business and might have some idea how to trace the original sales. But, Henry's threats deterred him. Henry would probably carry them out if Miguel confronted him with his chicanery and fired him.

Grandmother might have some ideas. She kept the accounts for grandfather's business. She might know how I can trace the information from the missing receipts, and how I can modify the accounting system to forestall future thefts. I must tell her about the money I used to set up the gallery. She's functioning better and showing an interest in things again. She needs to know what I've done.

Miguel was tired and anxious. He decided to go home and deal with it all another day.

— CHAPTER 29 —

Friday Evening, October 28

When Miguel arrived home, his grandmother was in the living room reading a book. He had hoped to avoid her today. He was tired, frustrated, and depressed. All he wanted to do was retire to the peace and quiet of his room.

Juanita looked up when he closed the door to the garage.

"Miguel, I didn't expect you so early."

"I was tired when I left the gallery, so I didn't stop for any dinner. Is there anything in the kitchen I can heat?"

"You've been busy with your show. With so much to do and the excitement, I'm not surprised that you're tired. Bessie left us several meals. I'll see what we have, then you can choose which appeals to you. I'll be happy to warm them since you're tired. We can eat together. I would welcome the company, and I've been wanting to talk to you. If you're too tired to talk, that can wait until another night. Why don't you sit and put your feet up while I warm the meals. Do you want a beer, or do you prefer something else to drink?"

"I would enjoy a beer, thanks. I've been wanting to talk to you for some time. Tonight is as good a night as any. I seem to be tired all the time lately. What did you want to talk to me about?"

"We left some loose ends when we last talked. I wanted to finish that conversation. I'll get dinner on the kitchen table and call you when it's ready. Juanita handed Miguel a beer, then returned to the kitchen.

Miguel had a few sips of his beer. He set it down, leaned back against the sofa, and then put his feet up on the coffee table. He tried to recall what loose ends his grandmother might be referring to. In moments, he was asleep. When Juanita returned to the living room to ask Miguel which of Bessie's entrées he would prefer, she saw that he had dozed off. She decided to let the boy sleep for a time before heating the meals.

I wonder what he had on his mind when he said he wanted to talk. Be patient, Juanita! You'll find out soon enough.

Juanita made herself a cup of tea while Miguel napped. Once she finished her tea, she put two meals into the microwave, and set the table. Miguel entered the kitchen as the microwave pinged to signal the food was ready.

"Sit down, Grandmother. I'll take those to the table. Thanks for letting me sleep. I can't believe I slept for half an hour!"

"Are you feeling better?"

"The nap took the edge off my exhaustion. Food will probably help even more. I ate little today."

Miguel sat down opposite his grandmother. "Let's enjoy our dinner. Bessie's meal looks wonderful. After we've eaten, you can get comfortable in the living room. I'll clean up, then we can talk."

Miguel finished the dishes and then joined Juanita in the living room. "What did you want to talk about, Miguelito? You sounded so serious."

"This is serious. I think I'm in over my head. I must make a confession, then ask for some advice. Please don't say anything until I've finished. I know you will be disappointed in me. Hopefully, when I explain what I was thinking, you can find it in your heart to forgive me.

"Shortly after I moved in here, you paid for my art classes. Later, you converted the room over the garage to an art studio. Then you had your stroke. Afterwards, you were so ill and depressed that you gave me your power of attorney and asked me to manage your affairs, including overseeing the work on your ground floor bedroom suite. When I tried to review expenses with you, you waved me away and told me to handle it.

"Eventually, I accumulated a body of paintings, but was unsuccessful selling many of them through the art cooperative. I concluded that exhibiting only a few of my paintings at a time, among those of so many other artists was not conducive to marketing my art. I needed a solo show. The art galleries in town show major, well-known artists. They weren't willing to even talk to an unknown like me.

"I became involved romantically with Henry during this time. He, of course, knew that I was managing your affairs. He suggested using some of the money from your account to develop my own gallery where I could show my work. He suggested that I could also earn money by holding solo shows for other artists and charging commissions on the sales of their paintings. He needed a job and had prior experience managing a gallery.

"The gallery was a good idea. I believed you might have loaned me money for the project if you weren't so withdrawn from life. I desperately believed that if I didn't do something soon, I'd have to give up my dream of being an artist. Then the property on Canyon Road was listed for rent. The building had once been an art gallery and the location was ideal. But, it was in need of substantial repair. Because of that, the rent was reasonable. It felt like fate was taking a hand.

"I'm ashamed to admit that I was able to rationalize using money from your account to cover the leasing expenses, repairs, and Henry's salary. I wanted it so much, I took the plunge. It solved several problems. I could get exposure for my art. By giving Henry a job, I could assure he would remain part of my life.

"I hoped that eventually the business would become known and grow. To support gallery expenses, I planned charge a standard commission of forty percent on sales when other artists held shows. I would continue showing my work in the back room. Eventually I hoped to support myself from sales of my paintings and running the gallery. I want to give up working as a cook, so I have more time and energy for painting. I always intended to pay your money back as soon as possible. I took out about fifty-five thousand dollars. I can show you all the expenses. I've kept careful records.

"No! Let me finish," exclaimed Miguel as Juanita tried to interrupt. "Today, I went to the gallery to look at the accounts. I wanted to see how much I've earned from sales during the show, hoping I'd have enough to put a chunk of money back in your account. I wanted also to determine how much I might be able repay each month in the future.

"Ten paintings sold since the show opened. Those ten should have brought in twenty-one thousand, and thirty dollars. I sold three small ones at seven hundred and fifty each, two medium ones at eighteen hundred and ninety each, and five large ones at three thousand each. When I looked at the accounts, I discovered that the listed sale prices reflected less for each painting than the price I put on them. Nineteen hundred and fifty dollars had been deducted.

"Even the two paintings I personally sold were listed in the account at a lower price than that at which I actually sold them. It appears that Henry is routinely skimming off money from each sale and falsifying the accounts when he enters the sale in the account book. The only sales slips I could find list the prices reflected in the account book. Henry must be making new sales slips for each sale. I couldn't find any others, or the credit card slips.

"I also learned that he closed the gallery several hours early one afternoon this week. This morning he called and asked me to cover for him at the gallery for a few hours. He finally showed up several hours later than he committed to be there. When I called him on it and threatened to fire him, he threatened to blackmail me by telling Dad that I am gay. You know what that would do. Just when I've gotten my family back, Dad would reject me forever! What am I to do? Do you hate me after what I've done?"

Miguel looked at his grandmother, tears running down his face. Juanita wanted to hold him in her arms and console him, but knew that she had to remain aloof. This was the time of reckoning. He knew what he had done was wrong and had planned to make restitution, but she must not excuse his deeds.

"Miguel, thank you for telling me what you did. You confirmed what I suspected since last Friday when I went to see my lawyer and my bank manager." Juanita glanced at Miguel and saw a look of surprise, then horror cross his face.

"At the lawyer's office, I signed papers to regain my power of attorney. You may recall that I told you I planned to do so. That means you will not be able to withdraw any money from the account after the end of this month.

"When I reviewed my accounts with the bank manager, we saw the pattern of withdrawals relating to renting and renovating the gallery. At least, that is what I assumed it must be when I saw the timing of the initial withdrawals and the ongoing pattern. I was to return to the bank the later this week, by which time the manager expected to have confirmation of who received the payments. I planned to ask you to explain it, once I had confirmation of what I suspected. So, I am relieved at your confession.

"Needless to say, I was in shock when I found out. Once I calmed down, I surmised that your rationale for using the money without asking permission would be similar to what you have described. I own some of the blame for asking you to take over my affairs, then showing no interest in your attempts to keep me involved. Since I encouraged your efforts at developing a painting career, I can understand how you might assume I would be willing to give you a loan to realize your ambitions. I would have done so, had you asked. Even so, what you did was wrong. I'm glad you realize that.

"You said you planned to make restitution. I expect that you will do so. I propose the following scenario. I will have my lawyer draw up a document that says I gave you a loan in the amount of fifty-five thousand dollars for the purpose of developing your gallery. This document will include a schedule of repayment, which you and I will discuss and agree upon before the document is drawn.

"Since you came to me voluntarily and told me what you have done, and you intended to repay the money, I will make this an interest-free loan. But, even with your plan to have solo shows for other artists and make commissions from those sales, I fear you will find it difficult to make a go of it. Continuing to pay Henry eighteen hundred dollars a month to manage the gallery will make it impossible, even without his theft. You need to be your own manager. I suspect you will continue to need income from your restaurant job until the gallery generates a reasonable and steady income. It is for you to figure out how you will manage. You have demonstrated creativity and a willingness to work hard, so I have no doubt you will find a way.

"Despite his threats of blackmail, you must fire Henry. Getting rid of that eighteen hundred dollar monthly expense will help a lot. The loan document I have proposed will protect you from Henry trying to blackmail you over your use of my money, should he decide to tell your father about that. I have no doubt he would try. How to prevent him from telling your father about your being gay is a more difficult problem. Sergio will find out eventually, you know. I agree that it is too soon after your reconciliation for him to learn about it now. Perhaps we can frighten Henry into keeping his mouth shut by confronting him with what you know about his stealing. We can threaten to report him to the police if he doesn't stay away from your father. You'll need to have evidence of his theft when you confront him. What do you think?"

"So we bargain? We don't say anything about his theft if he doesn't say anything to Dad about my being gay? It might work. He'll be furious about losing his job. I have no proof of how he managed to juggle the books. If he won't give me the original credit card receipts and sales slips, how can we prove he's stealing?"

"You will need to contact your buyers. I'm sure you have a list of their names and addresses so you can keep them informed of new works or shows. Contacting them will be awkward, but you have no choice. Tell them you've discovered that your manager kept inadequate records and you've fired him. Your accountant has asked you to retrieve whatever evidence of the original purchase is retrievable to back up what you report on your tax returns. You need the date of sale, amount of purchase, and credit card to which the purchase was charged. With that information, you can contact the credit card companies for documentation of the sale. Even if you can't get them all, we'll have enough to charge Henry with fraud if he doesn't cooperate. Do you think you can get the information by Tuesday?"

Miguel nodded. "I'll start calling buyers tomorrow, and will try to confirm the information from the buyers with the credit card companies. Next week I'll try to talk with some of the contractors who did our remodeling. I wouldn't be surprised if Henry found a way to skim some money from the remodeling budget."

"Have Henry meet us here at six o'clock on Wednesday evening. Tell him that I am serving as your accountant. I'd like to do that for you. I can prepare your tax returns and other necessary documents, and help you set up a more foolproof accounting system than the one you're currently using. Tell Henry I'm developing a new accounting system and want the three of us to meet and discuss it. Since he knows it is difficult for me to come to the gallery, he'll understand the request to meet here. Tell him to bring the credit card and sales receipts. If he brings fake receipts, when we compare those against the true sales information that you collect, it will show that he is cheating you. Fire him during our meeting. I will give him a check for one additional month's salary and we will extract his promise to stay silent about you being gay, in exchange for us staying silent about his theft. If he breaks his word, we go to the police. Agreed?"

"Agreed. Thank you, Grandmother. You're one smart lady! Thank you for everything--your forgiveness, all the help you've provided in the past, and your willingness to help solve this mess. I love you so much!"

"I love you, my Miguel."

— (HAPTER 30 —

Wednesday Evening, November 2

Miguel pulled his car into the garage. He was late. He had waited until Henry left the gallery, and then collected the documentation he obtained of the true sales data, and the account book that Henry maintained. *Grandmother probably offered Henry a cup of tea while they waited for me.* Miguel smiled to himself at the thought of Henry drinking tea.

He opened the door to the house and called out, "Hello. I'm here. Sorry I'm late. I was detained at the gallery."

Hearing no response, Miguel walked into the living room. He froze in shock at the sight that greeted him! Henry lay on the floor by the living room sofa in a pool of blood. His grandmother lay on the floor near the front door, her walker turned onto its side near her body. The front door was ajar. It appeared that Juanita must have gone to answer the door.

"Grandmother!" sobbed Miguel as he ran to her. He squatted and gently touched her face, calling to her urgently. "Grandmother, can you hear me? Grandmother?"

Receiving no reply, Miguel took her limp wrist and anxiously felt for a pulse. He was relieved to feel a pulse, although it was weak, He examined her more closely. There was a small amount of blood in her hair and on the floor by her head, but none elsewhere. He gingerly ran his hands over her head. A huge lump on the back of her head appeared to be the source of the blood.

Having ascertained that his grandmother was alive, Miguel went to check on Henry. He could feel no pulse. He touched the blood stains on the carpet. They were wet. Henry's shirt was soaked with blood.

Miguel grabbed his mobile phone and dialed 911. "Please, send an ambulance to 5467 Felida Street in Irvine," he pleaded. "Hurry! My grandmother is unconscious, but alive. I fear that my friend may be dead. I can't find any pulse! You'd better ask the police to come too."

Miguel returned to his grandmother's side. He wanted to put his arms around her, but feared he might do further injury. He sat down next to her on the floor, then dialed his father's number. He held Juanita's hand and waited for the ambulance to arrive.

"Dad, I have bad news! When I arrived home tonight, I found Grandmother lying unconscious on the floor, and Henry, my gallery manager, dead in a pool of blood! I think he's been shot. I've called 911 for an ambulance. Can you go to the hospital to meet grandmother when she arrives? I need to wait here for the police. Once they've finished with me, I'll join you at the hospital. I'll call you back as soon as I know for sure where they will take her."

He listened to his father's questions and offer to come and help, then replied, "No, I have no idea what happened. Grandmother and I had arranged to meet Henry here to discuss some issues relating to the gallery. It looks as if Grandmother went to answer the door sometime after Henry arrived and was shoved so hard she fell and hit her head against that marble pedestal that holds that bronze sculpture of the eagle she likes so much. She is lying near that pedestal. Her walker was overturned on the floor near the door. Her pulse is weak, but steady. But I can't get her to respond when I call her name.

"I appreciate your offer to come, Dad, but I don't think there's anything you can do here. It's better for you to be at the hospital when Grandmother arrives. I'll stay by her until the ambulance gets here. As soon as I have the information about the hospital, I'll call you. Bye."

Miguel got up and used his phone to snap several pictures of his grandmother and the areas of the room near her. They he took several pictures of the area where Henry lay. In the process he noticed a can of beer and a folder on the coffee table. He debated whether to take the folder, which he assumed Henry had brought for the meeting, but decided not to touch anything. He returned to sit with his grandmother, talking to her quietly and holding her hand as he waited.

About ten minutes later, Miguel heard sirens. He left his grandmother's side and looked out the window. An ambulance pulled up in front of the house. Once inside, the medics examined Juanita, and confirmed that she was alive. They examined Henry and pronounced him dead. A few minutes later, they had Juanita on oxygen, and loaded on a stretcher for transport to the Irvine hospital. A police car arrived as the medics were preparing to carry Juanita to the ambulance.

Miguel dialed his father. "The ambulance is just leaving. They will take grandmother to the Irvine Hospital. The police have arrived. I need to go talk with them. Bye."

Miguel was waiting by the door when two policemen came up the steps to the front entrance. The first officer extended his hand. "I'm Detective Stephens, this is Sergeant Molina. Our photographer and the rest of the team are close behind us. They should be here any minute. You are?"

"I'm Miguel Sanchez. I called 911 when I arrived home from work and found my grandmother and Henry on the floor. He was lying there where he is now. My grandmother was on the tile floor by the front door, next to that marble pedestal. The front door was ajar. I snapped a picture of her and that area before the ambulance arrived, because I knew they would have to move her. I thought it would be helpful for you to see the scene around where she was found."

"A good idea. Thank you, Mr. Sanchez. Please give me the names of the two victims."

"Henry Jenkins is the man on the living room floor. He was my gallery manager. I have an art gallery on Canyon Road. Juanita Sanchez, the other victim, is my grandmother. The ambulance just left to take her to the Irvine Hospital. She and I live here."

"Do you know where Henry Jenkins lived? Is there anyone we need to notify about his death?"

"He lived with a mutual friend, Nathan Stearns, in a house on Carmel Circle in Laguna Beach. I don't know the house number. Other than Nathan, I don't know of anyone to notify. I know nothing about his relatives. Henry never mentioned any. He would frequently say he is alone in the world."

They were interrupted by a knock on the door. It was the crime scene team. The officers excused themselves to consult with them. The team got to work and Detective Stephens returned to Miguel.

"Tell me about the circumstances of how you found them."

"I pulled my car into the garage at about ten minutes after six. I entered through that door over there," said Miguel, pointing. "It leads from the garage into the house. I called out that I was home, but received no response. So I went into the living room and found them."

"Were you expecting your manager to be here?"

"Yes. My grandmother asked that we meet with Henry about some accounting issues at the gallery. Since it is difficult for her to get out since her stroke, she asked to hold the meeting with Henry here at six p.m. I was a few minutes late, because I had to gather some documents for the meeting. On the way home, I ran into traffic."

"When did Henry leave the gallery?"

"Just after five-thirty. That's when we close."

"So, you don't know when he arrived here?"

"No idea, I'm afraid. If he came straight here, it should have taken him twenty to thirty minutes, depending on traffic."

"Can anyone confirm when you left the gallery? Or when you arrived home?"

"There was nobody at the gallery after Henry left, so no-one to confirm my departure. Perhaps, one of the young men who hangs around down the street saw me arrive here. You'd have to ask. But they're often drunk or stoned, so probably not."

"Did anyone else know that Henry would be here?"

"Not that I know of."

"Do you have any idea who might have done this?"

"I don't know anyone who would want to hurt my grandmother. Henry probably has some enemies, but I don't know them."

"What makes you say that?"

"Several things. Earlier this week, I was covering for him at the gallery while he went to an early morning appointment. When I came in that morning, there was a message on the answering machine. It was a male voice. He said, 'Henry, you son-of-a-bitch. Back off, or I'll see that you never bother me or anyone else again.' I've also heard a rumor that he has been blackmailing one of the artists at the art cooperative in Laguna Beach."

"I'm surprised you kept him on. Did you save the voice message?"

"No, I deleted the message, but told him about it when he came in. I routinely delete messages once I play them and record the caller's name, phone number, and reason for the call; that way the machine's tape doesn't get full. A business gets a lot of calls, and we don't have a secretary.

"What is your grandmother's involvement with the gallery?"

"I spoke with her last Friday about what appeared to be erroneous sales prices listed in the accounts. I thought she might have some advice; she maintained the books for my grandfather's business for many years. When I told her I suspected that Henry was falsifying the books, she suggested a way I could follow-up to confirm what the paintings actually sold for. She also offered to serve as my accountant and to develop a new system for documenting sales. She suggested that we meet with Henry once I had information about the actual sales prices."

"Do you own a gun?"

"No, I've never owned a gun."

"Okay, Mr. Sanchez. We'll have the body removed as soon as the team is finished here. Henry was shot, but there is no gun here at the scene. You didn't see any gun when you arrived?"

Miguel shook his head, no.

"Did you touch anything?"

"Only Henry and Grandmother, to check for a pulse."

"We'll start trying to locate the murder weapon. We'd like to talk with your grandmother when she regains consciousness. We'll stay in touch with the hospital. In the meantime, we'll contact this Nathan Stearns, Henry's room-mate, and maybe talk to some folks at the art cooperative. We may need to talk with you again."

"I understand. I hope you catch whoever did this."

— CHAPTER 31 —

Wednesday Evening, November 2

Sergeant Molina rang the doorbell. A short, slender, blond-haired man dressed all in black opened the door.

"Can I help you?"

"I'm Sergeant Molina. This is Detective Stevens. We're from the Irvine Police Department. I understand that a Mr. Henry Jenkins lives at this address. Is that correct?"

"Yes, Henry lives here. I'm Nathan Stearns. We share the house."

"We need to ask you a few questions."

"What is this about, Detective?"

"Do you own the house? How long have you lived here?"

"No, I lease the house. I've been here about three years."

"Are you related to Mr. Jenkins?"

"No. He pays me rent to live here."

"How long has Mr. Jenkins lived here?"

"Three or four months. He answered an ad I ran in the local paper when I was seeking someone to share the house."

"Did you know him before he answered the advertisement?"

"Not well, but we had met. He's an artist, so occasionally came into the art supply shop where I work to purchase oil painting supplies. I'd also run into him at the artists cooperative."

"What are your living arrangements here?"

"We split the rent. I pay one-third, he pays two-thirds. He pays more because the furnishings are mine and the utilities are in my name, so I pay those. We each have our own bedroom and bath, but share the rest of the house. Why do you want to know all this?"

"I'm sorry to tell you that Mr. Jenkins has been shot."

"What? Henry shot! When? Where? Was he badly hurt?"

"Mr. Jenkins has been killed. May we come in? We need to ask you some more questions, and we'd like to see his rooms."

"Yes, of course. Come in. I doubt that I can be of much help. I can't believe this has happened. Do you know who shot him?"

"When did you last see Henry?"

"This morning before he left for work. He came into the kitchen when I was finishing my breakfast. That must have been about eight-fifteen. I left for work shortly thereafter."

"How did he seem? Did you notice anything unusual?"

"No. I didn't notice anything different. He reminded me that he wouldn't be home until late because he had a meeting to review some accounts with Miguel Sanchez after the gallery closed. He manages ....managed the gallery for Miguel."

"Why didn't they discuss the accounts during working hours?"

"Henry said something about Henry's grandmother devising a new accounting system that she wanted to review with him. Apparently she's serving as Miguel's accountant."

"Were they meeting at the gallery?"

"No. Henry said that Mrs. Sanchez has difficulty getting out, so the meeting was to be held at Miguel's house. He lives with his grandmother."

"How did Henry get along with Miguel?"

"Generally okay. They had some sort of disagreement

recently. Several days ago, Henry said that Miguel had threatened to fire him if he didn't shape up. He told me he wasn't worried about being fired because he knew that Miguel had used money from his Grandmother's account to pay for gallery expenses. He also said Miguel's father didn't know that he was gay. Henry told Miguel that if he fired him, he would tell his father he was gay and tell his grandmother about him using her money."

"Did you believe him about the money?"

"I saw no reason not to. Miguel works as a cook at a local restaurant. Occasionally, he sells one of his paintings. It seems unlikely that he would have the personal funds to rent gallery space, remodel the space, and pay Henry to oversee the process. Apparently, he holds his grandmother's power of attorney."

"Where were you from four o'clock this afternoon until now?"

"The store closes early on Wednesdays, at three o'clock. I left shortly after three and came home. I've been wanting to do some housecleaning, so spent the afternoon and evening here. I figured that with Henry being late, I'd have a good chunk of time to accomplish something. If you're asking for an alibi, I have none. The store owner left shortly before I closed and I've been here alone all night."

"We need to notify Henry's next of kin. Do you know where we can reach his family?"

"I don't know anything about his family. Henry always gave the impression that he was alone in the world. He never kept any family pictures around or talked about family."

"Thank you, Mr. Stearns. May we see Henry's room, please?"

Nathan led the way up the stairs, then turned right. He opened a door and ushered the police into a high-ceilinged room, about fifteen feet by fifteen feet in size. The room overlooked the street.

"This is Henry's room. The bathroom is through there." Nathan pointed to a closed door on the other side of the room.

The room, painted in a light honey tan, was sparsely furnished. A queen bed was piled with multicolored pillows and sported a thick, cream-colored comforter. A worn, mirrored walnut dresser, a green recliner, a slatted-back walnut chair with a cane seat, a narrow walnut bedside table, and a small desk with a gooseneck lamp were the only other furnishings. The room was tidy. The closet door was ajar, displaying its contents, including a rack of neatly hung clothing, two suitcases on the floor, and two shoe racks on the shelf above the clothing, containing mostly dress shoes. There were two books and a lamp on the bedside table. Sitting on top of the dresser was an ornate brass box, which appeared to be a jewelry box. There were no personal pictures to be seen. Hanging on the walls were two paintings, both landscapes, reproductions of old masters. Detective Stevens motioned Sergeant Molina toward the dresser. "You check the drawers, I'll look through the bedside table."

While the sergeant sorted through the contents of the dresser, Detective Stevens tried to open the drawer of the bedside table. He turned to Nathan. "This seems to be locked. Do you have a key?"

"Do you have Henry's car keys? He usually kept the key to that drawer on his key ring."

"No, I'm afraid those are down at the station."

"I'll look for my copy of the key. I keep extra keys, because sometimes my tenants leave without returning theirs. It's just a matter of finding it. Let me do a search while you look at the rest of the room."

Nathan returned after about five minutes. "Here is the key. Please leave it in the lock when you're finished. This is the only extra I could find."

Detective Stevens opened the drawer. The inside was divided

into two compartments. One contained two check books, several credit cards, some bills in a money clip, and some loose change. The other side was empty.

"This seems odd. This large space is empty."

Nathan came closer and peered in. "That's where Henry usually kept his gun, his wallet, and his car keys. That's odd. The gun is missing. He rarely carried it with him. The last time I know that he kept it with him was during the gallery remodeling. He said some of the workmen made him nervous."

"We didn't find a gun on him, Sir," said Sergeant Molina. "We can check his car when we get back to the station. One of the guys drove his car there."

"You haven't seen his gun recently, Mr. Stearns?"

"No, like I said, he mentioned that he was taking it to work with him during the remodeling. He hasn't mentioned it since. I just assumed he returned it to the drawer."

"Do you know what kind of gun he had?"

"I'm afraid I don't know much about guns. It was a small handgun. That's all I know about it."

"Okay. Thanks for your help, Mr. Stearns. We'll be about another fifteen minutes up here. Then we'll be out of your hair."

"I'll be in the living room if you need me."

— CHAPTER 32 —

Friday Evening, November 4

The Conway family was eating their dinner when the telephone rang. Keith answered the phone. "It's for you, Monica. It's Delia. She sounds upset."

"Oh, I hope that nothing has happened to her grandmother. I told you about what happened at her grandmother's house and that Mrs. Sanchez was hospitalized. She was still unconscious when I talked to Delia yesterday." Monica took the phone from her father.

"Delia. What's happening? You sound upset."

"Oh no, Delia! Surely they can't believe that Miguel killed Henry and hit his grandmother! How is your father taking this? I see. Thank heavens for that. How is your grandmother? Still in a coma. I'm sorry. At least she hasn't changed for the worse.

"Grandfather? He's not here now. They went to San Diego for a few days. We expect them back later tonight. Grandfather and Grandma Susan plan to spend the weekend with us before returning to Seattle on Monday. Yes, of course I'll ask him. I do hope he'll say yes. I'll call you as soon as I talk to him. Bye, Delia."

Monica returned to find a sea of expectant faces in the

dining room. "The police came to the gallery to question Miguel today. Apparently, they think that Miguel shot Henry, his manager, and battered his grandmother! They said they will be wanting to talk to him further, and told him not to leave town. His family is frightened for him. They don't know how to begin to refute the belief of the police that he killed Henry and have no idea why the police think Miguel did it. I don't believe anyone could think that of Miguel! He's a kind, gentle man.

"Delia remembered that I once told her that Grandfather had been a policeman, and spent time working for the FBI. She asked whether he would be willing to help them figure out how to deal with this. I bet he would! I remember that he and Grandma Susan looked into that suspected murder in Hawaii last year."

"You can certainly ask, dear, but don't be disappointed if he says no. Grandpa and Grandma Susan have plans to return to Seattle. They have things to deal with back there. They've been gone for over a month."

"But, Mom. He liked Miguel. Surely he would want to help, if he can."

"I think I agree with Monica," said Keith. "I believe Dad would want to help if he is able. It certainly won't hurt to ask. Dad always got involved when he felt that justice wasn't being served. If he's not too tired when they get here, we'll ask him tonight. I'm sure Miguel's family would sleep better if they can count on some help. While we're waiting for your grandparents to arrive, Monica and James, go start on your homework. You'll want to spend time with Grandfather and Grandma Susan before they leave, so try to finish it off, if you can. I'll give Mom a hand with the dishes and call you when they arrive."

As they worked side-by-side, clearing the table and cleaning up the kitchen, Jan said to Keith.

"What if Miguel is guilty? Are you sure it's a good idea to get your father involved?"

"Relax, Jan. It will be his decision. If he should find evidence of Miguel's guilt, he'll have to share it with the police. He's dealt with similar situations before. But, can you really believe that talented young man we met at the gallery who painted those extraordinary pictures is a murderer? Why would he want to kill his manager? As for his grandmother, he's been looking after her for years. Monica has told us in the past that his grandmother was very fond of him, and that the two of them have been close."

"Even nice people do bad things when driven to it by extraordinary circumstances. I agree that it's hard to imagine him as a killer. Still, the police must have some evidence to believe him guilty."

"Dad has said that the police are often quick to jump to the conclusion that the person who finds the body is guilty. Because the person who found the victim is already in the picture, the police often start by tracking down information about that person and their relationship with the victim. The investigation can fan out from there. It's a bit like a cobweb, with all these interconnected threads. As the police investigation proceeds, they may uncover evidence that points them in a different direction. Unfortunately, their resources are limited. If Dad gets involved in investigating this, he may go after some threads that the police don't have time to deal with."

The sound of a car door closing interrupted their conversation.

"I think they're back," commented Jan. She went to open the front door. "Welcome back Walter, Susan. We just finished cleaning up from dinner. You said not to wait for you. Have you eaten?"

"Hello, Jan. It's good to be back. We stopped in Carlsbad on our way here. There is this Mexican Restaurant that Walter was dying to visit. Said it's been too long since he had one of their chili rellenos. I must admit that it was some of the best Mexican food I've ever eaten. The problem is, I'm still full."

"You must be talking about *Fidels.* We almost always take Walter to that restaurant when he's in town, even though it's a long drive. He says getting good Mexican food in Hawaii is almost impossible."

"We just saved you a long drive, then."

"How was your visit to San Diego?"

"I enjoyed it. We stopped in La Jolla on our way down. It's a pretty town. Walter was disappointed. He said both places have grown too much since he was last there. For him, their previous charm has been lost. I had never been to either before, so couldn't appreciate the differences that bothered him. I thought they were both scenic and charming places to visit."

"Mom. I heard voices. Is Grandpa here?" Monica came flying down the steps.

"Monica. Do be careful! You could fall and break your neck running down the stairs like that. Yes, it's Grandpa and Grandma Susan." Jan turned back to Susan. "We've had some excitement while you were gone. Monica will tell you and Walter all about it."

"Monica, give your grandparents a chance to put their bags in their room and get settled with a drink," said Keith, coming into the foyer. "Then you can tell them all about what's happened and make your request."

As Walter came through the door with luggage, Monica approached. "Hi Grandpa. Can I help you carry the bags upstairs?"

Walter set the bags down and gave Monica a hug. "Good to see you again. Why don't you carry Grandma Susan's bag for me?"

As Walter and Monica saw to the luggage, Jan turned to Susan. "What would you like to drink?"

"At this hour, I'd better stick to cold water, thanks. Perhaps with a slice of lemon."

"Actually, that sounds perfect for me too. You make yourself comfortable in the living room. I'll bring our drinks and join you. Keith, would you take your father's drink order when he comes down, please?" Keith nodded.

Soon, the adults and Monica were seated in the living room. James remained upstairs working on his homework. Monica looked as if she would burst.

"Go ahead and tell your grandparents what has happened, Monica," said her father. "I know you're anxious to get back to Delia."

The story poured out of Monica in a breathless torrent of words. The narrative concluded with, "So, Grandpa, will you help Miguel by looking into things? He really needs help. The family doesn't know where to start."

"I'll try to help. I really liked Miguel. I agree that it seems unlikely that he killed Henry and battered his grandmother. What possible motive could he have? No wonder his family is worried. This is like a thunderbolt out of the blue! You're sure the family wants me to stick my nose in? That isn't something you and your friend Delia cooked up, is it?"

"I told Delia about you working as a policeman and being in the FBI. She talked to her parents about asking you for help. They said they would be grateful for anything you can do."

"Alright then. You call Delia and tell her I will try to help. Then let me speak to her father. What is his name?"

"It's Sergio Sanchez."

Monica ran for the phone and dialed Delia. "Dee, its Monica. Grandfather says he will help! I know, isn't it wonderful? He wants to talk with your father. Is he there now? Will you put him on, please?

"Hello, Mr. Sanchez. It's Monica Conway. My grandfather says he'll try to help and would like to talk to you. I'll put him on." She handed Walter the telephone, then stood nearby so she could hear what her grandfather was saying.

"Hello, Mr. Sanchez. Walter Conway here. Monica filled me in on what has happened. I'm so sorry about your mother. Any good news yet?" Walter listened, then replied, "I'm sorry to hear that. It would be most helpful if she were able to tell us what happened. I gather that you don't know why the police think Miguel might have done it?

"Yes, well it's not unusual that they don't share their evidence or what they are thinking. It would be very helpful if I could interview Miguel tomorrow morning. I might get some idea of where to start looking into this. Can you set that up for me? Say around ten o'clock. It's probably better that I talk to him without your being present, if you don't mind. While I interview Miguel, perhaps you could obtain a lawyer to represent him. We may not need one, if the police discover some evidence that leads them in a new direction, or if your mother recovers and can tell her story. But, best to be prepared. If Miguel has a lawyer, he can be there in the event that Miguel is charged. Also, I can work with him and use that formal affiliation to help me in my investigations. If I can tell people I'm working with Miguel's lawyer they may be more willing to talk to me than if I must approach them as an unaffiliated stranger."

Walter listened as Sergio talked. "I do understand that you want to help, Mr. Sanchez. At the moment, you need to be available for your mother. Also, Miguel will need your presence and emotional support during the coming weeks until this is resolved. If there is anything you can do that will help my investigations, be sure that I will call on you.

"Compensation? No, I don't want to be paid. I'm doing this because I like your son; I met him at his gallery last week. And my granddaughter and your daughter are best friends. Consider this a family affair. We all want to see Miguel cleared of suspicion and the culprit identified. Call me on my mobile in the morning to let me know where and when Miguel can meet with me. The number is 619-233-4856. Good night, Mr. Sanchez."

As Walter hung up the phone, Susan interrupted, "Walter, can I..."

"No, Susan. You may not come with me to the interview with Miguel. It will be difficult enough for him to tell me what may be relevant. You would be a distraction. I'm sorry. You can help me sort through what I learn when I return, and perhaps interview some other players, once we know who they are. We made a good team on that investigation in Hawaii. I will welcome your ideas. But, this initial interview I must do alone. I'm sorry."

"I understand, Walter. You haven't hurt my feelings---too much," said Susan with a rueful smile. "What I can do is cancel our Monday morning flight to Seattle. We might be here for a while."

— CHAPTER 33 —

Saturday, November 5

Sergio Sanchez phoned Walter to tell him that Miguel would meet him at the gallery at nine-thirty. They would have time to talk before the gallery opened. Miguel had agreed to tell Walter everything pertaining to why the police might consider him a suspect in Henry Jenkin's death.

Walter arrived at nine twenty-five. As he got out of his car, the gallery door opened and Miguel walked out, hand outstretched.

"Mr. Conway. I heard your car. Thank you so much for agreeing to help."

"I only hope that I can."

Miguel ushered Walter into his office. "Would you like a cup of coffee? I just made a pot."

Walter nodded. Miguel poured two cups and set them on the table. "Please sit down, Mr. Conway."

"Your father told me you believe the police consider you a suspect in the murder of Henry Jenkins and the battering of your grandmother."

"Yes, sir. That is how it seemed when Detective Stephens came to talk to me here yesterday afternoon. He thought that

Henry was blackmailing me and that I shot him to keep him quiet. He warned me not to leave town."

"If you had wanted to shoot Henry, I wouldn't have thought you'd do it where your grandmother would be a witness. I don't believe you did it."

"Thank you for saying that, Mr. Conway."

"Please, call me Walter. Now, it would help me if you would describe what has happened. Start with Wednesday night when you found Henry and your grandmother in the living room. Describe the sequence of events from the time you entered the house until the police departed. Then tell me what has happened since then."

Miguel explained to Walter about the six o'clock meeting he had scheduled to meet with Henry and his grandmother. He described how he found them lying on the floor when he arrived home at ten minutes after six. He reiterated the conversation with Detective Stephens. "When they left the house that night, I had no idea that he suspected me!"

"Was yesterday afternoon the first time you thought you might be a suspect?"

"Yes. Detective Stephens came by the gallery just as I was preparing to close. He said he wanted to update me on the investigation and ask me some additional questions. First, he told me that he talked to Henry's roommate, Nathan Stearns. Nathan told Detective Stephens that Henry was upset with me, because I threatened to fire him. Henry told Nathan that to keep from being fired, he had threatened to tell my father that that I was gay, and to tell both my father and grandmother that I had stolen money from my grandmother to open the gallery."

"Was it true, what he said?"

"Yes, more or less. I did threaten to fire Henry; he has not been consistently on site when he was supposed to cover the gallery, and I recently learned that he was stealing from me. And Henry did threaten to blackmail me if I fired him. I am gay.

"It's painful for me to tell you about using Grandmother's money. I didn't think of it as stealing, but as a loan. I held Grandmother's power of attorney and had been managing her financial affairs since her stroke two years ago. Because she was depressed, she wasn't interested or willing to listen when I tried to discuss her finances after I took over. I borrowed money from her account to start the gallery. I kept careful records of what I used, so I could pay it back. I was finally able to tell her about it the week before Henry was killed. She said she would have her lawyer draw up a loan document and repayment schedule for me to sign."

"I am ashamed that I went ahead and used the money, but she did understand. Since she is now unconscious, I have nothing to prove my version of events. Unfortunately, she wanted to wait until after our meeting with Henry to contact her lawyer about drawing up the loan document. That document would have proved that what I say is true."

"Obviously, Detective Stephens thinks that the blackmail threat gives you a motive for killing Henry. It's a reasonable conclusion. With Henry stealing from you, if you can't fire him, you're between a rock and a hard place. But you have no motive for attacking your grandmother, except to eliminate her as a witness. What evidence do you have of Henry's theft?"

"Since grandmother and I talked last Friday evening, I've been calling customers who bought my paintings. I told them I've discovered that my manager kept inadequate records, and so my accountant asked me to retrieve information from buyers on sales price, date of purchase, and the credit card used. I've compared that information against what was recorded in the accounts and confirmed that there is a systematic reduction in the recorded sales price. I've since compared it with the credit card and sales slips that we asked Henry to bring to the meeting--they were on the coffee table in the living room. Those slips reflect the amounts entered in the account book. Apparently he was making new slips with the amounts he entered in the accounts. I don't know what he did with the originals, probably destroyed them. I can only assume that Henry was pocketing the difference. It would help if we could see his bank account. I'd be willing to bet there were deposits every time he made a deposit in the gallery account."

"You never contacted me for information about the painting Susan and I bought."

"No. The number you listed in the book was a Seattle number. I called, but got the answering machine. Also, since I sold you that painting, I knew I had charged the standard list price for that size of painting."

"Oh, of course. Susan and I had expected to return home on Monday. That number is our landline. We rarely use our cell phones except when we're traveling. Do you own a gun, Miguel?"

"No, I've never even held a gun."

"Do you know if Henry or Nathan owned a gun?"

"I don't."

"Tell me about Henry's roommate, Nathan Stearns."

"I don't know him well, just as a social acquaintance from art community events. He works at the art supply store. Like Henry and me, he is gay. Henry got involved with him when my grandmother told him it was time to move out of her place and get on with his life. Nathan was advertising for a roommate. Henry needed a place to live, so he responded to the ad. I guess they hit it off. Nathan accepted him as a housemate. I heard that they became lovers shortly after Henry and I broke up, but don't know it for a fact."

"Can you think of anyone who would have a reason to kill Henry?"

"Not really. I heard that he was blackmailing one of the artists at the art cooperative, Harry Gillis. It may be true, or just a rumor. There was a message on the gallery answering machine last week that is pertinent. The caller used the term 'son-of-a-bitch' in regard to Henry, then told him to back off or he'd make sure he did. I wish I still had that message as proof that it existed. I don't think Detective Stephens believed me when I said I routinely delete messages once I take down pertinent information. This caller didn't leave a name or number, so I didn't make any record of the call, although I did tell Henry about it. He brushed it off and I didn't pursue it because we were in the middle of a discussion about Henry's lack of responsibility.

"I think also that Henry may have been up to something with the contractors who did work on remodeling the gallery. They seemed upset and were short with me. Yet I had little to do with making arrangements or supervising their work. Henry handled all that. I had intended to talk to some of them this week, but with everything that has happened, haven't had a chance to do so. I'll give you a list of the companies that did work and copies of what they charged. Perhaps you could confirm that the charges are accurate and talk to them regarding any issues that came up."

"All right, Miguel. I believe your story. Give me Nathan's address and phone number. I'll try to talk with him. Then, I'll stop by the art cooperative and chat with some of the artists. Perhaps you can suggest the best times to go there. I'll also ask some of those fellows that hang around your grandmother's street whether they saw anything on Tuesday evening. Finally, I'll talk to the contractors. What do you know about Henry's past?"

"Very little. He never wanted to talk about his past. He said he's alone in the world. When I met him, he was living in his car. His car had Arizona plates, but he would never talk about his time there. He said that he had previously managed an art gallery, so when I decided to open this one, I offered him a job. That's about all I know."

"Okay, I'll see what I can learn about Henry's past. That might be helpful to us. Finally, I need to get back to your father. He will want to know why the police suspect you. What do you want me to tell him?"

"Please don't mention my being gay, or about my using Grandmother's funds. He doesn't know. Dad and I just reconnected several weeks ago, after several years of estrangement. I need my family's support and if you tell Dad about either of those things, he'll go back to having nothing to do with me. Can you just tell him that I have no witnesses to support my story, and the police think that Henry's embezzlement of funds from the gallery gives me a motive to want to kill him? Since they've found no other suspects to date, they're trying to make a case for my having done it."

"That sounds plausible. I'll do my best for you, Miguel. Before I talk to him, I'll look into Henry's background and talk to Nathan. Write down your mobile number. I'll keep you posted on progress. Try not to worry. My investigation could take some time. It's good news that they haven't yet arrested you. It indicates that they don't have much supporting evidence for their theory."

Walter called Nathan Stearns. Nathan was willing to talk to Walter, but couldn't talk at the store. If Walter would buy him lunch at *Sundried Tomato*, he would meet him there at eleven-thirty. Nathan instructed Walter to go early and ask for an outside table on the patio, where it would be easier to talk. "I'll be the short guy in black jeans and a black short-sleeved shirt, with blond hair and dark glasses."

"And I'm the grey-haired guy in khaki pants and a light blue tailored shirt."

Walter arrived at the restaurant promptly at eleven-thirty. He selected a table on the outer edge of the patio. At eleven thirty-five, he saw an older, light green Acura pull into a parking space near the end of the block. The man who got out resembled the description Nathan had given. The man walked down the block, then approached the table. "Walter Conway?"

"That's me," said Walter, standing and extending his hand. "Nice to meet you, Mr. Stearns. Please have a seat. Let's order then we can talk."

Once they had ordered and their beers were deposited on the table by a flirtatious waitress, Walter opened the conversation. "Tell me about Henry Jenkins, how you met, how long you've known him, what you think of him as a person."

"I met Henry about two years ago. He had ambitions to be an artist and would come into the store to buy art supplies. I would also see him at the art cooperative. He didn't have much talent. His paintings were flat and the colors muddy and depressing. However, he was good at organization, and played a role in helping to reorganize the art cooperative. He could be charming, so people tended to like him. They soon realized that he used his charm to manipulate people. He projected himself as a man of the world. Folks would confide in him and ask his advice. He would later use that knowledge to his advantage.

"Several months ago, I was looking for a new housemate; my current one was leaving town. Henry answered my advertisement. He had the job at the art gallery, so he had the income to pay his share of the rent. Since he was the only person who responded to the ad, I agreed to let him move in, even though I didn't like him that much. I think Miguel blames me for breaking up their relationship. But, that was already over as far as Henry was concerned. He wasn't one for long-term relationships unless he had something to gain."

"What do you think of Miguel?"

"I think that he's a talented artist and a hard worker. In the years since he got out of jail, he's stayed clean, worked hard, and built a life. He's been looking after his grandmother since she had a stroke. He's pleasant to be around, polite, respectful, and interested in what you are doing."

"The police seem to suspect Miguel of shooting Henry. Do you think that likely?"

There was a pause before Nathan answered. "A week ago, I've had said no. Over the weekend, Henry told me that Miguel had threatened to fire him. I said he better make sure that doesn't happen; if he can't pay the rent, he must move out of the house. Henry said, 'Don't worry. He won't fire me. I told him I'd go to his father and tell him he's gay if he did that. I also told him I'd tell both his father and his grandmother that he stole money from his grandmother's account to open the art gallery. He wouldn't want that.'

"That threat gave Miguel a motive to get rid of Henry. Henry also told me not to worry about the rent, that he had plenty in his bank account to live on. That surprised me. I know that Henry's lifestyle requires a lot of money. He spends freely and gambles. When he gambles, he usually loses. Last month, he was late with his rent payment. He got really nasty when I pressed him for the rent. 'It's not easy to get rid of me,' he told me. My income is limited. I need him to pay on time. Ever since that comment, I've worried about what he meant by that statement."

"Miguel says he has never handled, let alone owned a gun. Did Henry own one?"

"Yes, he did. A small hand gun, which seems to be missing. When the police came to notify me of Henry's death, they searched his room. Henry usually kept his gun locked in the drawer of his bedside table. It wasn't there when they opened the nightstand. Yesterday, I packed up his personal effects so I could dispose of them. I never came across the gun."

"He wasn't in the habit of carrying it with him?"

"Not so far as I know, except for when he supervised the remodel of Miguel's gallery. He said several of the workmen made him uneasy."

"Do you own a gun? If so, where do you keep it?"

No, I don't own a gun. They scare me."

"I ran an online search for information about Henry. Would it surprise you to know that he was once charged with blackmail in Arizona?"

"I didn't know Henry lived in Arizona. But, no, the blackmail doesn't surprise me. As I said, his charm induced people to share their secrets. Henry liked money. His pay at the gallery was modest. I heard a rumor that he blackmailed Sean Hilstrom, an artist at the art cooperative over cheating on his girlfriend with her best friend. A minor thing, but Sean really likes his girl, so it's possible he would give Henry money to keep his mouth shut. Unfortunately, it's probably never a one-time payment. He also tried to blackmail Harry Gillis, another artist. Then there are the threats that he made to Miguel."

"What secrets did Henry know about you?"

"What!" exclaimed Nathan. He rose from his chair. "What makes you think I have secrets?"

"Sorry. I meant it as a joke." Nathan sat down. "Did you know that Henry had an appointment to see Miguel at his house on Friday night?"

"Yes. No. What I mean is, he mentioned before he left that morning that he would be late coming home because he had to meet Miguel and his grandmother to go over some accounting changes. I assumed they would meet at the gallery after it closed."

Walter glanced at his watch. "It's almost twelve-twenty, Nathan. You said you needed to be back at work by twelve-thirty. Before you go, can you think of anything else that might be helpful for me to know?" Nathan shook his head. "No? Well, thanks for talking with me." They shook hands, and Nathan departed.

Since Henry and Nathan lived together, it's possible that Henry might know Nathan's secrets. We all have some. I wonder if Henry was blackmailing Nathan. I need to find out what kind of gun was used to kill Henry, and whether the police have the weapon. Nathan could have had access to Henry's gun. I don't know what it is, but something about what Nathan said doesn't quite fit.

Walter returned to Keith's house. Susan was waiting impatiently, eager to hear about the interviews with Miguel and Nathan. After he filled her in on what had transpired, they agreed that a logical next step would be to chat with the artists at the art cooperative. Miguel had said many of the artists were at the facility in the late afternoon. They decided to drive down immediately.

At the cooperative, a young man sat behind a desk at one side of the large open show room. He greeted Walter and Susan as they entered. "Welcome. Please feel free to look around."

They wandered slowly around the fringe of the room, examining the art hung in the large display space. As they completed the circuit of the room, Susan approached the young man at the desk.

"Do you have any work by Miguel Sanchez? We were told he is a member here."

"I'm afraid that Miguel moved all his art to his new gallery on Canyon Road for a solo show. It's called *Galleria de el Renacimiento*. You should visit it. He does amazing work. I think he will be a famous artist one day. Miguel is a great guy. He's offering selected artists from the cooperative a chance to have a month-long solo show at his gallery once his show is over. In fact, I'll be opening there next month. My name is Lawrence Tiller."

Susan shook his hand. "It's nice to meet you, Lawrence. That's your painting over there, the one of the sand dunes, isn't it?" Lawrence nodded. "My husband really liked that one."

Susan introduced Walter to Lawrence and they chatted about the painting. Then Walter said, "I heard that the man who was shot earlier this week in Irvine was a member of the cooperative. That must have been a shock to the artists here."

"We hate to lose a member, but I have to say that Henry Jenkins won't be missed. Henry wasn't a particularly good artist. While he could be charming, he was a real snake in the grass. Henry is..., sorry, was a blackmailer, among other things. He tried to blackmail several folks here. I think he may have been successful with Harry Gillis, but when he tried to blackmail Sean Hilstrom over an affair with his girl's best friend, he was too late. Sean's girl had already learned about the affair from her friend. We all learned to keep our mouths shut when Henry was around. I've never understood how Miguel got taken in by him. I wouldn't trust that bastard to run my gallery, if I had one. Of course, Henry did have experience as a gallery manager. He made some good suggestions to improve operations around here, I'll give him that."

"Is Henry's friend Nathan Stearns another of your members?" asked Susan. "I don't recall seeing any paintings by him."

"No, Nathan isn't an artist. He and Henry were housemates. I'm not so sure whether they were friends. Nathan works at the local art supply store and so, knows most of our members. He sometimes hangs out around here. But, he's another dubious character. Personally, I wonder about his mental stability. He's very passive/aggressive; one never knows which Nathan will show up. Sorry, I shouldn't be gossiping."

"Your group of artists represent an amazing array of media, techniques, and talent. We'd love to meet some of the artists and talk with them about their work. Are there any of them around?"

"Yes, many of them have studio space in the back of the building where we have our work areas. If you like, I'll give you a tour and introduce you to some of the artists who are around this afternoon."

"That would be wonderful, Lawrence, if you think they wouldn't mind."

"Mind? Of course not. I have yet to meet an artist who doesn't like to talk about his work."

Walter and Susan followed Lawrence to the workshop. Several artists were absorbed in their painting. "Heads up, fellows. These folks have been looking at the exhibit and expressed an interest in meeting some of the artists. I told them they could come look around and chat with some of you. Introduce yourselves as they stop by. I've got to get back on duty out front."

"Thank you," Susan said to Lawrence as he departed. The couple introduced themselves to each artist as they stopped by to watch and discuss their work. When they came to an artist who introduced himself as Harry Gillis, Walter asked if he could talk with him in private, indicating to Susan that she should continue to talk with the other artists.

Harry took Walter to a small office space in the rear of the workshop.

"What do you need to talk about in private?" Harry hoped that Walter wanted to talk about buying a painting.

"I'm doing a bit of investigation on behalf of Miguel Sanchez. Please keep this private for now, but Miguel thinks the police suspect him of murdering Henry Jenkins."

"Miguel? That's ridiculous! Miguel's the last person who would do anything like that."

"I agree. So, I need to find out more about Henry and who might want to kill him."

"I can think of a lot of people who might want to kill him, me included. I didn't, although the thought is tempting. He's a real bastard. Henry attempted to blackmail me after I tried to sell a painting that I based on a photograph printed in the local newspaper. I painted it as a practice exercise. Everyone around here admired it so much that I let them persuade me to hang it in the gallery. That meant it was for sale. In the art world, one doesn't copy someone else's work and then sell it as one's own. After a few days, I had second thoughts and told the guys that it was a copy of the newspaper photograph and took it away.

"Henry realized that it was a copy of the photo in the

227

newspaper. He didn't know that I removed it. When he saw it was gone, he assumed it had been sold. He threatened to expose me to the buyer and everyone here. He wanted me to pay him $300.00 to keep him quiet. I told him that I hadn't sold it, and I had informed my colleagues that it was a copy. He didn't believe me, of course. Eventually, he found out that what I said was true. That took the wind out of his sails! He also tried to blackmail another artist who is a member here—Sean Hilstrom. He was unsuccessful with that attempt as well."

"Thank you for sharing that, Harry. I did hear rumors that Henry was a blackmailer. There must be someone he successfully blackmailed who might want to shut him up and get him off their back. I just have to find them. Would you be willing to repeat what you told me to the police? I need to give them a reason to look beyond Miguel."

"I'd be happy to. Miguel's a good guy and there's no way he would kill anyone. The police are probably picking on him because he found Henry's body."

"Thank you, Harry. I'll suggest they talk with you." Walter handed him his card. They returned to the main room, where Susan was surrounded by three artists.

"Sorry to take you away from your admirers, my dear. But we're expected at Keith's home for dinner with the family. We'll have to come back and buy some art. There's a lot to like here! Thanks to all of you for your hospitality. We enjoyed visiting with you."

Walter and Susan walked slowly to their car. "Did you learn anything?" Susan asked.

"Yes, I was able to confirm that Henry tried to blackmail two of the artists here. Harry has agreed to speak with the police, so, if they continue to pursue Miguel, I can pass along what we've learned. Thanks for coming with me. It seems that the guys relax around you, and talk more than they might if it were just me asking. I had the feeling that Lawrence was showing off a bit for you. Not that I blame him. I'd do the same if I weren't married to you."

"Thanks for the compliment, darling. The artists did seem to feel relaxed with me. From what they said, it's pretty clear that these folks eventually recognized Henry for the disreputable person he was. They indicated that he was constantly trying to learn something he could use against them and others. There was precious little positive said about him. Miguel, on the other hand seemed to be universally popular, someone who always wanted to help others to achieve their potential."

"I think we're off to a good start. I feel like I have something to give the family hope that we can steer the police toward other suspects. I'll give Sergio a brief report when we get back to the house, then forget about crime for the rest of the evening."

— CHAPTER 34 —

Tuesday, November 8

Miguel was starving. He had been at the gallery since nine-fifteen this morning. It was now two o'clock in the afternoon. Traffic through the gallery had been moderate. Now there was a lull.

I shouldn't leave the gallery. That's what I got upset with Henry about. But I must get something to eat. Since there's no one to cover for me, I'll put up a sign saying I will be back at two-thirty. That should give me time to get to town, pick up a sandwich and get back here.

Miguel quickly made a sign, posted it on the gallery door, and then drove downtown. He parked his car and was walking toward the sandwich shop when he passed the art supply store. *I need some supplies if I'm going to start painting again. Since I'm here, I'll just pop in and grab a few items.*

Miguel entered the store. Nathan spotted him. "Hey, Miguel. How are you? I was talking to a friend of yours today, a guy named Walter Conway."

"Yes, he asked me how to get ahold of you. He's helping to gather information about Henry. The police seem to think I may have done it. What you told them about Henry saying he threatened to blackmail me seems to have convinced them that I'm their main suspect."

"That's ridiculous! You wouldn't do something like that."

"No, I wouldn't. But try and convince the police of that. Anyway, I haven't time to talk right now. With Henry gone, I've got to cover the gallery. I came into town to grab a sandwich, and remembered that I need some large tubes of Winsor and Newton's alizarin crimson and cobalt blue. If you'll get me two of each, I'll grab a few brushes. Several of mine are getting worn. I must start painting again, even if it I have to paint at night because of my job at the restaurant. I don't know how long I can juggle all of this!"

"You've got a lot on your plate. Losing Henry is clearly making things more difficult."

I'll find a way to manage as long as the police keep their distance. Now, if you'll get me that paint, please."

Miguel selected two new brushes and added them to the paint tubes on the counter. "I'll e-mail you a list of additional supplies I need when I have a free minute. If you'll order what's on the list, I'll come back later in the week to pick up the order. Let me know when it comes in. See you, Nathan."

At the sandwich shop, Miguel ordered a ham and Swiss-cheese on rye, one dill pickle, an apple, and grabbed a bottle of cold water. He paid, then drove as quickly as traffic would allow back to the gallery. A newer model Mercedes sat in the parking lot. Miguel got out of his car. Simultaneously, a slim, blond woman who looked to be in her sixties, and her companion, a grey haired man who looked as fit as a buff thirty-year old got out of the Mercedes. Both were clearly wearing designer togs.

"Hello. I'm Miguel Sanchez. I hope you haven't been waiting long. I ran into town to grab something for lunch. I recently lost my manager, so have no one to cover the gallery when I'm out."

"We've been waiting about ten minutes. I'm Samuel Ruben. This is my wife, Alicia. My brother bought one of your paintings during your show. We really liked it. We saw your note, and figured a short wait wouldn't hurt."

"Thank you for your patience. Please, go ahead and browse." Miguel swung open the door and motioned them into the gallery. "If you have questions, I'll be in the office having my lunch. Feel free to interrupt. A few bites should be enough to restore my energy."

Ten minutes later, Miguel returned to the gallery display room. The couple was discussing one of the paintings. "Is there anything I can tell you about the painting?"

"We were just admiring the way you use varying thicknesses of paint. That technique seems to be what gives your paintings such a vibrant quality. There is sort of a 3-D effect. Your colors seem to shimmer in light. You capture sunny southern California so well."

"Thank you. I'm glad you like the paintings."

"We'd like to buy this small one now. Do you do paintings on commission?"

"I have never done so. Since my work is not representational, but more abstract and expressionistic, I worry that clients who want me to paint a specific scene might be disappointed."

"What we had in mind is a painting of Laguna Beach crescent as seen from the cliff walk. That's what that large painting with the sold sign represents, isn't it? I know that artists often paint the same scene more than once. Could you paint us another version of that one, in the same size?"

"As is true for many artists around here, that particular scene is one of my favorite subjects. If you don't want it to be more representational than that one, I'd be glad to do one for you. Are you in a hurry, or can you wait for it? I must manage the gallery until I replace my manager. I'm not sure when I'll have a chance to paint off-site. If you leave your name and address, I'll contact you when I know I'll be able to do the painting. Would that be satisfactory?"

"There's no hurry. We'll buy this one now and wait to hear from you."

As Miguel finished writing up the sale, his cell phone rang. He glanced at it. It was Walter Conway.

"You take your call. We'll just finish writing our contact information in the book before we leave."

"Thank you for everything, Mr. and Mrs. Ruben. It was nice meeting you." Miguel handed Mr. Ruben his credit card receipt. He walked toward his office as he answered the call.

"Walter," he said anxiously. "Did you find out anything that may help me?"

"I've identified two people that Henry tried to blackmail. In both cases, the blackmail attempt failed. But, the fact that he tried is useful to know. It could offer the police a reason to look for other possible blackmail victims. One of them might want Henry dead. If you hear from the police, suggest that they talk to your fellow artists, Harry Gillis and Sean Hilstrom. Tell them you heard rumors that they had been blackmailed by Henry. I talked to Harry and he is willing to tell the police about when Henry tried to blackmail him. If the police visit the art cooperative and talk to the members, they might reconsider what they're thinking about you. The artists had little good to say about Henry. What they said about you was all positive!

"I talked with your father last evening. I told him that I was looking into other people with a motive to get rid of Henry, and relayed what I learned about Henry's attempts at blackmail. He seemed relieved. Tomorrow, he will contact an attorney to represent you. That will make it easier for me to talk with the police on your behalf. In the meantime, I want to look for information on Nathan Stearns. Something about that young man didn't ring true. I'll chat with the young men hanging around on your street before I check in with you again tomorrow."

"Thanks, Walter. I may even be able to stop worrying and enjoy dinner tonight with my family. I only wish that my grandmother had recovered and could be there. She's still in a coma. They said the blow on her head from the fall may have affected an area of her brain already damaged by her previous stroke. Say a prayer for her, would you, please?"

"Absolutely, Miguel. Susan and I will both keep her in our thoughts and prayers."

— CHAPTER 35 —

Wednesday, November 9

Walter drove slowly up Felida Street. He pulled up next to a group of young men who were smoking and chatting on the front stoop of a house.

"Excuse me. I'm looking for the Sanchez residence. Do any of you know it?" One of the men stepped toward the car.

"Yeah, we know it. It's that blue two story a few houses down on the right. But, you won't find anyone at home."

"I was hoping to talk with Miguel Sanchez. Do you have any idea when he might be around?"

"That must be the young guy who lives there. We don't really know him, and we haven't seen him around much since the shooting last week."

"The shooting?"

"Didn't you know? A guy was shot there one evening last week. The old lady who lives there was taken to the hospital."

"How tragic. Any idea what happened?"

The young man shrugged. "None. We were hanging out here as usual. Someone stopped in front of the house just before six o'clock and went in. A few minutes later, this light green sedan came roaring down the street and stopped near the house. Some guy got out, ran up the steps and banged on the door. When the door opened, he went charging in. We heard the sound of two shots, then the guy came running out, got in his car and took off. A short time later, the young guy came home and pulled into the garage. I guess he walked in on a pretty unpleasant scene, because it wasn't long until an ambulance came, then the police. That's when we moved on. We don't particularly like the police."

"They might be interested in what you said about the green car. Any idea what model? Did you notice the license plate number?"

"Nah. When he left, he drove on down the street, then turned left at the next corner. It was an older model car, maybe an Acura. As he passed us, I noticed a large decal on the back window, *Go Diamondbacks*. It caught my attention because my Dad lives in Arizona and is a Diamondbacks fan."

"What did the driver of the car look like?"

"I didn't notice him as he passed. When he got out of the car in front of the Sanchez house, I couldn't see him clearly. All I could see was that he was short, dressed in black, and had light-colored hair."

"Did you ever see the green car or the guy who got out of it before the night of the shooting?"

"Not me." He turned to the other men who had been listening to the conversation. "Any of you guys see that car or the guy before?" They shook their heads.

"Well, thanks for talking with me. I'll have to come back and look for Miguel another time." Walter rolled up his window and drove off.

A green sedan. Now where have I seen a green sedan recently? I remember. Nathan Stearns got out of a green sedan in Laguna Beach the day we had lunch! I really need to find out something about that young man. What possible motive could Nathan have for shooting Henry? And why would he go to Miguel's house to do it? Henry lived with him. That gave him lots of opportunity.

I suppose if he wanted to throw suspicion on Miguel, he might choose to shoot him at Miguel's house. He said he didn't know that Henry would be there. But he did know that Miguel's grandmother had a stroke. Did he know she couldn't get out to meet at the gallery? What could he have against Miguel?

— CHAPTER 36 —

Tuesday, November 15

Following a quiet Sunday evening with his family, Miguel's spirits improved so much that he was inspired to do some painting. The previous week, he had successfully negotiated with his boss at the restaurant for two weeks off, so he could manage the gallery alone until Lawrence Tiller's show opened. The contract specified that Lawrence would help him set up the show, then man the gallery twenty hours a week for the duration of the show.

Monday had been filled with errands and working at the gallery. Tuesday morning, Miguel woke at five a.m., as usual. By the time he finished his morning coffee and scanned the newspaper, dawn was breaking. The day promised to be bright and beautiful. Miguel decided to spend a few hours at his favorite painting spot on the cliff walk. He would begin work on the painting that the Rueben's had commissioned last week. Painting would distract him from worrying about being the chief suspect in Henry's murder. Completing the commissioned painting would bring in some income.

By six-fifteen, he was at the gallery to gather his painting supplies. He hoped to get a good start on the painting. He wanted to capture the feel of the morning light sparkling on the water before he had to return and open the gallery. It would feel good to be painting again.

Despite the early hour, there were people about when Miguel set up his easel. He had become accustomed to an audience when he painted *en plein air*. Today he chatted easily with a lady who had been on her morning walk when she came upon him. Her obvious admiration of his work was gratifying. He gave her a business card from the small stack he kept on the stool that held his paints. One never knew when an admiring spectator might become a future customer.

By nine-thirty, Miguel was hot and tired. His canvas was covered in bright colors and shapes. He decided that he had made enough progress to be able to finish the painting in his studio, Miguel packed his gear in his car trunk and headed to a local dive for breakfast. As he lingered over a second cup of coffee, Lawrence Tiller entered the restaurant and spotted him.

"Okay if I join you? I'd like to go over some details for my show."

"Sure. Have a seat." The waitress appeared and took Lawrence's order.

"What are you doing here at this early hour, Miguel? I thought you'd be working at the restaurant this morning. Instead, you seem to be relaxing over a leisurely breakfast."

"I arranged for someone to cover for me at the restaurant this week. With Henry gone, I've got things to attend to at the gallery. Since I woke early and it was a beautiful day, I decided to work on a commissioned painting at my favorite spot on the cliff. The gallery doesn't open for another hour."

"I know you're having to juggle a lot these days. Can I do anything to help out this week? Maybe I could work with you in the gallery for a day or two to learn how things work. That way, when I need to cover during my show, I'll know the ropes."

"Thanks, Lawrence. That's a good idea, and I'd appreciate

the assistance. I must start preparing for your show. If you bring a list of the paintings you want hung, along with their framed sizes, we can plan the layout for your exhibit, and design the format for brochures and posters to advertise the show. Do you have digital copies of several of your best paintings I can use for the advertisements?" Lawrence nodded.

"I need to meet with some of the other artists at the co-operative about future shows, procure supplies, meet with the printer, and place an ad in the newspapers for your show. If you can cover the gallery for a few hours, it would help a lot. I have other errands to attend to that should have been done last week. Once I've done them, maybe we can set up our easels and paint together in the back room during slow times at the gallery. I seem to be alone much of the time lately. I'm so busy, I never have time to just hang out with friends. Spending some time with you would do wonders for my morale."

"I'd enjoy that, Miguel. When should I report for duty? I could come by later this afternoon, say around two-thirty."

"That would work well. If we plan your exhibit layout and the advertising this afternoon, I can get the brochures to the printer and ads to the newspaper tomorrow morning before the gallery opens."

The waitress delivered Lawrence's breakfast and refilled Miguel's coffee. "Can I get you gentlemen anything else?"

"My check, please," said Miguel. Just then Nathan Stearns entered the restaurant.

"Hey Miguel, Lawrence. How are you guys? I'm on my way to work. I spotted you through the window as I was passing."

"Morning, Nathan. Lawrence and I were just having a business meeting. Would you like to join us?"

"Thanks, Miguel, but I need to open the store. I just popped in to let you know that your canvases came in yesterday afternoon. If you pull your car into the lot behind the shop after you leave here, I can help you load them."

"Thanks, Nathan. That will save me another trip downtown. I appreciate it. I'll be there is about fifteen minutes."

"See you then. I'd better get a move on before that old grouch I work for gets in ahead of me and complains that I'm late for work."

"I can't figure that one out," said Lawrence nodding toward the departing Nathan.

"What do you mean?"

"Sometimes he's so abrupt and unsocial, seems to hate the world. Other times he seems so considerate, like today, making the effort to let you know your order is in. I guess none of us knows what burden everyone else is carrying."

"Probably better that way." Miguel paid his check. "Sorry to leave you, Lawrence, but if I'm to open on time, I'd better get over to the art supply store and pick up my canvases. See you this afternoon."

"Two-thirty, then. I'll bring those lists and digital copies of some paintings."

Miguel pulled into the lot behind the art supply store, as instructed, and entered the shop through the back door. "That's your order over by the register," said Nathan, as he loaded some tubes of paint into empty slots on the rack.

"I hadn't realized it would be such a big load. I'll go move my easel and the painting I worked on this morning to the back seat. Hopefully, we can fit all that stuff in the trunk." Miguel headed out.

Nathan stacked some of the larger canvases and carried them to the car. "Just put those in the trunk, Nathan," said Miguel from the back seat, where he was carefully positioning the wet painting so it wouldn't shift. I'll go get the next load."

Miguel picked up the medium sized canvases and headed out to the car. Nathan returned for the final load. When Nathan returned to the car, he glanced at the nearly full trunk. "I left the invoice on the counter for you to double-check, Miguel. I'll figure out how to pack all these in while you review it. Just sign it and leave it on the counter if everything is okay. Do you mind if I put some of these smaller ones on the floor of the back seat?"

"Put those that don't fit in the trunk on the front passenger seat, if you don't mind. Thanks."

Miguel returned to the car, just as Nathan closed the front passenger door. "I only had to put four medium frames on the passenger seat. Everything else fit snugly in the trunk."

"Thanks, Nathan for your help. I signed the invoice. I should be able to pay the balance on the account at the end of the month. Now all I need to do is to figure out where at the gallery to store all these. Space is tight. Lawrence's paintings go up in the main gallery space next week. I've got to store my paintings that don't fit on the wall of the small showroom. Running a gallery seems to be a constant juggling act! Have a good one, Nathan, and thanks again for saving me a trip to town."

"Happy I could do it, Miguel. See you soon."

Back at the gallery, Miguel and Lawrence spent a productive afternoon. They planned the upcoming show layout and developed the publicity campaign. Miguel showed Lawrence where the sales receipts and credit card forms were kept. He reviewed how to process sales, and how to approach customers when they came to the gallery. He also discussed the need to get contact information so buyers could be notified of future showings and special events. Miguel gave Lawrence a key to the gallery so that he could start bringing in some paintings for his forthcoming show at his convenience when the gallery was closed.

Miguel stayed on at the gallery after closing time to organize the storage area. Before leaving for home, he called his father for news about his grandmother. "No change, unfortunately," said Sergio. "At least her vital signs remain strong. They can't understand why she hasn't regained consciousness."

"A friend has offered to cover for me at the gallery for a few hours this week. I'll try to stop by and see her. It will make me feel better to be with her, even if she doesn't know I'm there."

— CHAPTER 37 —

Wednesday, November 16

Miguel dropped off brochure mockups at the printers and took his ads for the upcoming Lawrence Tiller show to the newspaper office. Then, he stopped by the hospital to see his grandmother.

"Hello, Grandmother. It's Miguel" He sat down in the chair beside her bed and took her hand. He looked sadly at the old woman in the bed.

She looks so old and frail. She's losing weight. Those IV's and the feeding tube don't seem to supply enough calories. I wonder if she can hear me if I talk to her?

"Abuela, it's me, Miguel. We all miss you. I miss you! Please get better. Now that Dad and I have patched up our differences, we want to have the family together again. You're the center of that family. There's a big hole when you're not there. Our house is so empty when I get home at the end of the day. I now realize how you must feel when I'm out.

"I'm really busy trying to keep the gallery afloat without Henry. His death has solved some problems, but created others. I could really use some of your excellent advice.

"I still can't believe that Henry is dead! The police haven't found out who shot him. They seem to believe that I did it. I feel as if they might arrest me at any minute. They know about Henry's blackmail threats and think those threats and his embezzlement gave me a motive to kill him. You, and the person who shot him, are the only people who know what happened. The police want to talk to you.

"Bessie and Micah asked to be remembered to you. They returned from their visit to her sister and called me when they saw the article in the paper about Henry's death. They said they are praying for your recovery. The hospital won't let them visit, since they aren't relatives.

Miguel stood slowly and released his grandmother's hand. He leaned over and kissed her on the cheek. "I love you, Abuela. Please get better. I'll come back to see you again, very soon."

Miguel returned to the gallery. He had only been there for forty-five minutes when two police cars pulled into the lot. Detective Stevens and Sergeant Molino came into the gallery and handed Miguel a search warrant. Three other policemen followed them in.

"We had an anonymous phone call this morning at the station. The caller said that we would find the gun that killed Henry Jenkins either here in the gallery, or in your car."

"What? That's ridiculous!"

"Be that as it may, we need to conduct a search."

"Please be respectful of the artwork, Detective Stevens. That represents my livelihood."

"I'll try to insure that my officers do no damage."

"Thank you."

Miguel stood by helplessly as the policemen swarmed over his facility. They searched drawers in his office, removed art from the walls to check behind the paintings, shifted furniture, moved the stacks of art supplies, and generally turned the gallery upside down. Having found nothing, Officer Stevens asked for the keys to his car. Miguel handed them over and followed them outside. After a brief search of the empty trunk, two officers began searching the interior, reaching under the seats to feel for anything hidden there. Then one man opened the unlocked glove compartment. "Here it is!" said the policeman, gingerly lifting a small handgun with his gloved hand.

Detective Stevens carefully took the gun from him and looked at it. "A twenty-two. That's what killed Henry Jenkins. I'll bet this is a match. We'll order the ballistics tests this afternoon." He turned to Miguel. "You'd better come down to the station with me."

Miguel stood frozen in place, a look of horror on his face. He jerked away from the officer who tried to take his arm.

"No! This can't be happening! I had nothing to do with Henry's death. I never put that gun in my car. I never saw it before!"

"We'll talk about this down at the precinct station."

"I need to post a notice that the gallery will be closed for the remainder of the day."

Detective Stevens nodded. Miguel quickly wrote a note and taped it on the front door. Then he locked the gallery door and his car, and got into the police car.

At the station, Miguel was booked and put in an interrogation room. About twenty minutes later, Detective Stevens and Sergeant Molina joined him there. They entered to find him sitting at the table with his hands together in front of his face, apparently praying.

"Praying isn't going to help. Only the truth can help you now. You had the murder weapon, a motive to kill Henry to stop him from blackmailing you, and you knew where he would be at the time he was shot. Weapon, motive, and opportunity."

"My grandmother would tell you she loaned me the money. We also had a plan to keep Henry from telling my Dad about my being gay. She would gladly tell you all that."

"Sure, sure. You made certain she couldn't talk, didn't you?"

"I didn't hurt my grandmother. I love her!"

Sergeant Molina read Miguel his rights. Miguel declined to

ask for a lawyer to be present. "I haven't done anything. I'll just answer your questions honestly."

"We have checked the registration number on the gun. It is Henry's gun. Tell me how you obtained it."

"Everything I've told you is true. I know nothing more. I didn't even know that Henry owned a gun."

"How do you think the gun got in your car? Who has had access to your car since the murder?"

"No one that I know of. That's the devil of it. The car is parked in the garage of my house at night; nobody can access it there. I'm at the gallery during the day, and some evenings. I park my car at the side of the building. Usually, I remember to lock it. When I run errands and when I work at the restaurant, I park it in the street or in a lot, and lock it."

"You're making a case for why you are the only person with access to your car; that makes it a safe place to hide the gun. Think hard. Is there anyone else who might have been in your car, either as a passenger, or for some other reason?"

"I think the only passenger I've had in the past month was my grandmother, but that was before Henry was killed. Early yesterday, I parked at *Las Brisas*, the Mexican Restaurant, when I went up to the cliff path to do some painting. The restaurant wasn't open and the valet wasn't in yet, so I left my keys with one of the waiters who was setting up. But they don't know me. There hasn't been anyone else."

"Are you sure? If you didn't put the gun there, someone else must have had access to your car."

"I can't think of anyone." Miguel frowned, trying to think. "Wait! When I stopped at the art supply store to pick up my order yesterday, Nathan Stearns helped me to load my order. But Nathan! No. It's not possible! Why would Nathan put the gun in my car? Why would he have it in the first place?"

"Were you present the entire time that Mr. Stearns had access to your car?"

"No. He finished loading the supplies while I went inside to sign the requisition order."

"So, he could have put it there without your knowledge?"

"I suppose it's possible. By why? Nathan and I aren't especially close, but neither have we had any disagreements. Even if he had the gun, why would he want to try and frame me? It makes no sense. He and Henry were housemates. Why would he want to kill Henry?"

"Why indeed? It still seems like you are the only person with a motive."

"Unless it was someone else that Henry was blackmailing."

"Do you know of someone else?"

"Not first-hand. After you came and told me that Nathan said Henry had threatened to blackmail me, I felt like you suspected me. I asked this ex-cop and FBI agent, Walter Conway, to help me find evidence that would show I didn't do it. Walter talked with some of the artists at the cooperative. They told him that Henry tried to blackmail two of the members, unsuccessfully, as it turned out. If he threatened to blackmail me, and tried to blackmail those two, there must be others around. Maybe he was successful at blackmailing someone else. They would have a motive."

"Do you know the names of these two guys?"

"One of them was Harry Gillis. The other was Sean Hilstrom. Walter told me that Harry said he was willing to tell the police his story. Would you talk to them, please? It would, at least support the idea that there are others out there with a motive to kill Henry. They are at the art coop most afternoons. If they aren't there, the cooperative will have their contact information."

"And your friend, Walter Conway. How do we reach him?"

"I'll give you his phone number. He's from out of town. He recently came to visit his family in Laguna Hills."

"So, how do you know him and why is he helping you out?"

"My sister and his granddaughter are friends. My sister told me about him when you started asking questions about Henry blackmailing me. She said he is an ex-New York City police detective and that he had been involved with helping to solve a murder in Hawaii last year. She suggested I ask him to look for information that might help find Henry's real killer."

"All right. I'll get in touch with Conway, and will talk to the artists at the coop. You may feel that I've been picking on you, but I'm just trying to do my job. So far, everything seems to point to you. I don't want to convict the wrong man, so I'll do some more looking around. But, I will have to hold you, until you have a hearing and can post bail."

"I understand, Detective Stevens. May I call someone to arrange coverage for my gallery? I also need to contact my lawyer."

"I'll arrange for you to make the phone calls."

Miguel called Lawrence Tiller. He agreed to cover the gallery until Miguel was released on bail, and promised to restore order to the disarray the police had left behind from their search. Since Miguel had given Lawrence a key to the gallery yesterday so that he could bring in his paintings at his leisure, access would not be an issue. Next, he called Walter.

"Hello, this is Walter Conway."

"Walter, this is Miguel."

"Miguel! How is it going?"

"I'm calling you because I've been arrested. The police showed up with a search warrant this morning. When they searched my car, they found Henry's gun in the glove compartment. They said it is the murder weapon. I have no idea how it got there. As far as I know, no one had access to my car except for the valet at *Las Brisas* restaurant and Nathan Stearns."

"What led them to search your car?"

"They said they received an anonymous phone call."

"That's very odd. Suggests to me that the call may have come from whoever put the gun there. Did they trace the call?"

"They didn't say anything about that."

"Well, if they didn't, they should. Did you tell them about the blackmail threats Henry made?"

"Yes, I did. They agreed to go to the art cooperative and talk with Harry and Sean. They also plan to contact you."

"I'm glad they plan to follow-up with Harry and Sean. When they contact me, perhaps I can throw some doubt on their theory. I've been snooping around and have some information to share with them. I was trying out to figure out how to approach them to tell them what I've learned. Now, they're giving me an opportunity to do so. Did you call the lawyer your Dad found for you?"

"No. Would you call him for me? Ask him and my father to arrange bail, please. The police did allow me to call Lawrence Tiller. He agreed to cover the gallery for me until I'm released and will try to restore order from the mess the police left after their search. Fortunately, I had given Lawrence a key and oriented him to the procedures at the gallery."

"Okay, I'll call the lawyer for you. Hopefully, by tomorrow morning you'll be out on bail. I'll keep in touch. Don't lose heart, Miguel. You have many of us out here who believe in you."

Walter closed his phone, then turned into the street on which his son lives. He parked in the driveway and went into the house. "Anybody home?"

Susan appeared in the family room doorway. "It's just me, darling. Everyone else is out. Jan thought she'd be back by five o'clock. The kids are doing homework at the library. Keith isn't yet home from work. I have you all to myself! We don't get much alone time anymore."

She came to Walter, hugged him, and then gave him a lingering kiss.

"I get the feeling that maybe you missed me."

"I did. I got used to having you around. I'm dying to hear how you made out today. I feel out of the loop on this investigation."

"We seem to have switched roles. During our Hawaii case,

you did most of the field work and I reacted to what you learned. Here it's the other way around. Let me get something wet to drink, then I'll bring you up to date. First, though, I must contact Sergio and arrange for him to contact Miguel's lawyer and arrange bail."

"Arrange bail? He's been arrested?"

Walter nodded. Ten minutes later, Walter brought his beer and settled on the sofa next to Susan. She snuggled up next to him. "Now, tell me about what's going on, please."

"The bad news is that Miguel was arrested today. Sergio will work with the lawyer to post bail. An anonymous caller told the police to look for the murder weapon in Miguel's gallery and car. When they searched, they found a gun in the glove compartment of Miguel's car. Turned out to be Henry's."

"But Walter, if Miguel had done it, how would anyone know where he hid the gun? Miguel is a bit of a loner. Who has a grudge against him and would want to hurt him? Those artists we talked with at the cooperative had nothing but good things to say about him."

"This whole thing doesn't make sense, Susan. I have a feeling that whoever called the police with a tip about the gun is the murderer, and is trying to deflect attention away from himself. He must be feeling vulnerable. I have a hunch that all this is somehow related to Henry's blackmailing. But, so far, I haven't identified anyone who had been successfully blackmailed. We have only those two artists we identified from the coop who said that Henry tried, but didn't succeed. Miguel told the police about them, and they will interview them. They will also be contacting me. I hope to be able to point the police away from Miguel."

"What have you learned?"

"This morning I followed a suggestion from Miguel to talk with some of the contractors who worked on the remodel of Miguel's gallery. They had little good to say about their experiences working with Henry during that process. It seems that he demanded kickbacks to award them a contract. Those companies that provide specialized services unavailable locally didn't agree to the kickbacks. There was nothing Henry could do; he needed them to do the work. But things have been slow in the construction industry since the recession, so several of the local companies that provide non-specialized services, like painting and dry-walling agreed. They needed the work.

"After the job was finished, Henry threatened to spread the word in the local community that those companies paid kickbacks to Miguel. That would begin a vicious spiral for those contractors, as others might also demand kickbacks. So, several of them have been paying Henry to keep his mouth shut."

"That's some scheme. First he uses extortion, then black-mails them for paying! That would give them a motive for getting rid of Henry."

"It could, if they couldn't find some other way of dealing with it. No doubt they are glad Henry is gone. I also talked with one of the young men who hangs out on Felida Street, several houses down from Miguel's house. On the evening of the shooting, he saw a green, older-model sedan come tearing down the street and stop in front of Miguel's. He said that a man with light hair, dressed in black jeans and shirt, got out and pounded on the door of the house, then rushed in when the door opened. A few minutes later, the man came running out, got in the car, and drove on down the street to the next corner, where he turned and disappeared from sight. Nathan Stearns is blond, often wears black, and drives an older green sedan. Nathan also helped Miguel load some art supplies in his car yesterday. He could have put the gun in the glove compartment."

"What possible motive would he have for doing that? Nobody mentioned antagonism between Miguel and Nathan."

"I agree, Susan. The only motive I can think of would be to keep police attention away from himself. When I interviewed

Nathan over lunch, I felt that he might be hiding something. Just before we left the restaurant, I jokingly asked him what secrets he had that Henry found out about. His reaction seemed excessive. Just out of curiosity, I ran a search on Nathan. It turns out that he lived in Tempe, Arizona, around the same time that Henry was briefly held on a blackmail charge there."

"Would Nathan have allowed Henry to move into his house, if he knew about what happened in Arizona? We were told there were rumors that he and Henry were lovers for a brief time after Henry moved in. It doesn't make sense!"

"I know. I don't see any motive there. But, I'm pretty certain it was Nathan's car that night, and he did have access to Miguel's car yesterday. He knew that Henry owned a gun, and he potentially had access to the gun. It's all circumstantial, but until we find someone else, perhaps someone Henry was blackmailing, he's the best alternative to Miguel as a suspect. Hopefully, after the police interview me, they will question Nathan again."

"I do wish Miguel's grandmother would recover consciousness. She could throw some light on what happened."

"Miguel said that he visited her this morning and there had been no change in her condition."

Walter put his arm around Susan's shoulders. She moved closer and laid her head on his shoulder. He kissed her forehead, then rested his head against hers. "Let's enjoy a few quiet moments together before the family gets home. I'm so grateful that our biggest problem is figuring out where we want to live the rest of our lives. I feel so sorry for Miguel and his family."

— (HAPTER 38 —

Thursday, November 17

Detective Stevens was interviewing Walter Conway when an officer interrupted.

"There's this lady outside who insists on seeing you. She says she works for Mrs. Sanchez, the old lady who's in the hospital. She says she has some information that may be helpful in finding out who killed Henry Jenkins. Her name is Bessie Jones."

"Ask her to wait. I'm just finishing up here."

He turned to Walter. "Do you know this Bessie Jones?"

"No, I've never met her."

"I guess I'd better talk to her. I need something more concrete than what you have to offer, although I do agree that Nathan Stearns is worth looking at. We'll interview him again.

"We talked to Gillis and Holstrom from the art cooperative. As you said, since Henry Jenkins was trying to blackmail them, there may be others around with whom he was more successful. The contractors you talked with who say Henry was blackmailing them come to mind. We will talk to those on the list you gave me. Miguel Sanchez did say there was a message on the gallery answering machine that seemed to be threatening Henry. Someone who was being blackmailed would definitely

253

have a motive. Unfortunately, we have no name. I suppose there may be others out there. How to find them is the question.

"I probably shouldn't admit it, but I like Miguel Sanchez. I'd be pleased if he turned out to be innocent. Unfortunately, he remains our main suspect. Keep me appraised of any new information that you uncover, Mr. Conway. We're short of resources. Any information you can share will be helpful."

"That I will do happily, Detective Stevens. I also like Miguel, and I believe him to be innocent. At the moment, he seems to be a victim of circumstances. I'd be mightily pleased to find some evidence that would exonerate him."

Walter shook hands with the Detective and departed. The desk officer brought Bessie Jones into the room and introduced her to Detective Stevens.

"Now Mrs. Jones. You said you might have something to help us solve this crime?"

"Yes, sir. I've been Mrs. Sanchez's housekeeper for the past several months. My husband, Micah, did some handyman work for her. Just before we left to visit my sister, he installed dead bolts on two doors. While he was at it, he convinced her to let him install a security camera that is focused on the front of the house. When we first got back and read about the murder, we didn't think about the camera. When we read this morning that Miguel had been arrested for the murder of Henry Jenkins and assaulting his grandmother, we couldn't believe it! Then Micah remembered the security camera. It might show something from the night of the murder that would be helpful."

"It might indeed. We never thought to look for a camera. I will send an officer over to the Sanchez house to retrieve the tape. Thank you for telling us about it, Mrs. Jones. You sound like you find it difficult to believe that Miguel could have done this."

"He seems like a kind, gentle man, Detective. He and his grandmother love each other. He might be self-involved, but I can't believe he would physically harm her!"

"What do you mean about him being self-involved?"

"I shouldn't have said that."

"But you did. Please explain why you thought that."

"Although he has been looking after his grandmother since her stroke, he had recently gotten so involved in his painting and preparing for his solo show that he became neglectful of his grandmother. That's why I was hired to cook and clean."

"Is that the only reason for your comment? That hardly seems like enough to justify thinking he is self-involved."

No. Recently, a few weeks before Micah and I went on vacation, I drove Mrs. Sanchez to see her lawyer and her banker. She had given Miguel her power of attorney after she had her stroke several years ago. Now that she was feeling better, she planned to take over managing her own affairs. When she went over her accounts with her banker, she discovered money had been withdrawn during the past year, above and beyond the usual recurring expenses. She thought the timing and pattern of the amounts withdrawn implied that Miguel was using her money to rent and rehab the gallery, and to pay the manager."

"In other words, he was embezzling from her accounts."

"She didn't see it that way. She was going to talk to him about it. My husband and I left on our trip before she had talked to him, so I don't know the outcome of that conversation."

"I know you came here to try to help Miguel Sanchez. What you've just told me confirms some previous information we had been provided that gives Miguel a motive for killing Henry. Let's hope that tape provides something to raise doubt about Miguel being the killer. Thank you for coming in."

Later that afternoon, Detective Stevens and Sergeant Molina were reviewing the tape taken from the camera at the Sanchez house.

"For just a moment, you can just glimpse a green sedan in the corner of the picture. Do you see it, Molina? It's coming down the street, but quickly moves out of camera range. Now there is a man running up the front steps and pounding on the door. He has blond hair and is dressed in black. Fits the description Conway was given by the loiterer down the block. The time is right around six o'clock. The door is opening. He shoves it hard and rushes in. That could have knocked over the old lady, if she answered the door.

"Too bad we can't see what is going on inside. There he comes, running out the door and down the steps. We can't see the car, unfortunately. One must presume he drives away, continuing in the direction he was going when he came in. We need to get a man over to that neighborhood and interview some of those guys who hang out down the street. We must get a signed statement to confirm what Conway says he was told.

"Let's watch more of the tape. Maybe we can glimpse Sanchez driving in around ten after six like he told us. This may be the first evidence we've got to support his story."

Just then, an officer entered the room and handed Sergeant Molina a sheet of paper.

"What have you got there, Molina?"

"It's the results of the ballistics test. The gun found in the car of Miguel Sanchez is not the gun that killed Henry Jenkins!"

"Whoa! Are you sure?"

"That's what it says on the report. It's the same type of gun, but the ballistics don't match."

"I'll be darned! It looks like someone is trying to frame Miguel Sanchez. Give the kid a call and let him know. He deserves a break. Then we'll go talk to Nathan Stearns again."

"Will do."

What do you know! So someone put Henry's gun in Miguel's car to throw suspicion onto him. Now, who had access to Henry's gun? His housemate certainly could have. I wonder what Stearns will have to say about this. When we interviewed him the night of the shooting, he mentioned that Jenkins owned a gun. When we unlocked the bedside table where he claimed it was usually stored, it was missing. The car that arrived at the Sanchez house was a green sedan. Conway said that Stearns drives a light green Acura. The man who got out had blond hair and was dressed in black, like Nathan Stearns. He also had access to the Sanchez car. We may have ourselves another suspect. But what about motive?

Sergeant Molina returned to the room. "I spoke to Miguel Sanchez. As you can imagine, he was relieved to hear the news that he is no longer our major suspect. While I was in the office, a call came in from Irvine Hospital. The Sanchez woman has regained consciousness. We can talk to her in the morning."

"Everything seems to be happening at once! It's late. I'm sure your wife would be happy if you were home for dinner tonight. I know mine will be. Let's delay our interview with Stearns until after we talk to Juanita Sanchez. It may be useful to know what she has to say before we talk with him. I don't think he'll be going anywhere. See you tomorrow at the hospital, say around nine a.m."

— CHAPTER 39 —

Friday Morning, November 18

Sergio, Dolores, and Miguel Sanchez entered Juanita's hospital room. Juanita lay in the hospital bed. Her eyes were open. She smiled when she saw them.

"Mother, we're so glad to have you back with us!" Sergio kissed his mother on her forehead, followed by Dolores, then Miguel. They gathered around her bed. Miguel held his grandmother's hand.

"How do you feel, Grandmother?"

"Happy to be able to talk with all of you. While I was in my coma—the nurses told me it had been nine days—I could hear all of you talking to me. I just couldn't seem to wake up. The fog was so thick and it was too much effort. On his last visit, Miguel talked about what was happening to him and how much it would help if I could only tell the police what had happened. I knew I had to find a way to wake up. After that, every time I felt a trace of consciousness but started to slide back into the fog, I forced myself to push forward. Finally, yesterday afternoon, I succeeded. I'm tired, but so happy to be back among the living."

"We were worried about you, Mother. The doctors said that the blow on the head you received may have further damaged an area of the brain injured by your stroke. That was their explanation for why you remained in a coma."

Just then, Detective Stevens and Sergeant Molina entered the room, escorted by a nurse. "You're not to tire her," she instructed. "Try to limit your questions to ten minutes."

They introduced themselves. "We're glad to see that you are doing better, Mrs. Sanchez. Sorry to interrupt the family gathering, but we need to talk to you about what happened the night that you and Miguel were to meet with Henry Jenkins. Henry was shot in your living room and we're searching for his killer."

He turned to the family. "I'm afraid I must ask you to step outside for a few minutes. We don't want your presence to influence what Mrs. Sanchez has to say."

After the family left, Detective Stevens said, "Now, Mrs. Sanchez, tell us what you remember about last Wednesday evening. Start with the arrival of Henry Jenkins."

"Well, Detective Stevens. Henry arrived around six o'clock, as requested. He came in and I offered him a cup of tea. He declined, but said that if I had beer, he would enjoy a glass. I sent him into the kitchen to get one out of the refrigerator. He returned to the living room with a can of beer and sat down to wait for Miguel. We made small talk while waiting.

"Maybe five minutes later, we heard banging on the door. It was loud banging, not knocking. I went to the door. It took me a while with my walker. When I started to open it, the door was shoved hard by someone on the other side. I was knocked off my feet by the force, lost my grip on my walker, and fell backward. I remember my head hitting something hard, then everything went black. That's all I remember. I didn't see who came in. I didn't hear any shooting. That's all I remember until last night when I woke up here in this bed."

"So you can't tell us who it was?"

"No. Like I said, I never saw anyone. It all happened too fast."

"Did you hear anything before the pounding on the door?"

"Yes. Henry and I both thought we heard a car door slam just before the pounding started."

"Did Henry seem nervous or worried?"

"No. The only thing different I noticed about him was that he was more polite than he had been when he lived there."

"Okay, on another topic. Did Miguel have a conversation with you about using funds from your account to remodel his gallery space and to cover his rental and management expenses?"

"Yes, he did. I had given Miguel my power of attorney after my stroke, when I was too ill to manage my affairs. I refused to discuss my finances with him after that. When he finally was able to get me to listen to him about what he had used my money for, I told him that I would make it a loan. It would be interest-free, but he would have a regular schedule for repayment. I had planned to get a loan document drawn up later in the week, after we met with Henry."

"Thank you, Mrs. Sanchez. What you have told us corroborates the information we have been given. We hope you will recover quickly. I will have what you said typed up in a statement that you will need to sign. Sergeant Molino will bring the statement by the hospital for your signature later today."

Once outside the room, Detective Stevens stopped by where the Sanchez family was sitting. "Mrs. Sanchez was very helpful. I don't think we'll need to bother Miguel further. You can go back to Mrs. Sanchez now, if you like."

— CHAPTER 40 —

Saturday Morning, November 19

Nathan Stearns sat at the table in the interrogation room of the police station. He held a foam cup of coffee tightly in his hands, gripping it as if his life depended on not letting go. Detective Stevens and Sergeant Molina sat opposite him. A tape recorder was running. They read him his rights.

"Do you wish to have an attorney present?"

"No, that's not necessary."

"So, Nathan, your story is that you were at home on Friday after four o'clock. You never left the house, you had no phone calls, and no one else was there until we arrived to give you the news about Henry. No one can confirm your alibi. Is that correct?"

"Yes, sir."

"Why was your car on Felida Street in Irvine around six o'clock? You knew that Henry would be there."

"What! That's impossible. My car was parked in my driveway."

"We have signed statements from two witnesses who said they saw a light green Acura sedan drive down the street and park in front of the Sanchez house around six on Friday night.

It had a *Go Diamondbacks* sticker on the back window. We checked the DMV records. Only nine green older model Acura sedans turned up in this general area. Yours is the only one with the sticker on the back window. Witnesses also said that the man who got out of the car had light-colored hair and was dressed all in black. He was about your height and build. You have blond hair. When we came to your house on Friday, you were dressed in black. Other individuals have told us that you often wear black. You lived in Tempe at the time that Henry lived there. Did you know him when you lived there?"

"No, I told you. I met Henry at the art supply store in Laguna Beach."

"Why did you put Henry's gun in Miguel Sanchez's car?"

"What makes you think I did that?"

"You were the only person who had access to Miguel's car in the past several weeks. When you were loading his canvases and he was in the store, you had every opportunity to hide the gun there. You also could have taken Henry's gun from his bedside table; you had a key. When we were at the house, his gun wasn't there."

"Why would I do that?"

"I wish I knew. Why did you kill Henry? I assume you did it at Miguel's house to throw suspicion on him. If you had done it at your own house, you would have been our first suspect."

"I wasn't at Miguel's house. I didn't kill Henry."

"We have a tape that shows you going up the front steps of the Sanchez house just after six o'clock."

"No, that's not possible."

"There was a security camera on the Sanchez house that focused on the front door. It was you pounding on the door. Would you like us to show you the tape?"

Nathan buried his head in his hands, sobbing. Finally, he looked up. "That's not necessary. I killed Henry. I'm sorry I did it. I lost all sense of reason at the time."

"Why don't you start at the beginning and tell us what happened from the time you left the art supply store."

"I went home, like I told you. I wanted to do some work around the house. When I got home, I organized the kitchen pantry and cupboards, then vacuumed the living room. At about five-fifteen, I picked up the mail. There was a letter addressed to Henry from an attorney in Tempe. I hadn't known that Henry had connections there.

"I had been getting increasingly uncomfortable with Henry living in my house, especially after I pressed him when he didn't pay his rent on time and he told me that it will be hard to get rid of him. Then, when Henry said he would blackmail Miguel if he fired him, and I heard stories about him trying to blackmail someone else at the art cooperative, I wanted to know more about who was living in my house. So I decided to open the letter."

"And....."

"It was a letter from a lawyer saying Henry still owed him money from two years ago when he had defended him against an accusation of blackmail against someone named Trent. The lawyer said he had only recently succeeded in tracking Henry to his present address. That made sense to me, because Henry lived in his car for some time after coming to Laguna Beach. Then he lived for nine months at Miguel's house. Since he expected that arrangement to be temporary, he didn't register an address with the post office. I believe he finally registered his car in California after he moved into my place.

"The letter went on to say that a Jennifer Cortina had recently approached the law firm about legal actions she might take against Henry for blackmailing her brother. She said the blackmail had led her brother, Enrico, to take his own life. Even though it had occurred in the past, she was asking if anything could be done to make Henry pay for what he had done. The lawyer's letter said they were looking into whether she had a case. They no longer considered Henry their client.

"I knew Jennifer Cortina and her brother, Enrico. He came to this country illegally. He found a job working on a ranch and sent most of what he earned back home to his family in Mexico. Enrico had been an engineer in Mexico, but couldn't earn enough there to support his mother, brother, and three sisters. His father had been killed in an accident at the petroleum processing plant where he worked. The family was in desperate straits. So, Enrico found a way to cross the U.S. border illegally. Farm work was readily available to illegals in Arizona at the time. Other Mexican immigrants put him in touch with the rancher. He earned more on the ranch than he had been able to earn as an engineer in Mexico.

"Enrico and I met at an accounting class I took at a local night school. Enrico was a remarkable person, bright, funny, ambitious, hard-working, and loyal. He was taking the night course because the rancher had taken a liking to him and told him that if he learned accounting, he would hire him to help with the ranch accounts.

"Enrico and I became lovers. We had been together two years when he told me that someone was blackmailing him, threatening to turn him in to immigration authorities if he didn't pay. The amount demanded was almost half of what he was making. Over the next months, Enrico became increasingly angry, then depressed.

"Shortly before the blackmail started, Enrico's sister, Jennifer, immigrated legally. She found employment as a nurse in a local hospital, where she earned a decent salary with benefits. Sometime after Jennifer came here and began sending money back to the family, Enrico told me he was ashamed that his sister was sending more to his family than he was. He couldn't see any way out of his predicament. Then the blackmailer raised the amount of money he demanded. Enrico was furious and confronted his blackmailer. He tried to negotiate some arrangement to make a single large payment and end it. He told me that the blackmailer told him to 'shut up and pay up', that this was a lifetime arrangement. The next night he killed himself. I was devastated! Still am. I'll never forget him. I loved him so much. He never told me who was blackmailing him.

"It was too painful to remain in Tempe after Enrico died. I left and eventually established a new life here. Recently, I've settled into a routine and was beginning to feel content with my life, although the emptiness in my heart has never gone away. When I read the letter, I was consumed by rage. I've never hated anyone the way I hated Henry at that moment. I knew he would be going to Miguel's house at six. I took Henry's gun out of his side-table, intending to kill him with his own gun. I thought that would be a kind of justice. But, it wasn't loaded and I couldn't find his ammunition. I put his gun in the desk where I store my gun, and grabbed my own.

"I told you I don't own a gun, but I do. It isn't registered. I took my gun, loaded it, and headed for Irvine. I pushed my way into Miguel's house. I didn't mean to hurt his grandmother. I guess I knocked her off balance when I shoved my way in. I wasn't thinking at that point, just acting on instinct. Henry got up from the living room sofa when he saw me come in. I fired twice and he went down. I rushed out the door, ran to my car, and drove home. When I got home, I was quite shaken by what I had done. I sat there in a state of shock for a long time. I had finally gotten up to make something to eat and think about what I should do when you arrived at the house."

"Why did you put Henry's gun in Miguel's car? You called us anonymously didn't you?"

"I guess I thought that it would deflect attention away from me if you kept pursuing Miguel as your major suspect. I didn't want to get Miguel in major trouble. I figured eventually you'd realize that Henry's gun wasn't the murder weapon. Since my gun isn't registered, I suppose I thought you might pursue some other leads, like people that Henry might have blackmailed.

That could keep attention away from me until I could figure something out, which I never did."

"Your story is poignant and I can understand why you felt terrible anger toward Henry. But, murder isn't a solution. It always creates a whole new set of problems. Nathan Stearns, I am arresting you on the charge of first degree murder. I suggest you hire yourself a lawyer. Sergeant Molina, please take Mr. Stearns and book him."

— CHAPTER 41 —

Sunday Evening, November 20

Keith pulled the van into a parking space in front of a spacious contemporary ranch house with a tile roof, set on a beautifully landscaped, oversized lot. "This is the address Miguel gave us. Looks to me as if Sergio could use his home as an advertisement for his landscaping service."

"He's used xeriscaping very effectively", said Susan. "I usually find that form of landscaping too spare; it doesn't appeal to me. But the way this is done feels lush. Sergio has some unusual plants among the specimens he used."

"Susan, I didn't know you were an expert on xeriscaping as well as all your other talents," said Walter with a grin.

Susan poked Walter in the ribs. "You still have a lot to learn about me, husband. I have lots of surprises for you."

Keith opened the passenger door for Jan. Walter, Susan, Monica, and James exited the rear seats of the van. They followed the walkway to the front door, through a garden of flowering cacti, and grasses that swayed in the breeze.

Miguel opened the door. "Welcome. My parents are eager to meet you."

Sergio and Dolores joined the group. Miguel made the introductions.

"We're so glad you could join us for this celebration. Keith and Jan, it's nice to meet you at last. Delia has talked so often about her visits to your home." Dolores, shook their hands. She turned to Walter and Susan. "We're grateful to Walter for his help in clearing Miguel. And to Monica for connecting us."

"Please come in and make yourselves comfortable." Sergio waved his hand toward a spacious seating area in the living room."

As they walked toward the living room, Delia ran to Monica and hugged her. "Thanks for persuading your grandfather to help us. It's so wonderful not to be worrying about what will happen to Miguel."

Monica returned the hug. "I'm just glad it all worked out. I never believed that Miguel could have done it."

"I appreciate your faith in me, Monica," said Miguel with a grin.

As they took their seats, Sergio introduced them to Juanita. "I'd like you to meet my mother, Juanita. She was released from the hospital Saturday morning and will be staying here with us until we're sure she's ready to manage by herself at home. She's feeling a bit weak, but agreed to join us for dinner, since she wanted to meet all of you."

Juanita smiled. "I'm so happy to meet Monica's family, and grateful to you for helping my grandson. Mr. Conway, you were a lifeline for him when he felt the depths of despair. Isn't it wonderful that we've seen the end of this episode?"

"It is indeed, Mrs. Sanchez. We're all relieved that you have recovered. You gave everyone quite a scare!"

"What can I get you all to drink?" asked Dolores. "We have sangria, Corona, a pinot grigio, or a cabernet for the adults, and lemonade or Pepsi for the young folks." Dolores refused an offer of assistance from her guests, but asked Delia and Fernando to help carry drinks.

The doorbell rang. Miguel went to answer the door. Soon he reappeared. "Our final guests have arrived. I'd like to introduce Bessie and Micah Jones. They're important contributors to this celebration. If Micah hadn't persuaded Grandmother to let him install the camera above the front door, and if Bessie hadn't alerted the police to the tape that proved Nathan was at the house that night, this nightmare might not be over!

"Bessie and Micah, I believe the only person you know here is Grandmother. Let me introduce our other guests."

After Miguel completed the introductions, Bessie went to Juanita and gave her a hug. "I'm glad to see you up and about. Micah and I have been praying for your recovery ever since Miguel told us what happened."

"Thank you. It's wonderful to see you Bessie. And Micah. I'm so grateful that Micah thought of installing that camera! It turned out to be an important piece of evidence. I look forward to us having some time to chat when I get back home next week. I want to hear all about your visit with your sister. Tonight I'm just going to sit here quietly and be an observer, so I have enough energy left to enjoy the celebration dinner Dolores has prepared."

The young people, Delia, Fernando, Monica, and James, excused themselves, and retired to the family room to get acquainted. The adults began conversing, feeling their way as they got to know each other. Sergio and Micah soon found common ground; both their businesses dealt with property maintenance, Micah's of the house, Sergio's of the landscape. They soon saw advantages to referring business to the other when their clients needed work done in the other's specialty area. Walter and Keith occasionally interjected their thoughts into that conversation, when they weren't conversing with Miguel about his efforts to grow his gallery. Susan, Dolores, and Bessie chatted about their families, while Juanita listened.

Conversation continued over dinner. Everyone complimented

Dolores on the feast she laid before them. Fare was down-home American: roast pork tenderloin, mashed potatoes and gravy, a corn casserole, glazed carrots, and a green salad, with hearts of palm and tomato wedges.

After dinner had been cleared, Dolores asked Sergio to pour champagne, while she brought in the desert.

"This is a tres leche cake. It's traditionally served at celebratory events in our family. Tonight we have a lot to celebrate. Juanita is recovering from her illness. Miguel's name has been cleared, and he is free to return to building his promising career as an artist. Our family is together again, and we're making new friends. We are truly blessed. We thank all of you for everything you've done for our family. We hope we will see you often in the future."

Sergio raised his glass. "To friendship and the future!"

"To friendship and the future." Glasses touched as guests returned the toast.

— CHAPTER 42 —

Tuesday Evening, November 22

Susan and Walter snuggled on the family room sofa in her house on Lake Washington. They had returned earlier that afternoon, on a flight from California. The fall air in Seattle was chilly and damp from the misty rain. They lit a fire after dinner, and were sipping a warming glass of brandy.

"I miss everyone, Walter. We had such a lovely time. On the other hand, being alone together again is heavenly. We've had little time to ourselves these past seven weeks!"

Walter gently kissed Susan on her forehead. "I missed time alone with you. I look forward to lots more of this. But, I must agree that our visits with our children and grandchildren were lovely. Our children went out of their way to make us welcome and to integrate us into the family circle. You and I merged seamlessly into each other's families, as if we've always been there. You were so good with the grandchildren. They all love you. Both Jan and Celia commented on what a great guest you are; you anticipate how you can be helpful. It's like you've been part of their routine forever."

"You did pretty well with the grandchildren too, Walter. Kristin's boys, Alex and Jack acted as if you were an old pal. I was tickled when you played basketball with them. I never knew you played! And Brendan seemed quite taken with you. He's usually shy around people he doesn't know well. He seemed quite comfortable talking with you. What did you two find to talk about?"

"Well, we talked a lot about his job. He's able to explain the technical aspects in simple language that a layman like me can understand. I was fascinated by the prospective applications of the work. Did he tell you about the promotion he's been offered?"

"No, he didn't. I wonder why? Maria certainly arranged for us to have time together. But he never mentioned it."

"He didn't tell me not to mention it to you. He mentioned it to me because he wanted some advice. Maybe he didn't tell you because he hasn't yet told Maria. The promotion would require a transfer to San Diego. He's worried about how it will affect her. You saw how close she is to her family."

"It all begins to make sense. Maria told me that she thought Brendan was worried about something he wouldn't share. She was quite concerned. I urged her to press him to share whatever it was with her. I can understand why he might be worried about taking Maria away from her family, but I think he underestimates her."

"I told Brendan he must share this with Maria as soon as possible. I suggested he discuss their options, including offering ways to minimize the impact on her family relationships. I advised him to point out the effects on his career and his morale if he turns down the promotion. They're both sensible individuals. And they're very much in love. I have no doubt that we'll soon hear from them about how they've resolved their dilemma. So don't get all worried, Susan, please."

"I'll try not to. I know you're right. They will find a solution they can both live with."

"We're very fortunate. Our children have turned out to be

responsible adults. More importantly, they are nice people and good, caring parents. Both our children and grandchildren are healthy and happy. What more could one ask for?"

"It would be greedy to ask for anything more, Walter. We have been blessed."

"It will be fun to have everyone together this winter in Hawaii." Walter felt tension run through Susan's body. "Relax, Susan. I know the logistics seem overwhelming to you. I remember that I promised to take care the arrangements. All you need to do is enjoy the event when it happens."

"Thank you, Walter. I know you will keep that promise. My anxiety reaction is instinctive. Hopefully I'll outgrow it one of these days! I'm grateful that you're so patient with me."

"You come as a package, Susan, idiosyncrasies and all. I love you just the way you are."

Susan kissed him, a long lingering kiss. "I'm very blessed to have you for my husband. I do love you so."

She snuggled closer. They sat watching the embers die, reminiscing about the romantic fire they had enjoyed in Neskowin that had played a key role in securing their relationship.

Barbara Valanis began writing fiction after she retired from her career as a professor, epidemiologist, and health services researcher. Although she spent much of her life in Washington State, she and her husband now live in Melbourne, Florida, closer to their family.